creek god

creek god

BY

LEE McALLEN

ISBN: 9798600863330 (paperback)

ACKNOWLEDGMENTS

* * *

I want to thank my wife and my friend Barry. They both motivated me to pursue my writing plans. I hope this is the first of many times I am thanking them.

CHAPTER 1

✳ ✳ ✳

THE GREAT RAINS

I look back at where it all started, a simple third grade camping trip. It sounds innocent enough, but this trip was the start of something much bigger than tents and campfires. This trip was the "tip of the spear," as we said in 3/7 CAV. I had heard my brothers speak of the magical land of "Oh Shit," and I had to experience it for myself. For some reason this time they allowed it. I don't know why, but maybe it was because I wouldn't ever shut up about it, or maybe it was because my parents made them. In the end the reason doesn't matter. I went, and I was never the same again.

After school let out, I got onto the bus, because we lived on the outskirts of the school district. This meant that all grade levels rode this bus, which sucked for a third grader. The only way to survive was to keep your head down and hope that the high schoolers didn't notice you. Most days they didn't. They had their favorite targets, and I wasn't perceived by them as fat or ugly, so I mostly evaded their radar. I swore that one day I would take these jackasses down a peg or two, but I was presently in no position to do so. Anyway, they were busy tormenting a pair of fourth graders a few seats behind me, so I was able to focus on the night's grand adventure. The day had finally arrived. I would be going on my first creek mission tonight. No parents and no rules, just fun.

An hour or so after I got home, I grabbed my sleeping bag from the back of the Oldsmobile station wagon. I also had my mini-igloo cooler. In the cooler was a six-pack of Dr Pepper and three packs of strawberry Pop-Tarts. This would prove to be a winning combination over the years, and I can't think of many subsequent creek missions that did not include at least these basic supplies. My mom had dropped us off at my brother Brett's friend Mike's house. Brett was in ninth grade at the time, so we didn't have the advantage of non-parental auto travel yet. Mike's house was about a hundred yards away from the entrance we used to the creek. There were several houses on the street that could have been used, but we used the Shermans' property as our launching point. This never changed over the years. I don't think they were big fans of us trudging through their four acres down to the creek, but my brother had been nice to their oldest son, who had faced some social problems. Later in life, I became friends with their daughter, so they just let us use their property as the pass-through. Most of our subsequent expeditions had an average of four participants, but that was not the case on this day. If my memory serves me correctly, we had eight campers on this historic outing.

The Shermans' home was set about an acre back from the street. There were huge cedar trees on the property. Normally, in my later missions, these would serve as great cover. We would meet behind these trees in the dark and gather our thoughts about the night's events. Cars passing by wouldn't even notice us, and this was one of our goals. Cedar trees were all over this neighborhood. In fact, they could be found in nearly every corner of the great town of Waynesville. As this was my first trip through this vast yard on my way to the creek, the trees created a fitting backdrop for the coming adventures. We journeyed on a well-worn path from the street out front, through large gaps between the cedar trees, past the spacious home, to the edge of the creek. I looked down when I got to the edge. The water was moving quickly through the creek bed. I peered down at the water and pictured myself being rushed along toward something, but I wasn't sure what. I also pictured myself tumbling down the side, with my gear ending up soaked and scattered.

"Has anybody ever fallen down the side?" I inquired. Brett looked at me with an annoyed expression, which relayed to me that I was to be seen and not heard on this trip.

"Have you heard of anyone breaking a leg, or their back even? No, so nobody we know has lost it here," he said. His buddy Mike looked at me and made the obvious dig:

"You'll be the first if you don't shut the hell up and pay attention."

I pulled back inland from the edge of the creek walls, careful not to fall the twenty or thirty feet down to the rocks and water below. The rest of the crew was busy crossing over a fence to a stretch of land known as the Kirks. We called it this simply due to the last name of the owners. Did they allow us to use their property? I didn't know at the time, but our pathway was at the back of their property, and they couldn't see us traveling through from their house. I suspect they knew someone used their land as a shortcut to avoid the steep drop of the creek by the fence, but I was never sure if they knew it was us. Quite frankly, I didn't care, because we lived in the moment, and the Kirks were known as good people who probably wouldn't have cared all that much anyway.

When I think back to this pivotal day in my life, I see parts of it as a blur. I mean, I remember the "forest" but certainly not all the "trees." I can picture my brother and Mike, and a few of the others, but the rest of the people's faces escape me. I know others were there; I just am not sure who. There are several possibilities, and if I were to guess the players, I could probably get close to the truth. However, the main player in this event is still fresh in my mind, because he became a mentor that helped get me through my school years. I remember him slowing me down as we neared the next obstacle on the long walk to our campsite. We called him Beetle.

Beetle was a family friend from down the block. He lived within a few minutes' walk of my house. He was three years ahead of me at the elementary school known as Alex Bields, which was just on the edge of the Possum Fields school district. He was a hang-along of someone else on this trip, but he was older and more respected than me. I think he felt sorry for me, so that night he took me under his wing. The Kirks was a dense, thick forest on the edge of the creek. It had a few stray cows every now and then that would come down to drink from the pond between us and the main house, which was several acres up from where we were. The cows would get stuck in the mud by the pond and not know what to do or how to get out. The pond drained into the creek. There was a cement drainage slide that led down to the creek bed below. A fence was designed to keep you from slipping down this moss-slicked, smooth cement downgrade into the creek. However, the fence was not well thought out, because it was barbed wire and had been destroyed long ago, so only remnants of it remained. At the pond end of the drain the cement could be carefully crossed. It was deceptively slick, and I saw many people unwillingly ride it like a water slide over the years. As I was crossing without thinking, Beetle told me to slow down and to step over the two feet of water running down toward the creek. I did what he said and was able to avoid falling on my ass, like one of the other campers did. We always pictured someone killing themselves on this ride, because if you followed it to the end you would see a metal fence pole protruding out of the creek below. This view was enough to make you consider crossing at another point. Yet we always crossed right here, because we were too lazy to navigate the steep downward path to the creek bed below, although it led straight to one of our favorite creek camping sites. Beetle told me a story later that night of another expedition that had failed to cross the drainage feature as skillfully as we did, and that mission ended in lost food, broken skin, and family blows thrown. Thankfully, we avoided those on this night.

After we made it past the pond, the brush cleared a little into a worn path, and we moved further from the creek into the woods. We passed a small fence about one foot in height. We walked another few hundred feet and came to one of the most famous landmarks of my childhood, simply known as the "ravine."

This was a smaller, dry creek bed that at some point fed into the larger creek. This was the first real test of manhood for a creeker. Could you make it down and up the ravine with all of your stuff without dropping it or needing human assistance? It was not an easy feat because the ravine was pretty steep on both sides. If you could make it close to the top of the other side, there were several roots you could grab to finish the job. If it was muddy, you could forget it: you would need to either drop some stuff and go back to get smaller loads or form a human chain to defeat the ravine when slick. My first time here was intimidating, and my brother grabbed my cooler, leaving me with the sleeping bag alone. He had only a jam box and my cooler, and he made it up with no help.

"You need me to get your bag?" Mike inquired.

"No thanks, I think I can make it," I answered.

Beetle had already ventured down the slope to the bottom, but his tent had fallen out of his rucksack. He reached down to grab it but had a much tougher time going up than some of the others, because without momentum it was a much more difficult climb.

"C'mon now, we ain't got all night," my brother yelled from the top of the other side. I held tight to the sleeping bag and slowly started down the hill, picking up steam as I neared the bottom. I headed quickly up the other side and lost my concentration. I began to slow down and I felt gravity working against me. At the last second, I saw a big root sticking out of the ground about halfway up. I grabbed it.

"Yes, grab it and pull yourself up!" I'm not sure who said it, but it got me to the top with no assistance. I had passed the first test. Not bad for a third grader going on twenty.

I stepped up out of the ravine and into a large field. I could see about five or six cows off in the distance. On the other side of the field were some dense woods, or the "forest" as we called it. We were now a good bit away from the big creek. You could still hear it, but you couldn't see it anymore. This field was another monumental spot for my teenage development years, but more will come on that later.

The crew traveled through the field toward the forest. We still had about an hour of daylight left at this point. The whole journey may have been a mile, but with the fences, brush, and other obstacles it sometimes seemed much further than this. Beetle led the way with his rucksack on his back, although I got the feeling he was new to this realm as well. My brother and Mike followed closely behind. I could hear them talking about a lady named Ms. Woy, saying that she had a wandering eye. I didn't know what that meant, but I later found that with her it had a double meaning. She favored the men and she had what they used to call a "lazy eye." They also spoke of a new band director named Mr. Jotts, and they bantered back and forth about whether he was gay. I tagged along as closely as I could. The field was big and you could easily see everything, but I still was afraid I might get lost. The cows looked up from their grass meals as we passed by, but they paid us no mind.

When we reached the edge of the field before heading into the woods, Beetle spoke up: "That fence to the left leads to the white rock." I knew that meant the big creek, but that was not our destination on this trip.

We marched into the forest at a quick pace. Brett looked back to make sure I was still keeping up. There was a broken platform about a foot off the ground at the entryway to the forest. I wondered what purpose it served, because it seemed an odd place for a platform. Yet, it somehow belonged as well. Mike walked back in my direction.

"See the marks on the trees?" he asked.

"Yep, it looks like someone hit them with an axe or something, "I said.

Mike seemed impressed with my elementary-level knowledge. "That's exactly what they are. They are marks on the trees that lead to our campsite, which is sometimes hard to find in the dark. Just follow the marks."

Over the years, I added to these marks and kept them alive for future generations.

The group spread out through the woods, and I could see we were getting close to the camp. A few minutes later we were putting our stuff down.

"Welcome to the New," Mike said. The campsite was situated around a firepit next to a tree that was bent over naturally in the shape of a bench. This tree made a great seat for two or three kids hanging out by the fire. The camp was also well positioned at the top of a path that led to a mini-pond or spring that fed off from the main creek about a half-mile away. Sometimes this water was swimmable and sometimes it wasn't, from a depth perspective. Not many dared to actually get in this water because it had its share of snakes, mostly of the water moccasin variety. However, we always walked down the path to make use of the water running into the pond. It was great for putting out fires and cleaning pots and stuff.

With only a few minutes left until dark, Brett started a fire with some paper and a lighter. The flame shot into the sky as someone doused it with lighter fluid. We quickly began to set up the two tents that had made the trip with us. Mike was clearly perturbed by this.

"Creekers rarely sleep in tents," he exclaimed. I knew enough not to question the alpha male. I learned in later years that tents are rarely needed in this area of Texas because the weather usually cooperates. Also, we sometimes had to make hasty exits, and a tent made that hard to do. But this night, the tents went up fast, no thanks to me. However, I did notice that they were an easy setup.

Darkness came quickly and the fire was mesmerizing. I had been around fires, but never campfires with no parents. Brett threw a small grill top on the fire and placed several hunks of meat on it. The sizzle sounded alive and the smell was intoxicating. He was able to provide this treat because he worked part time at the Waynesville Market, a convenience store that also sold some meat and produce. It was locally famous for its barbeque, which fed the growing community. The owner of the market had another store over in Possum Fields, about a mile from the high school. Brett worked at both of these, but there was no question where the money was made. Waynesville was a growing community, and the construction workers lined up at lunch for burgers, fries, and the BBQ. If the town had been "wet," it might have grown even faster, but you had to drive thirty minutes just to get beer. This was probably a good thing, or I may have gotten in more trouble growing up.

"Grab some steak and have a Dr Pepper," Brett suggested.

I didn't need to be told twice. Only Mike and I were taking the meat, so I learned it was every man for himself at dinner time. The meat was hot and overcooked, but I was living the dream. It tasted delicious, and my first creek dinner was one of the best ever. When it was over and I had cleaned my hands in the creek below, Mike tossed me a pack of strawberry Pop-Tarts. They made one hell of a dessert. If only I could eat like this every night! Everyone else was busy cooking stuff up. Beetle had a can of SpaghettiOs, and someone else was eating beef and country vegetable soup. The place smelled amazing. The last can I saw on the ground was Wolf Brand Chili. Any container that would burn ended up in the fire within the next thirty minutes, which meant we had very little trash to carry out. Someone turned on the jam box, and the night's soundtrack soon became the Bee Gees, Elton John, Billy Joel, and even a little ELO. This trip was going well. Nobody really talked much to me at first – not surprising as I was still just a little kid. However, I didn't feel that way. Tonight, I felt older and somehow cooler. People had their own conversations going on all over camp. I just tried to stay out of everyone's way and enjoyed the night. Only Beetle was quieter, and I saw him climb into his tent with a knife and a stick. I climbed in as well, and he never told me to leave. We still talk to this day, over thirty-five years later.

Everything was starting to wind down for the night, although the radio kept providing the night's soundtrack. I had been in the tent for about an hour. Beetle had a propane lamp that lit the place up nicely. The door of the tent was positioned so we could see the fire, which Brett and Mike faithfully kept rolling for us. I could hear them yapping on and on about "Big Daddy," the owner of the stores they both worked at. He was a local legend because of his temper and juxtaposed big heart.

Beetle worked on a stick with his knife, creating a sort of spear. It was clearly a timewaster, but he still did a pretty good job of it. It wasn't too cold, so I brought my sleeping bag into the tent and just lay on top of it. Beetle told me stories of his "classic" soccer team tournament trips, and how some of the team members were jackasses. Beetle was a good athlete, but I always thought he didn't belong with that crew. I played soccer as well, and my team was really good, but we were a public team.

"We won the Dallas Morning News Tournament of Champions, but the competition was pretty weak last year," Beetle explained. I was just hanging out, happy an older kid was talking to me, and every now and then I would throw something in.

"My team is set to go next year. Some dude's dad is paying the entry fee for us and buying us Umbro uniforms and gear. He owns a bunch of gas stations." I tried to stay on subject with this comment, but I had already run out of soccer talk.

"Yeah, every kid on my team is rich, except me and Winston," Beetle advised.

The night had worn on and it must have been close to midnight. The radio was still humming, but the volume was much lower than it had been. A few people were already asleep. Brett stoked the fire and paid little attention to me. A cigarette or two had been smoked, but I was not sure if it was him or not, and I didn't care either way. We were at the creek, and it would take much more than that to ruin my night. Beetle turned the light out, and he talked softly about the stars and his upcoming camping trips down to Glen Rose, the dinosaur area. I had heard of it before and thought maybe my parents could take me someday. Some thunder played off in the distance, but at this point it was far away. The clock soared past midnight, which was late for me, but I wanted the night to go on. It took maybe another hour, but I drifted off to sleep, with my eyes drowsy from the soft glow of a dying fire. Beetle was out as well.

"Shit!"

Panicked, frustrated noises rocked the calm night. I could hear people scrambling around outside, all using choice words to protest the night. Thunder and lightning ushered in the chilly night air. My face was covered with wet tent. It had rained so hard the tent sagged and was touching our faces. Beetle was already moving around inside the tent. I had fallen asleep on top of my bag, so it was dry where I had been lying, but an inch or two of water lined the inside perimeter of the tent. I looked at the red glow of the coals in the pit and wondered how long it could last under this pounding. Flashlights lit up the night as people moved around trying to find a dry spot under a tree. This was not light rain; this was a full-on ass-kicker of a storm. I pushed the sagging tent up off me. Beetle was climbing through the doorway out into the night. I followed him.

"How long has this been going on, Brett?" I asked.

"Long enough to ruin sleep and make this a miserable trip," he exclaimed.

"What do we do?" I asked.

Brett must have been through similar situations because he was not as panicked as some of the others. "Ride it out. There is nowhere within a mile safer than here. Just go get under the tarp Mike has strung up," he said.

I walked over to the cooler and grabbed two drinks. I threw one to Beetle, who was looking down the path to the creek. The pond had already risen, and the creek rushing into it looked like Colorado rapids I had seen on TV. The path was already muddy. I wanted to go down to the creek but decided to get under the tarp. It wasn't completely dry there either, but I was able to ride out the storm. Mike had had the foresight to bring some wood in under the tarp. It rained another forty-five minutes or so, and my wet clothes stuck to my body. It then just stopped.

"Man, that was the worst storm I've ever seen," Mike said.

"I know, and most of my shit is ruined," somebody complained.

It was cold but we were able to exit the tarp area and mill around a bit. The fire was dead. Brett dug down into the pit and stirred up some coals. Mike got the wood ready, and lighter fluid did the rest. We had fire! The warmth was a godsend. We scrambled around camp gathering stuff the wind had blown, mainly clothing. My Pop-Tarts box was drenched, but I was able to salvage a few of them. It must have been 5:00 a.m. or so by now. I sat on my cooler by the fire. Smoke burned my eyes, but I was so happy the rain was done. The creek below us rushed into the pond, sounding like a raging river. Beetle sat on a stump next to me. Nobody was talking really. We were all blown away by what we had just been through. The place looked like a tornado had passed close by, warning us but not defeating us.

I had never been that tired up to that point in my life. We had many all-night creek sessions after that, but none for me until after sixth grade. I had slept a few hours I guess, but the way we were woken up seemed to weigh on everyone. We were out of dry wood by 7:00 a.m., and everyone was ready for some dry clothes.

"Let's pack up our shit," said Mike.

"Burn the rest of the trash and make sure we don't leave anything," Brett exclaimed.

I rolled up my wet sleeping bag and drank the last of my sodas. The cooler was pretty light at this point, and I figured the trip home would be easier than the trip there – besides the tired-and-wet factor, of course. After thirty minutes or so the motley crew was ready to venture back to civilization, soaked as we were.

"Hey, Beetle, when are you coming back?" I inquired.

"Don't know," he said.

I decided to leave it at that. I didn't want to push my luck with the older kid. Brett surveyed the campsite one last time and proclaimed it clear enough. I didn't see anything we had left, but it had been windy during the storm, so I'm sure we must have missed something. Anyway, it was clean enough, so we were ready. Mike and a few of the others made sure the fire was put out, and the acrid smell of urine betrayed how, even to a third grader. With no further words, Brett and Mike headed into the forest, back toward the real world.

My sleeping bag was cold on my arms as we made our way toward the field through the woods. Somehow, the trip seemed to go a little faster this time, and I rather quickly found myself standing on the broken-down platform at the edge of the woods. The field was wet but not muddy, and when the entire crew made it to the platform, we proceeded to walk the longest (and easiest) part of the journey. The sky was gray and it began to sprinkle some. The light rain might have been refreshing if we weren't already soaked and miserable. I didn't see any cows out here this time, and I assumed they were huddled up under some tree or other shelter. For a minute, I thought it must suck to be an animal stuck in the rain, but that thought quickly left me. Brett picked up the pace, and I could tell from his demeanor he was ready to be done. My parents weren't going to pick us up until 11:00 a.m., so I knew we'd be walking the half-mile or so back home once we hit the street. I wasn't worried about it, because I felt like a big kid, and the final leg was the least of my worries. As we neared the edge of the field, I remembered the ravine, and I wondered if the addition of mud to my super-wet clothing would make me any less comfortable than I already was.

"Throw your bag down to the bottom, and drop the cooler as well," Brett ordered. I did as he said, and just as quickly he was no longer standing next to me. He took a step down the ravine and his feet got away from him. He was sprawled flat on his back, but he had managed to grab a root a few feet down. This kept him from a total wipeout, but I knew I was in trouble. Brett laid out a few choice words and then let go of the root. He slid down the ravine and into the bottom. He stood up after a minute and his entire back was covered in mud. Two others had ridden down the slope on their butts, deciding it would be better to muddy their pants than their entire outfit. The rain picked up. Brett picked up his muddy jam box and my cooler and trudged sideways up the other side of the ravine. He'd slip a little here and there, but there were a few roots sticking up close to his path that he used to keep heading in the right direction. He finally got near the top and was able to throw the cooler up into the brush on the other side. He then grabbed a root and pulled himself the rest of the way up. He was filthy but he had made it to the top. Mike slid down the ravine like he was on skis, and he didn't get that muddy, until he slipped going up the other side. Mike managed to get his stuff and himself to the top, and he was probably the cleanest of the bunch of us. Beetle had figured out how to get down using the ski method, but his rucksack threw off his balance and he busted at the bottom. Fortunately, his backpack took most of the blow. He was slightly muddy, but his sack was caked! One way or another, everyone else made it down and up the ravine, with the final group of three making a chain going up the other side that enabled the last two to avoid much of the muddy clothes effect. Brett yelled for me to hurry up. I stepped to the edge of the ravine and began to slide down.

Mike had grabbed a root and lowered his arm down for me. I just needed to make it halfway up the other side and I would be golden. I slid sideways down the muddy hill, and I picked up a good bit of speed. I began to think I might make it unscathed. As I reached the bottom, I crouched down and one-handed my wet sleeping bag. The wetness made it easier to grab, and I was able to pick it up and keep moving. I hadn't counted on the fact that I was sliding and not running, and that I would need to actually take some steps to climb the other side. I switched to running mode, made it four good steps, and reached out for Mike's hand. We made contact, but my hand was too slick from the light rain of the last few minutes. I couldn't grab on and I slid backwards. I then lost all balance and fell flat on my face at the bottom of the ravine. I was completely covered in mud, and I had scraped my leg on a root on the way down.

"Good attempt, but the creek god has denied your request!" Mike shouted. A few of the others laughed as I stood there soaked and defeated.

"Throw me the bag, John." I did as my brother wanted.

"Screw it," I said. I headed back up the ravine. I wasn't going to allow defeat to set in. This time I would make it! Mike held out a lifeline and I grabbed his arm. He latched on and pulled me up. I made it to the top, bruised and a little embarrassed, but a little wiser because of it. Most of the others were already making their way through the brush toward the cement drain and home. I picked up my shit and followed.

The cement drain into the big creek was a much more dangerous place this morning than the night before. The rainwater the pond had collected overnight rushed down the drain toward the white rock below. As I said before, this drain was basically a big slab of concrete waterslide. Still, we either had to cross here or swim through the snake-infested pond. We chose to cross. It would have been foolish even for kids to cross alone, so we formed a human chain. One end held tight to a tree and we eased everyone across. The water rushed hard, and a few people almost lost it, but we all made it across with little damage. My feet actually came out cleaner on the other side, as the ravine mud below my calves was washed away.

Once we reached the other side of the cement, we were on the downward slope. I crossed the final fence and entered the Shermans' backyard. The creek below was higher than I'd ever seen it. It must have risen three or four feet overnight. It actually looked like a fast-moving river. We made our way up to the street, heading toward Mike's house. If anyone was watching us through the windows, they didn't say anything. We were filthy and tired, and we looked like a group who had come through a hurricane or a war zone. I was happy to have made it through the night, and I now had a notch on my belt.

As the group crossed from the street into Mike's yard everyone was saying their goodbyes. Nobody had cell phones yet, so people would need to call for rides the old-fashioned way – the landline in Mike's kitchen. We lived about a half-mile away, so we readied ourselves for the final walk home. Beetle grabbed his stuff and began his walk home, which was a little shorter than mine.

"See ya next time," he said to me.

This was encouraging, because I still felt lucky to have been invited at all. That quick, he was around the corner and on his way. Brett started heading home and told me to hurry up. Mike looked at me and laughed.

"So, how was it? You did pretty good, kid." I was happy. I was sure Brett didn't want me tagging along on the next mission, but at least Mike wasn't too annoyed with me. I answered as I slowly moved through the yard toward the street.

"I loved it, and I love the creek, but, man, I need a shower," I remarked. Mike and a few others chuckled at that one.

"Dude," Mike said, "that's the understatement of the year."

CHAPTER 2

✳ ✳ ✳

WIFFLE

I didn't get to go to the creek nearly as much as I would have liked over the next few years. I mean, at ten years old I was lucky ever to get to go at all. In fact, I can't remember any additional, memorable creek camping trips after the one I just described until sometime in sixth grade. However, that doesn't mean I didn't have my share of fun. Overall, I think I lived a pretty normal middle-class suburban life. I had friends down the street and rode my bike around the neighborhood a lot. I had a mom and dad, a couple of older brothers, and a little sister. This made up the Decker family. We lived in a four-bedroom house on Brightwood Street in Waynesville, Texas, just thirty minutes or so south of Dallas. My dad worked five days a week, and my mom took care of the house. She also ran a community theater in the county square, which was in the city of Indian Lake. I was in elementary school still, but my brothers were four and six years older than me, respectively. Joel was in ninth grade by then, and Brett was in eleventh. Joel was class president material and a little goofy. Brett was drum major of the high school band and a National Honor Society member. My sister, Shelly, was just starting her school journey in kindergarten. Like I said before, we were a normal middle-class family. Except for one thing.

Sometime around my fifth-grade year my Dad got tired of the local Baptist church. Another man, Larry Devins, felt the same way and they pulled us out of the church. They decided to hold a service at my house on Sunday mornings. My dad played guitar and led the music. Larry was supposed to have the gift of teaching, so he did the preaching. I remember my brother Brett conveniently arranged to have to work the early Sunday shift at his convenience store job. He never attended a home church service that I recall. My brother Joel also played guitar, and he helped out some. We started out with about nine people at the house each Sunday morning for church. Over the next two years, this grew to over thirty people and many fun times. (It also ruined me for traditional church, but that's an entirely different story.)

The home church ran at my house for its first two years. We then began to rotate among the houses of different families for the final year. This was enjoyable because we had a different venue each week. However, once this change occurred, the normal church power struggles began and the church started the downward spiral toward closure. This didn't affect the kids. We all had a blast. The main reasons for this were the food and games. At the end of each service, we had a potluck meal. While this was going on inside, the kids would be outside playing games and having a good time. The games of choice were polo and Wiffle ball. Polo involved yellow Wiffle ball bats and an underinflated kickball. It was basically soccer using plastic bats. We also allowed a little tackling and pushing. I know our rules didn't match the official polo guidelines, but we didn't care. Polo played itself out in a few months, but Wiffle ball gave us hours of fun throughout the entire two years that church remained at my house. The fun began as a simple after-church activity but grew into the phenomenon of the neighborhood.

Wiffle ball was simply baseball played with a plastic bat and ball. The field was much smaller to accommodate the shrunken team size. In fact, we normally played one on one, or two on two at most. Many from my generation will remember the long, skinny yellow bat. There was also a thicker black bat that was allowed when more power was required. The only ball allowed was the official Wiffle ball. On this we did not compromise. We tried imitation balls, but they did not pitch or move the same, so as a group we agreed to use the standard Wiffle ball. We had a lawn chair for the strike zone to avoid arguments. The rule was simple: if the ball hit the chair anywhere, it was a strike.

We rarely finished any games as a group on Sunday, since parents were ready to go home soon after finishing the meal. But those of us who lived in the neighborhood would finish the games, and this is where the real fun began.

It seemed like we played Wiffle ball every day the summer before I entered fifth grade. I was on a traditional Little League baseball team that won the local championship, but that somehow didn't compare to the backyard competitions at the house. By this time, it wasn't only home church kids playing the game; it was people from all over our neighborhood. I remember playing against kids I didn't even know. It was a great advantage to have the host field because we took it a lot more seriously than most other kids. Those of us who played a lot got very good at pitching, so it was hard for neighborhood kids to beat us.

I remember the day when the inevitable next step was conceived. Beetle, Joel, Brett, Benton, and I were present for the conversation.

"Let's start an actual league. We've already had enough players come through to make six two-man squads," Joel stated.

Benton from two doors down was a serious athlete and a regular at our games. He had a different idea. "Screw a league! Let's have a tournament!"

Our eyes lit up at this idea. Beetle and Joel had a little side conversation going, so I jumped into the main conversation while I had the chance. "We can do both a singles and a doubles competition. We can get a trophy for each and everything. I bet we get a lot of people to sign up," I said.

"This sounds good. Let's get some poster board and make the brackets," Benton declared. Brett went inside and brought out poster board, which was a staple in our house before the glorious days of PowerPoint. Within a few hours, and with a lot of bike riding, we had filled out the first round of the tournament. It was due to begin the next morning at 9:00 a.m.

The rest of the day before the tournament was amazing and exciting. We planned the games down to the minute, and we somehow got my mom to go buy a few floodlights to put in the big tree out back, because the final game would start right about 9:00 p.m. This was to be our first (and last) nighttime Wiffle ball game. I think my parents were just excited that we were doing something besides sitting on the Atari, which was basically the king whenever we were inside the house. In fact, I had just finished a game of M Network baseball against my dad when I went out back to check on the progress of the preparations. My brother Joel was acting like the head groundskeeper at Arlington Stadium.

"A little to the right. No. Back to the left a bit. Hold it. Brett, plug in the light," Joel ordered. Beetle was up in the tree placing the lights. They had waited till close to dark to do this, so it wasn't all that easy.

"How does it look? Can we see the chair and the mound?" Beetle inquired.

"Looks great! Tape them up," said Joel.

"Awesome," I added. You could see the chair better as it got darker, and the mound was fairly lit up as well. This all seemed like a great idea but was really just a novelty. Beetle climbed down out of the tree and we all went inside to play some more Atari. I could barely sleep I was so excited.

The 9:00 a.m. start actually happened. Everyone that had signed up had checked in. Many chose to hang out while waiting for their game to start. We had mini-Atari brackets going on inside as well, so it was an all-around master of a day. When I think back to my childhood, this day always ranks toward the top. I actually won the M Network baseball bracket going on in the TV room. I had logged so many hours on that game I rarely ever lost. People who dared to play me usually got embarrassed (except for those who lived close and played a lot as well). The Wiffle tournament trudged on outside through the heat of the day. I won my first-round game against a kid from down the street named Justin. I was frankly surprised he even came, because he wasn't part of our normal circle. I lost in the next round to an older kid in Beetle's grade. The singles battle wrapped up about 3:30 p.m., with my brother Joel winning it all. He pitched so fast the ball never really made it into play, and he could hit spots on the chair better than Nolan Ryan. The real fun kicked off at 4:00 p.m. with the doubles.

The first game was over in thirty minutes. Beetle and Joel had paired up to beat the Good brothers from the edge of the neighborhood. If anyone had a chance against Joel and Beetle, I thought it might be the Goods. They could fight and play football, but Joel sent them home quickly that afternoon. His pitching was just too good. Brett and me were up next against Benton (we called him by his last name, but don't ask me why!) and his little brother. Benton was better than me, but Brett was as good as him at Wiffle due to experience and the home field advantage. They cancelled each other out, and because I was so much better than young Benton, we beat them easily. We moved on to the semis against Joel and Beetle. Another semifinal match took place before ours. It involved a high school kid named Kilyar, who rivaled Joel. Kilyar hadn't played in the singles round, or it might have been a game. His team won and secured its place in the 9:00 p.m. final. There was one game before that to decide who they would play: The battle of brothers! And a battle it was.

Joel and Beetle were up first, and Brett was on the mound. I was somewhere behind second base ready for Joel to start pounding us, but Brett actually struck out the side in a masterful first-inning performance. We played two outs per inning instead of the traditional three, so the game moved at a good pace.

Beetle started the game pitching; they clearly were trying to keep Joel fresh after they saw Kilyar could actually play. I hadn't ever seen Joel hold back on the Wiffle field (or at any game of any kind for that matter), but Kilyar clearly had him rattled. He hadn't expected any competition that day. Brett got walked, and I rocked a double that brought Brett home. Brett then doubled to bring me home and we were up two to nothing. Beetle struck me out and walked Brett, and then I popped out to end the inning. Brett then struck out Beetle, and we got Joel on a ground ball to first. It appeared we actually had a chance. Brett came to the plate and hit a single off of Beetle. Joel was clearly frustrated at this point, and he came to the mound like a pitching coach in the World Series. After a minute Beetle went to the outfield and Joel took over the mound. "Here we go," I thought, and soon all hell broke loose.

Joel blew the first two right by me, hitting the bottom left corner of the chair. Yes, these would have been balls in any other baseball game, but the chair ruled here. Joel could usually hit any spot on it at will and at high speed. I was nervous as I waited for the inevitable strikeout. I had hit him before, but extremely rarely. I choked up on the bat and realized I had nothing to be scared of. I had been hit by a Wiffle ball many times in the past. It hurt, but the pain always went away. Joel was pitching out of the stretch, keeping Brett close to first base. I was ready. Joel let his arrogance get the better of him in an attempt to dominate me and teach me a lesson for having hope. Because of this, he ripped a fast ball right down the middle. I barely had time to get the bat out, but I did get the swing down. It was perfect! The ball hit my bat right in the sweet spot and rocketed on a skyward path into the tree above the mound. According to Decker Wiffle ball rules, this was an automatic home run, because the tree stopped the forward progress of the ball and kept it from going over the fence. This had led to many arguments over projected path, popup versus line drives, and such, but there was no arguing this one. Even Beetle was impressed.

"Good shot, John," Beetle yelled.

"Four-nothing," Brett added as he strolled around the bases. Joel was seething. His competitive nature got the best of him, and I soon saw a side of both brothers I hadn't known existed.

"That's bullshit," yelled Joel. "You know that wasn't going over the fence!"

"It was, but it doesn't matter anyway. Rules are rules," Brett countered. I knew enough to stay out of it at this point.

Beetle was a peacemaker (as Joel *usually* was) and spoke up to try to smooth things over. "It's a home run and it's only four-nothing. Let's get going so we can stay on schedule."

"Fuck that, I quit," yelled Joel. This was shocking because I had never heard him use that word, and I couldn't imagine him quitting anything. However, I then remembered many times he'd shown similar anger when I beat him on the Atari. I had just never seen him lose anything physical before. We were only in the second inning, so he had plenty of time to still beat us. Joel threw his glove at me and walked off the field toward the house.

Brett followed him. "Get back on the field! We're not done yet." Joel turned around with a look on his face I hadn't seen before.

Joel tackled Brett and started whaling on him. He landed a few blows before Brett was able to wrestle him off.

"What are you doing? Stop," yelled Brett.

"Come on, guys, let's just play the game," Beetle interjected. Joel wasn't having it. He lunged at Brett again and landed a good shot square in the jaw. I could tell it hurt as tears of anger welled up in Brett's eyes. Brett launched a fury of body blows and Joel went down. Brett moved in for more as Beetle and Benton grabbed him to restrain him while Joel got to his feet.

"Screw you," yelled Joel as he walked away into the house. He disappeared inside and we lost sight of him. Just when we thought things had calmed down, we realized we had lost sight of Brett, too. I looked inside and they were throwing blows in the living room. My mom and Shelly were out for the day, and my dad was not yet home from work. It was an all-out brawl at this point, with both brothers fully, willingly engaged. We managed to get them apart. Brett went outside to cool down, while Beetle tried to calm Joel down. Two minutes later, the back door flew open and Joel was standing there with a good-sized rock in his hand. He launched it straight at Brett. It hit Brett in the ribs, and he yelled out in pain.

"Shit!"

All this seemed to do was intensify the anger, and Brett slammed Joel onto the cement back porch. He pounded Joel pretty good as Joel struggled to regain the upper hand. Within a minute, our neighbor Mr. Dunegan was in the backyard pulling the two warriors apart. He succeeded where we had failed. The fight was over, and my admiration for Joel was as well.

Joel and Beetle had forfeited the game to Brett and me. We were in a groove and thought we would have won anyway. Nine o'clock came and the first night game got underway. Kilyar and his teammate beat us handily, seven to two. The lights worked, but it was still much harder to see and just too difficult to play in the dark. Joel could have beaten Kilyar on a good day, but we will never know how things might have turned out if Joel had stayed the course and tried to beat Brett and me.

A piece of my innocence was lost that day. I knew Brett wasn't an angel, but I was shocked to see Joel cuss like a sailor and physically attack his brother. I was sorely disappointed. Getting past this event was a challenge, but it wasn't enough to ruin the great Wiffle ball summer in Waynesville. In fact, the fight only enhanced the reputation of our street for being a place of great competition and fun. My brothers were grounded a week or so, and that was it. I never really saw them speak much after that until they were adults.

Beetle and I became even better friends that summer; he basically became my third brother. It was a year or so later when Beetle invited me on a creek mission that I still remember vividly to this day.

CHAPTER 3

✳ ✳ ✳

THE THREE QUESTION MARKS
???

Few nights of my early years had such a profound effect on me as the one I'm about to describe. This night had adventure, mystery, intrigue, and most of all, fear. Those who grew up close to me know that it was nights like this that led to the creation of the one known only as the "creek god." Some things, good and bad, can only be attributed to this entity.

It had been about three years since the wild night of the great rains. I was almost finished with sixth grade. I basically ruled Alex Bields elementary school. (This was back when sixth graders were still considered "elementary" age; now, they are included in middle school.) However, the time was looming when we would have to join all the kids from the other side of the tracks, from Possum Fields Elementary. They were somehow rougher, more mysterious – at least in our minds. In reality, the economics weren't all that different, but we thought they were. The next stop on my journey would be Possum Fields Junior High. I remembered stories from both my brothers, and I imagined this might be a horrible place. It wasn't.

Over the previous three years, since the great muddy adventure I described earlier, I had begun to hang out with Beetle. I was still a little kid at times, and he was already busting out his freshman year in high school, but he tolerated me for some reason. It wasn't like he had too many options on our street, so I guess I was one of the best (only) choices. Over the years, he taught me how to ride a lawn mower (we had a sweet course in his hilly backyard next to the creek), and he taught me a lot about fishing. During the summers, we rode our bikes or walked the mile or so over to the Two Ponds. These were exactly what they sounded like. We never caught much, but one fish per trip made it all worthwhile. We also had an old canoe out there, so we had loads of fun. Anyways, the night I'm about to describe includes Beetle and his friend Steady. (The name just did not match the dude, which made for good irony.)

We began the night by grabbing our stuff and cutting through the back of Beetle's yard and the small creek bed to the cul-de-sac behind his house. This led us to the road out front of the Shermans', from where all creek missions launched. Steady had more bags than I was used to seeing and a PVC pipe cannon. The guy can best be described as a science geek – the kind of guy that is rich and pulling a lot of women at age forty. But back then, the thought of Steady pulling girls seemed ludicrous. His company always made for a wonderful time, and his family owned a sweet pool we frequented during the summer. I hoped I would get to hang out with him more, but he was Beetle's friend more than my own. Steady's real name was Freddy. People used to call him Steady Freddy, and then they got lazy and dropped off the Fred part. He had been called Steady ever since. Steady loved science, planning cosmic destruction, and the Cars. The rock band that had sung "Shake It Up" and "Drive" was his favorite. He would have been a good host of that show that tests out theories and such, if I could only remember the name.

Anyway, Steady was talking about something in freshman science class when Beetle interrupted. "We're here, just through these trees," said Beetle.

"I gathered that from the ample description you gave me in English last week," Steady shot back.

We set our stuff down behind a cedar tree to take a breather. I pulled a drink (DP) out of my cooler.

"Which site are we camping at tonight, Beetle?" I inquired.

"The New-New," Beetle answered as he picked up his bag and started toward the campsite.

The creek of our youth had multiple campsites, but none was more argued about than the New-New. Some of the old-time creekers didn't recognize the New-New as a legitimate site. However, to the newer generation, it was the best one. It was furthest from the creek and from our houses, yet closer to the landowners and danger. It was as if we were sleeping behind enemy lines. The site was brilliant, cut out from inside a grove of large cedar trees. If you passed by the outside of the grove without looking too closely, you couldn't even see the fire inside. We rarely were quiet there, so I doubt we would have gone undetected by any serious efforts to find us, but this night was different because we later had a reason to be quiet.

We set our bags down at the campsite. Beetle got working on the fire. "Get me some wood, dude." I did as commanded. Steady set his stuff down and immediately got the tunes cranking. Yes, the first song was something about keeping it going till the sun fell down, but a casual observer might have been expecting to hear Devo's "Whip It." Within twenty minutes or so we had a fire to be proud of. Beetle was already opening a can of Franco-American ravioli, one of our favorites. I was munching down cherry Pop-Tarts and Doritos. Things that didn't go together at home made perfect sense at the creek. Steady was busy prepping his cannon for a night mission soon after the darkness arrived. Beetle and I were just sitting back taking it all in. The fire, the food and drink, and the moment were perfect. It seemed weird that Beetle would bring me on a mission with one of his older friends, but I think I knew why. The next night was also a big one for us. Phil Keaggy and Randy Stonehill were coming to Southern Methodist University (SMU) and my brother Joel had tickets. I would be going to my first concert, and Beetle would be there too. I guess he was just letting me come along as a favor to my brother, and I appreciated it. I knew I could be annoying at times.

Darkness fell and the glow of the fire made the night brilliant. Steady grabbed the cannon and I grabbed the jam box. We were listening to 106.1, which was the soundtrack to much of my younger years. We pushed through our cover of cedar trees and into the large field surrounding us. We walked a good fifty yards to an open spot.

"How big will the explosion be?" I asked. Steady liked it when people showed an interest in his experiments.

"Louder than a .22 gun," he stated.

Growing up in Texas, I had heard a few guns, so I had an idea of what to expect. Steady grabbed an orange golf ball and put it in the end of the cannon. He poured in the water and told us to step back. We were in a field with nothing around for a good 200 yards, so it felt safe. He dropped in a black rock and the solution started to fizzle, or maybe even sizzle. A few seconds later, an explosion ripped through the night air. We actually heard the golf ball exit the PVC pipe with a SWOOSH!

"Shit! What the hell?" I shouted. I was thrilled. Steady and Beetle were dancing around like fools, high-fiving each other.

"I told you it would be louder than a .22," Steady threw back at me.

"This is the high school camping mission. You now understand our dominance," Beetle joked.

I was in love with a cannon. We set out to find the golf ball. We gave up after thirty minutes or so. We found it about 200 yards away during another camping mission a year later.

"Can we do it again?" I asked.

"Too loud. Once per trip if we want to stay out of the limelight," Beetle answered. The night was going so well. The cannon would be a part of many missions over the years and will be mentioned more than once in this story. This was the first night I witnessed its glory!

After the blast, we took the equipment back to camp. We all opened drinks and sat around laughing about the great display we had just seen.

"Does anyone want to hit the neighborhood?" Beetle asked.

"I do," I answered.

Steady grumbled some reply but reluctantly agreed to the night mission. It was about 9:45 p.m. now, so most things in Waynesville were settling down. We almost always walked the streets in search of adventure, and found it – at least in our minds. Tonight was different because adventure actually found us.

We were unsure what to do when we hit the streets, so we headed to Steady's pool. We could at least take a dip to cool off before we made any additional plans. We had to make sure we were very quiet because Steady's dad would be pissed if he caught us out there this late when we were supposed to be at the creek. The parents never knew where we were. Only my dad and maybe Mike's had ever been to any of the campsites, and I doubt either could have found our campsite if the chips were down. I guess they figured one of the older boys would show them if they needed to find us. That was probably true.

I stripped down to my boxers and slowly lowered myself into the water. It was still close to ninety degrees, so it was very refreshing. Beetle and Steady got in as well. We swam around quietly and talked of dreams and the future. It was going so well.

After drying off we decided to leave through the gate at the front of Steady's house. We crossed through the gate area undetected and made it to the road. Our group was in no rush, but I figured we would soon head back to our camp. We were about a mile away at this point.

BOOM! BANG! BAM!

The night's calm was broken by three loud crashes. It was a fierce sound like the banging of metal. We looked in the direction of the noise and saw three dudes jump into a yellow Camaro and slam the doors. They peeled off into the late-night air. I don't know if they saw us, but my heart was pumping as house lights came on up and down the street.

"Shit, let's move," Beetle yelled.

I didn't hesitate, but I didn't make it very far. I saw Steady was already sitting on the ground at the feet of Mr. Mavis, his next-door neighbor. My full sprint had me moving in the same direction. I had been seen, and there was no point in running as Mr. Mavis was a friend of my dad and I knew his kid. He was mad and leery, and I could see why. The stop sign on the corner near the end of his yard was now bent and defaced. The dudes had damaged the metal bar that held up the sign. I had no idea how they'd done it, but I understood that I was getting the blame right now, so I thought I would tell Mr. Mavis the truth. There was a chance he would believe me. He did.

Right about that time, Beetle came wandering up to meet us and the angry adult. Beetle had a way of getting away when no one else could, but once he realized we were in decent shape, he knew it was safe to come out. Mr. Mavis told us to go back to the creek and to avoid yellow cars – and the drunken idiots he assumed had destroyed the stop sign. We said thanks and left, relieved that we knew the man.

On the way back to the creek, we spotted the yellow Camaro parked in a driveway a few houses down from my brother's friend Mike's house. Don Waters lived there. It was a nice ranch-style home on about an acre of land. I had always heard weird things about this family. Gary Waters was the youngest boy, and he was in my class. He was considered a weird little kid by much of the school. However, that was not because he did goofy things. I think it was just really unusual that he was chubby with confidence. He had a little weight in the wrong places but acted as if he was a Greek god. His self-image level was off the charts.

Anyway, the car was parked out by the street, and we were happy to see it was empty. However, we could see three or four dudes through the garage windows. They were a little noisy. I couldn't stand it any longer; they had broken public property, so I would break something of theirs. No, that wasn't right, no matter how much I wanted to. But I would leave them a message.

"Anybody got the Shoe Goo?" I whispered.

"Back in my garage," Steady whispered in response.

"How can we get it?"

"Just open my garage slowly. My dad is on the other side of the house and sleeps like a log," Steady said.

I ran the half-mile or so back to Steady's house, which was made quicker by cutting through the small creek behind Beetle's house. I then crossed the field across the street from Beetle's house and walked into another small field that led to Steady's. I decided it was worth a shot, so I slowly opened the garage door a bit. It wouldn't stay in place unless I took it up at least halfway, so I did it quick. I lit up the garage with my flashlight and located the white mischief cream. "Shoe Goo got you" became one of my taglines later in high school, but for now I just needed it to help me call out some jackasses. I grabbed the bottle and backed out of the garage. As I did, the inside light popped on, and I knew I was in for it. I slammed down the garage door in the interest of speed and sprinted out into the night, back to the Waters' house, where Beetle and Steady were waiting for me. At least I hoped they were.

Now that I look back on things, I was pretty bold for a sixth grader. I mean, we really had no idea who had been driving the yellow Camaro, and we knew nothing about these guys. All I knew at this point was that I had Shoe Goo in my hands for the first time. I left a pretty straightforward, pointed message for the car's occupants:

Replace the sign, Jackass.

Beetle and Steady were heading back out into the street when I bolted toward the front door. I just couldn't call it a night with those dudes running around thinking they had not been detected. I hit the doorbell eight times – and I heard it ring, so I knew it was working. Lights shot on inside the house, and I could see people scrambling around. I heard a few choice words being yelled about me, the mysterious man at the door. Just wait until they saw the car! I dashed from the scene, only to see the backs of Beetle and Steady 75 yards ahead of me already. We had about 200 yards to go to get to the safety of the cedar trees at the Shermans' house. We made it.

We sat in the trees for a few minutes catching our breath. We saw a few random cars pass by.

"We solved the case, just like the Three Question Marks," I stated excitedly.

"Only halfway though, because we didn't see it through with arrests and admissions," Beetle mused. Steady looked lost at this point. Beetle filled him in with the needed information.

"You never read the book series *Alfred Hitchcock and the Three Investigators*?" Beetle inquired. "They were some cheesy mysteries we read in elementary." I didn't tell Beetle, but I was still reading them. I loved them.

"Well, at least we know Don Waters is involved. What do we do now?" I asked Beetle. Beetle was about to answer when we heard a loud engine coming slowly down the road.

"Oh shit, they're coming," Beetle whispered sternly. This was a lot more action than Steady was used to.

"Why did you ring the doorbell, you idiot?" Steady asked.

"I just did, because they deserved it," I answered.

We heard yelling as lights came on up and down the street. These guys gave "bold" a new meaning, making this much noise this late at night. The yelling grew closer, and things started to get a little scary.

"We're gonna kill you. We're gonna crush you …"

I knew when to leave well-enough alone, so I dashed out of the trees toward the entrance to the creek. In no time, I was in the Kirks' field and headed across the cement drain toward the ravine. Beetle and Steady were close behind, and we could still hear the yelling. It grew fainter as we got closer to the campsite. I made it to the New-New in record time. I wasted no time in putting out what was left of the coals and getting into the sleeping bag. Beetle and Steady did the same, and we grew still. As far as we knew, nobody outside of our circle knew where this place was, so we thought we were pretty safe for now. The yelling finally disappeared, and our heavy breathing eventually stopped.

As I sat in the sleeping bag, I had never been happier to hang with Beetle. Yes, I was scared, but Beetle was like a big brother who actually paid attention to me. As long as dependable Beetle was around, I knew we would be all right. A few years later, Beetle moved in with us for a year when his parents went through a nasty divorce. He basically was my brother, so it was like being on a family adventure.

The yells from the street were already fading from my mind, and I was drifting off to sleep. I imagined this was a mystery on TV or an adventure from the *Three Question Marks* books. The camp grew quiet, and we were all basically falling asleep. After a few silent moments, the calmness was overtaken by a faint, but building noise off in the distance. The yelling had started again and was moving in our direction.

I don't know if you've ever been terrorized by haunting voices in the middle of the night, but those voices still hit me sometimes to this day. Growing up in Baptist churches in the eighties meant that I'd heard my share of warnings about devil worship, heavy metal music, and how these two things were explicitly linked. I'd also heard many stories about the famous "goat man" that lived in the woods outside a church camp about ten miles from where I lay at this very moment. Even at my young age, I was normally able to write this stuff off as extremism and dismiss it. However, it's different and not as easy in the dark of night. The rational side of our brains was not really in play on this night – but from a sixth grader and two freshmen in high school what could you expect? We were pretty sure we knew at least one of the voices and possibly two of them. We thought we could take those two between the three of us, but it was the unknown quantity we were worried about.

"Shhhh. Shut up," Beetle whispered aggressively. My heart was beating a thousand miles a minute by now.

"What do we do now?" I whispered back to Beetle.

"Shut it, dammit," Beetle responded. I tried hard to comply, but fear was overcoming me. I looked over at Steady, and he was literally zipped completely up in his bag. Was he actually asleep, or was he scared shitless like I was?

The sound was increasing in volume, but I still couldn't make out the words. It was past midnight now, and the night was dark and quiet, so the noise sounded like a hum every minute or so. It grew louder, and we lay there petrified in the dark cover of the cedar trees. Had they seen this place? Did they know where we were? I couldn't answer those questions. I wished Mike was there, or my brother Brett. Mike would light the fire and start yelling back at them. We were not that bold at this stage in our lives.

Time passed. The night grew darker, and the noise grew louder. I could begin to make out what they were yelling. Steady was up, and we all huddled together around the currently un-used firepit. This was sad, as one of the biggest thrills of the camp was chilling around the fire, and yet we were sitting by an empty pit. As I sat there, the fear grew exponentially.

"Bitches beware, we're coming to kill you! We're going to screw you! You're gonna die! Get ready to eat shit!"

By now it was all we could do to stay put. The otherwise dark, silent night made the noise sound like an army was on the way. I pictured a mob with pitchforks, guns, and torches making their way through the field toward me. I couldn't take it much longer. The fury was increasing by the minute, and the group really sounded like they were coming to kill us. Beetle had heard enough. Not taking any more chances, he told us to stand up.

"Get up! We're leaving. Follow me," Beetle exclaimed.

I didn't hesitate. We stepped out of the cover of the cedars and we were exposed. I looked about fifty yards in front of me and saw what appeared to be a mob with lights heading toward us. The lamps were heading our way fast. Beetle took off toward the forest in the other direction, which led to the New. Steady and I followed. I thought I was faster than him, but he proved me wrong. I was eating his dust. With no light, the forest in front of us was difficult to navigate. The yelling increased, and I heard the posse enter the forest.

I finally caught up with Beetle and Steady, who were hunched over catching their breath at the New. This was a great campsite, but it was better known for sure. I always felt like maybe we weren't the only ones that used it.

"What now?" I asked Beetle.

"I don't know," he answered.

Steady was mumbling something about needing to be indoors by dark Friday night or something like that. I can't exactly remember. I do recall thinking he was losing it.

"What about the dunes you told me about?" I desperately inquired.

Beetle stood up, and he was breathing easier than me. It must have been all the classic soccer he used to play. As he was getting ready to speak, a noise broke through the night.

"There they are! Get the Fuckers!"

Beetle tore off down the ravine that led to the pond by the camp-site. We followed. I slipped as I passed through the creek on my way to the hill going up the other side. Steady and Beetle were already at the top. The noise grew closer, and I figured they must be about twenty yards away. I rushed up the side and saw Beetle was stretching the barbed wire fence so I could squeeze through the middle of it. It rattled as he let go, and we all ran for our lives through the field leading to the backside of the Old campsite on the white rock. I looked back and saw people carefully navigating the fence. The fence saved me. They took a while to get over it. I hauled ass while they blundered their way through it.

We came to the Old and looked around. This was the camp-site of legends. In fact, to this day, I have not seen a spot so well laid out for a sizable camping group. When the big creek had water, this spot made you feel like you were on some river in Colorado. We didn't have much time to enjoy it, but I could tell Steady was wondering why we didn't camp here in the first place. I figured we would have been screwed if we had, because they'd probably checked here first. I think all the neighborhood kids knew about this place.

Beetle headed down the rock and crossed the creek. We fol-lowed. Steady wasn't happy about crossing the big creek.

"My shoes are getting wet," he complained.

"Better than getting your ass kicked," I countered.

We made our way across and up the other side, where we negotiated another fence. The noise of the angry mob could still be heard, but it was further behind than it had been. Beetle took off at a sprint across another field. He headed east, and we struggled to keep up. A few minutes later, we were huddled silently in the middle of some Texas rock dunes. This was a series of tiny hills that were a hell of a place to play capture the flag. Beetle had camped out here once before, and I made a note that I wanted to camp out here as well.

We sat in silence for what seemed like an hour. We heard no yelling. I figured the group had given up. I hoped they had, but I was still really scared. Beetle seemed pretty calm. Steady was the first to break the silence.

"What now? Do we go back?" he whispered.

"Not me," Beetle answered.

With that he got up and headed south. We followed. We traveled through some more of the dunes and then entered another field. The walk took a while, but we ended up on a county road. I had never been on this road before. We took a left and headed back to civilization. After a few minutes, we began passing a few houses with land. I didn't recognize anything. It was about 4:30 a.m., and yet I was wide awake. My fear subsided as we walked along. I remember thanking God that Beetle was with us. Nobody knew that land like he did. Later in life, I became the standard for creek navigation. But in the early years, Beetle was the trailblazer. We eventually made it to the ball fields behind Waynesville City Hall. We sat around jaw-jacking until the sun came up. Once we felt secure, we walked the couple of miles back to camp. All I could think about was sleep and Pop-Tarts.

The New-New had clearly been violated in our absence. My sleeping bag had been cut into shreds, and my drinks were now just empty cans on the ground. Fortunately, my Pop-Tarts were still there, so I had a few. Beetle's jam box was crushed and in pieces. Steady's clothes and extras were scattered all over the site. Considering the rage in the voices we'd heard the previous night; I remember thinking we'd got off easy.

"John, are you missing anything?" Beetle asked.

"Just the Dr Pepper that should still be in my cans. Everything else is as I left it," I answered. "Steady, the idiots left your bitchin' cannon," I exclaimed.

"The ruffians were probably perplexed by it, and they simply couldn't understand its value," Steady replied.

Beetle chuckled at the last comment and countered with "Or they were just drunk and took it for a plumbing anomaly!"

We picked the place up, gathered our things, and prepped for the long walk home. I often marvel at our human ability to switch gears so quickly. The night had been traumatic and exhausting, and yet we acted as if we were getting ready to head home from a normal camping experience. Beetle led the way out through the cedar trees and we followed.

"John, what time is Joel picking me up?" Beetle asked.

"The show starts at seven, so I guess around five," I replied casually.

"Cool," Beetle proclaimed.

The long trip home calmed any nerves I still had. I was looking forward to my first concert. Randy Stonehill had a song about American fast food that I loved, and a song about keeping out the devil that *everybody* loved. It seemed we hadn't been able to keep evil from our camp, although we had escaped relatively unscathed. I felt like the "Three Question Marks" had a good idea who the vandals were, but we never heard another thing about it. We had made it through the night, and I was ready to hit the sack. In a little over seven hours, I would be heading to my first concert, and I wanted to be ready. I never told my brothers about that night, and I'm not sure if Beetle ever did. God knows I never informed my parents, or that would have been a premature end to my camping career (and any writing career as a result).

I made it home and dropped my dirty camping stuff in the garage. My mom was sitting watching a show and barely acknowledged me as I quietly passed behind her seat on the couch. I took a quick shower, hit the bunk beds, and passed out. I dreamed of adventures to come and drifted further away from the terror of the previous night.

CHAPTER 4

❋ ❋ ❋

FIRST CONCERT

It was about 4:30 p.m. when my brother Joel barged into the room we shared and woke me up. I had passed out around noon, so I had managed four-and-a-half hours of sleep – not much considering the previous night's adventures. "We're leaving in forty-five minutes," Joel said. He was gone as quickly as he had arrived. I lay in bed really tired, wondering how I would make it through the concert. I was excited, but to be honest I knew of only four or five songs between Randy Stonehill and Phil Keaggy. When wide-awake, I would be pretty excited to see just about any group, but I was groggy and out of sorts. I made my way to the bathroom and got ready.

I then traveled to the kitchen, where my mom had made "home-made" pizza. It was pretty good, and I was glad to see Beetle sitting at the table with Joel. Joel was asking about our camping trip.

"How did it go?"

Beetle quickly glanced at me as if to say, "I got this."

He looked over at Joel and said, "Pretty standard trip. Steady brought the cannon, so we had a little fun. There were no issues due to the loud explosion, so that was good. Basically, an uneventful night."

At that moment, I understood that what goes on at the creek stays at the creek. I figured after more than thirty years I could print the truth, but even now it feels a little weird recounting all these stories for other people. My mom sat down and grabbed a slice of pizza. She looked at me and asked the obvious mom questions.

"Did you not get any sleep last night? You look dead on your feet."

"Yeah, Mom, I slept. I guess I don't always sleep too good on the hard ground," I answered.

"Okay then, just make sure to stay with Joel at the show," Mom advised.

My dad drove us the forty-five minutes or so up to SMU. He dropped us off at a place called the McFarlin Auditorium. (I am not 100 percent sure of this name, but I think I am pretty close.) "I'll be back to pick you up right here at eleven," he said. He then handed me a twenty and drove away. I remember feeling excited as I walked in, but it wasn't like I was walking into a secular concert. Things were pretty calm and well lit, and there was no stale smell of grass in the air. No smoking or drinking was going on, which I guess made it a pretty safe place for a sixth grader to hang out for an evening. Still, I would rather have been walking into a Van Halen or Michael Jackson show. If my memory serves me correctly, this was the year of "Jump," "Hot for Teacher," and

"Thriller." These were all great tunes, and no Christian song I remember even came close to their level of quality. However, Phil Keaggy could play the guitar as well as anybody, and there was even a rumor that he had been in Jimmy Hendrix's backup band. I never researched this to see if it was true, but that didn't matter: I would know as much as I needed to within a few hours, when the concert was done.

When I got in the door, I remember seeing quite a number of people in the lobby. Randy Stonehill was the opening act, but the guy had just put out a song that all the Christians I knew loved: "Shut De Dó." This song got people in the door. His album *Equator* had done well in Christian circles. Phil Keaggy was on the *Underground* Tour, but the early energy I saw was based on Randy. This was also my first experience with the "shirt tables." To the right of the doors into the concert hall were several tables with people selling shirts, tapes, and pins. (These small, round artist pins were popular in those days). I stood in line a few minutes and bought a Keaggy shirt. It was a white jersey with red sleeves and cost me twelve bucks. I then made my way down front to my seat. Surprisingly, my brother had bought good seats. We were on the fifth row to the right of the auditorium. It had to be at least thirty minutes or so before the concert was due to start. After going to many concerts since that night, I have learned that the more things change, the more they stay the same. Yes, even Christian bands made the audience wait forever at concerts. I don't know if it is supposed to build the excitement or give more time for T-shirt and concession sales, but it drives me crazy. This night kicked off at least forty-five minutes late.

As I sat there tired in my seat listening to Beetle and Joel's small talk, I couldn't help but think back several weeks to the local Baptist church's New Year's Eve youth group party. My brothers had maintained ties there even after we had joined the home church. I had never gone to that youth group, primarily because I wasn't old enough yet. However, they had a big event that they wanted people to see, so they opened up the doors to parents and kids alike.

I don't know if this was a Christian community thing or an American eighties culture thing, but it sure was a big deal for a while in our town. What do I speak of? The Air Band competition. Basically, groups of people would form "air bands." They would make fake guitars out of wood and decorate them to the nines. They would put a real set of drums on stage as a prop. Each group would lip-synch to two songs by the band of their choice. The teams were judged on energy, prop uniqueness, lip-synch skill, and general audience response. The main bands I remember from the night were Petra, Whiteheart, Rez Band, and Randy Stonehill (because his *Equator* album was really popular that year). My brothers both had a band in the competition, and they seemed to have a good time. I at least got a few cool air guitars to use in my room for my high school years. I'll never forget this goofy teen lip-synching to "Shut De Dó." He tried to get the New Year's Eve crowd to sing along with the chorus, and nobody responded. It was embarrassing but funny. I was shaken out of my daydream by a drop in the theater lights, and then I heard Randy Stonehill sing the song for real.

The song was great, and the crowd was really into it. He sang three or four more songs and was done. All of the songs were pretty well received, and the guy knew how to work a crowd. I saw him once more that night, when he came out to sing a duet with Keaggy ("Save the Children"). After Randy Stonehill's set, it was about 8:30 p.m. and I was dead tired. It was another thirty minutes before Phil Keaggy came out. He was really good, but I had never heard most of the songs. I remember thinking that Keaggy rivaled Eddie van Halen's guitar skills on a song called "Full Circle." However, after that song I remember no other. I actually fell asleep in my seat at my first concert. Beetle understood and let me sleep because he knew I wasn't really a big fan of either of these performers. I remember Beetle waking me up when it was over and handing me a Coke to drink. We made our way out to the curb to catch a ride with my dad, who was on time, as always.

The ride home was a blur because I could barely keep my eyes open. We drove down 75 to I-35 South. I stayed awake long enough to see downtown Dallas. I loved the big city at night, especially the Reunion Tower Ball. Somebody had told me there was a restaurant at the top! Beetle and Joel were analyzing the guitar skills of Phil Keaggy and relaying a report on them to my dad. This wasn't really my thing, since I was the only guy in the car that didn't play the guitar.

"Is he as good as you thought?" Dad inquired.

"Better," Joel exclaimed.

"Right, the guy is a genius on that thing. His acoustic sets were brilliant," Beetle added.

This kind of talk carried on the whole way home I presume, as I could hear a constant hum while I drifted in and out of consciousness. I remember thinking I would have had more fun if it had been Petra, Rez Band, or even Amy Grant, who at least had more songs I knew. Still, this is a good memory because it was the first real concert I went to. Through the years, I ended up seeing Rez Band, Mylon Lefevre and Broken Heart, Petra, and Stryper. These were all great Christian bands, and I enjoyed them more because I was older and understood more of what was going on. However, my real fun came in high school after getting a car and the freedom to go where I wanted to. I saw some really great shows in the late eighties, including George Michael, the Cure, Oingo Boingo, Depeche Mode, and the Smiths. I had tickets for Bon Jovi but ended up grounded for that one and didn't get to go. Even so, concert opportunities in the Dallas area were abundant.

We finally reached home, and I had never been so happy to hit the sheets. I think I was out like a light within three minutes. I woke up feeling good the next day and got ready for school. I put on my Phil Keaggy concert shirt and hit school excited for the new day. A few people asked me who Keaggy was, and I did the best I could to explain, but with no radio tunes to point them to, they quickly lost interest. I felt pretty good and started wondering when I would get to camp at the creek by myself, with no older kids. My parents were noncommittal each time I asked. It was about a month later when I got invited for the second time that year. I was ecstatic that Beetle wanted me to come along. I hoped it would go better this time than before. It did.

CHAPTER 5

✳ ✳ ✳

THE INITIATION OF INITIATIONS (FARMER BROWN)

f I haven't mentioned it already, I was (and am) part of a network of people called "creekers." This network is made up of individuals who regularly camped at our designated creek campsites. The key word in this description is "regularly." Those of us who lived for these missions make up an elite fraternity. The core of our unit comprises four people. Several others are also creekers but are more loosely associated with our group. These men and women are important to our existence, but they are not "voting members." Many came on a single mission and never came back again. One likely reason for this might have been our high entrance standards. The first such standard was a simple "initiation." College fraternities and sororities have entire weeks dedicated to these rituals, but we needed just one night to sort the wheat from the chaff. I was not the creator of this policy, but I happened to be around for the first confirmed initiation mission. I later brought the institution to a whole new level, but the purity of the night I'm about to describe laid the groundwork for a legacy.

It was a month or so after the angry mob had chased us from our camp. I was almost afraid to go back, but Beetle encouraged me to take the plunge. He said the group that had chased us was probably a bunch of drunks that wouldn't have known what to do if they had caught us. I wasn't so sure, but if he was going back to the creek so was I. We had maybe a month of school to go, and I needed some adventure. The concert had gone okay, although I had fallen asleep as the night wore on, thanks to my adventure of the previous night. To cut to the chase, it was just time to go back. I was lucky Beetle had asked me back, and I wasn't going to blow the chance I had been given. The cast wasn't that different than on our last trip. This time it was Beetle, Steady, myself, and Dillen. Dillen was a skinny giant from the other side of town. He must have stood six feet four but weighed only 175 or so. He bulked up later in high school.

We made it to the New about 6:00 p.m. It was still daylight, but we had a fire already. Steady and Dillen had argued the whole trip, about stupid things I can't even remember. Dillen was friends with my brother Joel, but he had no use for me. I had been to his house multiple times because our moms were friends. He was an early version of a video game master. I usually sat and watched him play Space Invaders or Warlords. Every now and then he would let me take a shot, but that was rare. Beetle and Dillen had already made several creek trips as a duo.

He was much more comfortable outdoors than Steady was, and he was relentless in his needling of Steady.

"Does anyone have a can opener?" Steady inquired.

"Ask your mom," Dillen answered.

"How sanitary is this cooking pot?" Steady continued.

Dillen couldn't help himself; he just had to poke at Steady. "How sanitary is your mom?"

This kind of ribbing continued the whole trip. Some of it was funny, and some of it was not. Steady was a smart guy, but he was out of his league dealing with Dillen.

We sat around the fire experiencing the endless banter. Dillen let up on Steady for a few minutes while Beetle told us about seeing a dude in a cowboy hat down here a few weeks ago. The guy had looked rough but was just feeding the cows something out of his beat-up Chevy truck. He had seen Beetle and told him to get off the land or he would call the cops. Beetle had run down the ravine and wasn't sure if the guy tried to follow him. There was no way some old man could catch Beetle on this property without help. For some reason, this encounter that should have frightened us away made the place even more magical. Beetle was in a good mood, so I figured I'd talk while I could.

"Seems pretty calm tonight."

Beetle let out a satisfied sigh after finishing off his Dinty Moore stew.

"Good night for some fishing, if the creek had anything to fish for," said Beetle.

I'd seen Beetle pull a few out of the creek, but that had been closer to the Shermans' part of the creek than here. I always assumed the pond by the New had some fish, although it looked more like a swamp befitting Yoda's home world than a bustling interchange for fish. To this day, I have never seen anyone pull a fish out of that small pond. We had a few spots around town that yielded some fish, but we never really caught a bounty. The Two Ponds was a great spot, but I believe it was overfished. Another great visual spot was called Rocky Falls. This was closer to Waynesville city center. It had a small section of rapids that you could actually raft over in early spring, before the creek dried up. Anyway, Beetle had pulled a few bass out of there as well.

I scanned the camp for a fishing pole and realized it was just small talk.

"We can go home and get some poles. I'm game," I said hopefully.

"Naw, the fire is rolling and the Eagle is putting out tonight," Beetle answered. The Eagle was a local rock station, and Beetle was right: it was providing a great soundtrack for the night. So we basically just sat there humming along to the music and watching Steady parry Dillen's insults. It was quite entertaining. It grew dark, and the moon was nearly full. I was happy to be back at the creek and vowed internally that I would never let anyone run me off again.

"Why are you even here? I thought you couldn't come out on Saturday night, right?" Dillen asked.

"That's Friday night, and what am I supposed to do, stay at home and play video games or basketball?" Steady shot back. Steady was clearly learning how to respond after a couple of hours of dealing with Dillen's bullshit.

"Sorry, I can't always keep my 'cult' timetables straight," Dillen replied.

"It's not a cult. We're Christians just like you," Steady stated.

"Whatever, jackass," said Dillen.

I was interested in this line of conversation because I had heard of the Seventh-day Adventists but knew nothing about them. It was clear Dillen didn't know much either. Beetle kept the fire rolling as the two continued their banter. I think they were both enjoying the intellectual stimulation. I just hoped it wouldn't end up in a fight, or worse. Maybe they would even become friends. I quit paying attention when Quiet Riot's "Cum on Feel the Noise" started to play. This was one the parents would object to, I was sure. The night went on and we must have heard every current hit at least once. Yes and REO Speedwagon were regulars. I was having a ball.

Out of nowhere, Beetle emptied a canteen to put out the fire and began waving his arms around.

"Shut up. Shut up, dudes," Beetle whispered very loudly.

I did as Beetle commanded. It felt like déjà vu to me.

"Can you hear that?"

"I can't hear shit," Dillen responded.

"What is it?" Steady asked.

"Quiet. I don't know yet. Listen," Beetle warned.

We sat in the dark. I could hear trees rustling and brush moving. The sound was faint but definitely real. There were voices on the wind as well, but they weren't as menacing as the last time we'd been approached. No, these voices were a little scary as well, but they seemed to be much more controlled. I couldn't quite make out what they were saying. Several minutes passed as we sat in silence. The sounds grew closer. I could start to make out some of the words.

"Land ... Mine ... Fire ... Trespassing ..."

There was also a dull, thumping noise. What was going on? Had the landowners figured out we were on their land. Why now? As far as I knew, camping had been going on out here for at least a few years. Beetle then shot me a look that instantly calmed me down. I don't know exactly why, but it did. Steady was packing his stuff quietly and was almost done.

"What are you doing?" Dillen whispered to Steady.

"Getting out of here. I'm never doing this again," Steady answered.

Steady was moving quickly, and he seemed almost panicked. He finished up and sat down.

"Are you coming? I'm not sure if I know the way home. Are you coming?" Steady asked Beetle.

"Maybe he doesn't know where we are. There is a good chance he will miss us," Beetle answered with more confidence than I was feeling.

"Who's on my land? I know you're there. I'll find you. Just come on out. I won't give up till I know who you are" the voice yelled clearly.

The guy had to be within fifty or sixty yards. I couldn't tell if there was another voice, but there was also a banging on the trees. It sounded like someone was hitting them with a pole or something. When Steady heard the voice this last time, he grabbed his stuff and took off running through the woods. He was not heading toward home. His running was panicked and sporadic. He turned on a flashlight and was making a bunch of noise. He was scared out of his mind, and it was rubbing off on me. Beetle jumped up to follow him.

"Stay here, John," Beetle whispered as he ran in Steady's direction.

"What? Why would I stay to get caught?"

At that moment, I noticed Dillen laughing. He wasn't even bothering to keep the noise down. He grabbed my arm as I got ready to run toward Beetle.

"Dude, it ain't Farmer Brown. It's Joel," Dillen told me.

I breathed a huge sigh of relief. I could hear "Farmer Brown" still yelling and beating on trees in the distance.

After a few additional minutes of yelling and acting the part of Farmer Brown, my brother Joel came strolling into camp. Joel and Dillen were friends, and they had clearly coordinated this as an initiation of Steady. I didn't know where Beetle and Steady were now, as I could no longer see Steady's light or hear his frantic rustling through the woods. Dillen and Joel high-fived.

"That was classic. You almost even had me fooled," Dillen exclaimed.

"You did have me fooled," I added to the conversation.

"Not some of my best work, but it got the job done," Joel responded.

He grabbed one of my Dr Peppers out of the cooler and sat on the overhanging limb east of the fire. He then began relating some story I don't remember about football to Dillen.

Joel was a sophomore at Possum Fields High, so he was a year ahead of Beetle, Dillen, and Steady. He was a National Honor Society member and one of the stars of the school drama department's one-act play. The school's drama team made it to state one of his high school years. Joel had played a role in *To Kill a Mockingbird*, and he'd won some All-Star cast award along with it. Besides being a pretty good student and actor, he was a decent athlete. He played both offense and defense on the football team up through his tenth-grade year, until he realized he was limited by size and would never make it in college football, much less the pros. If all that wasn't enough, he was also a pretty good guitar player. He liked to make up goofy songs and play them wherever and whenever he got the chance.

Joel was a genuinely good guy, so the initiations were the extent of any marginal behavior for him (other than being a little too competitive in recreational sports, as I demonstrated in an earlier chapter). He plays a role in some later missions, so I figured I'd give you a little more background info on him. Joel was a good brother, but it was a rare thing for me to be in on a creek mission he was part of. The fun of being on one of my big brother's creek missions didn't last long, as his presence was gone almost as soon as it began. Although this wasn't the last time I would camp with him in life, it was one of the last times I would see him at the creek.

Twenty or so minutes later, Beetle and Steady came walking back into camp. Beetle had clearly pulled off a masterpiece of personal counseling and manipulation to get Steady to come back. I figured the initiation would have been the last straw, after having to deal with Dillen's taunts all night. Anyway, they were back and ready to continue with the trip.

"You didn't hurt yourself in the woods, did you?" Joel asked.

"No. Why did you do that? What problems have I ever caused you?" Steady asked.

"None, man. We're good. It's just a rite of passage. Consider yourself eligible for creeker status," Joel replied.

"I'm not sure I want creeker status if you guys do this kind of stuff," Steady lamented.

"Come on, dude, you know we're just having some fun! We all went through the initiation," Dillen teased. (This may have been a lie, because I had heard the creek history stories and I didn't think any of these three had gone through the trials. In fact, as far as I knew, they created the "tradition").

Steady was clearly upset, and I didn't think this trip could be salvaged for him. My brother Joel was almost always a peacemaker, so he tried to get Steady feeling good.

"You took it better than some have. I mean, I've seen people just grab their stuff and leave. You came back. We're having a fun time. The next time you can be Farmer Brown."

Steady frowned as he considered this proposition.

"No thanks. I won't participate in this activity again."

"Don't blow it out of proportion, dude. It's no big deal," Beetle downplayed.

As if on cue, the radio began to play Queen's mega-hit "Another One Bites the Dust." The subject changed, and Steady sat by himself messing with his cannon. Joel and Dillen joked about the "penny races" both had gone through at Possum Fields High. The penny races were legitimate races in which two freshmen pushed a penny with their nose on the cement for a certain distance. Victory was the only way out of the initiation. This left an impression on me, as I realized they had endured initiation somewhere – just maybe not at the creek.

After another hour or so, Joel said bye and left for home. Steady was still not very talkative, so we let the fire go down and hit the sack. The next day would be a good one even for Steady, and this entire trip became the foundation for my journey into the creek history books. This was the night I learned of the initiation. The next day I learned the joy of Fox and Hounds, which morphed into Capture the Flag later in my career. I also got the idea for the creek "honor circle" as a way of fighting to settle differences. It all came to me on this trip.

We woke up to sunshine. The radio was playing, and all seemed good. Even Steady was in a good mood. Beetle was down the hill messing around at the pond. Dillen was eating a Pop-Tart and loading a BB gun. Steady was cooking some ravioli over the fire. All was well, and the transgressions of the previous night seemed to be a distant memory for Steady. I finished off my Doritos and joined Beetle. Dillen had gone down the mini-ravine and up the other side. He'd crossed the fence and was scanning the trees for birds.

"What are we gonna do now?" I asked Beetle.

"Whatever. I guess we can hunt birds," Beetle answered.

"Cool. Can I get a few shots off yours?" I asked. Beetle was the only owner of a BB gun in the crew.

"When Dillen's done you can," he answered.

Steady was still at camp polishing off his Franco-American.

"Hurry up, Steady. The birds won't hang around all day. Crank up the cannon," Beetle said loud enough for Steady to hear him up the hill at the campsite.

"The cannon has always been ready. That's not the problem. I didn't bring the sodium rocks," Steady replied. "Unfortunately, there will be no explosion this morning."

Dillen seemed to have been listening all along from the other side of the creek.

"Then why are you here? Without the cannon, your mom can't save you," Dillen yelled. "The cannon is the only reason I told Beetle to bring you. Why don't you go home?" Dillen inquired.

Beetle didn't seem happy with this line of conversation. He was jockeying two diverse types of horses with these two.

"Tone it down, Dillen. No reason for that shit," Beetle stated with authority.

"I got to take it from his mom and now you? Hell no, dude needs to go back to the Boy Scouts," Dillen shot back angrily.

I don't think Steady fit the scout stereotype, but I didn't know him all that well.

"My mom has nothing to do with this. My cannon is reserved for elite purposes, and you are not worthy of the cost of the sodium ammo. So go back to the barbaric practice of hunting birds for sport and leave me alone, please," Steady stated calmly.

I wasn't sure how Dillen would take Steady having a set of balls, and I was right to be concerned.

"Really, I'll hunt you. Shut up, jackass," Dillen yelled as he popped off a shot at a robin in a tree. I didn't see any feathers fly, but I'll never forget what I did see.

Steady slowly set down his drink and tossed his granola bar dessert aside. He calmly started down the ravine to the bottom and then made the turn and very uncalmly raced up the side. He got to the fence line and tried to leap over, but his foot got caught at the last minute. Beetle and I watched in disbelief, while Dillen was laughing so hard he dropped the BB gun. Steady untangled his foot and bum rushed Dillen, tackling him to the ground. He threw a few punches that landed, but Dillen was still overcome by laughter as they wrestled on the other side of the fence line.

"Stop!" Beetle yelled as the two grappled. I would call the fight more a test of strength and will than a traditional fistfight. The two were on their feet, and Dillen still had a smile on his face. I think he was honestly impressed that Steady had stood up for himself. The smile quickly vanished when Steady grabbed his hunting knife. He held it in a threatening manner toward Dillen. Dillen bent into a fight launch stance as Steady moved in. Dillen grabbed the arm holding the knife, and they fought for it. I was starting to get concerned. Beetle raced up the side toward the fight, and I followed. We both crossed the fence in record time. Dillen had somehow flipped Steady to the ground on his back. Steady was holding the knife between him and Dillen. This was the reverse of what you normally see on TV: normally the person on top is holding the knife, and the person on bottom is desperate to keep the knife from engaging the target. Here, Steady was holding the knife up toward Dillen, who was holding that arm with both hands. The struggle continued. Beetle tried feverishly to get the two to stop. The whole event was surreal, and I guess I never believed either of them really wanted to stab or hurt the other.

"Quit it. Stop it now!" Beetle demanded again.

Dillen wrestled the knife away from Steady and tossed it to the side. He now had a "ground and pound" position on Steady, but he didn't take advantage of it. He just sat there as Steady tried to maneuver his way out of the horrible fight position he was now in. With the knife gone, Dillen's smile had returned. Beetle and I rushed in to grab him. I am not sure we could have moved him if he hadn't let us. Steady breathed a sigh of relief. Like nothing had happened, Dillen picked up the BB gun and headed through the field toward the Old campsite.

"You okay, dude?" Beetle asked.

"It seems I miscalculated the strength of my opponent. That won't happen again," Steady stated, almost jokingly.

"You want to go home?"

"Of course not. The trip is not yet complete." Steady surprised us.

Beetle and Steady headed toward the Old, and I followed, not understanding what had just taken place. Now that I look back as a man, I see they were simply involved in a dance for supremacy. Neither really wanted to hurt the other, but Dillen wanted to be the clear alpha. Steady wasn't so concerned about that, but he didn't recognize Dillen as the alpha, and that was the problem. Creek history will later reveal that neither of these foes was the actual alpha on the scene that day. Beetle just didn't care about such things.

We finally caught up to Dillen at the Old campsite on the white rock. He had a bird at his feet. I wanted to hunt, but the moment was over.

"Wanna play Fox and Hounds?" Dillen inquired.

"That would be incredible," Steady answered, as if they were friends and the previous events had not taken place.

"Who will be the first fox?" Beetle inquired.

"Steady gets to pick," Dillen answered.

"I'll be the fox," Steady confidently confirmed.

If you've ever played Fox and Hounds, then you know it is basically a reverse version of Hide and Seek. Instead of one person looking for everyone else, everyone else looks for just one person. The game is enjoyable enough in a large house and a few acres. Imagine playing the game on hundreds of acres. Then it can be loads of fun – and a lot of exercise as well. We gave a three-minute head start, and Steady raced off down the white rock away from the campsite. He cut up a trail to the left and was then out of sight. The clock was ticking, and I was already anxious to give chase. We heard a fence rattle and then nothing. Steady must have been in the field before the New and the platform, but who knew where he might travel from there. We waited another minute and then took off down the creek at a brisk walk.

"Where do you think he went?" Dillen asked Beetle.

"Who knows? He's only been here three times, so he may get lost," Beetle laughingly answered.

"I bet he goes back to the New to get his stuff and heads home. He could keep us looking for hours," I mused.

"No, that's a clear violation of creek code, so that's out of the question," Beetle made clear.

"All right, where then?" Dillen liked to be in control, but he didn't know the land as well as Beetle.

"I think we should hit all the campsites, because he is going to stay in the areas he is comfortable in," Beetle stated.

"To the New we go," Dillen decided.

The New was still where we had left it. I was clearly wrong, because all Steady's stuff was where it had been prior to the fight. Beetle looked around approvingly and headed through the forest toward the New-New. It would take us about eight minutes at a normal pace, and there was no reason to waste our energy when we weren't sure where Steady was. I was loving this game, although I bet it could be nerve-racking if you were the fox, especially if people quit looking for you in a large area like this but didn't tell you. I wondered what other spots Steady could be in as we wandered into the New-New.

It was bright and warm as we searched. Steady was not at the New-New, but he had been there. In the middle of the camp, which had been home to our terror during our previous outing, was a message scrawled in the dirt:

You'll never find this fox!!!!

It had been nearly an hour. I could tell Dillen wasn't used to losing, because he was starting to get stressed out.

"Where could he be? This is screwed up," Dillen muttered.

"He is winning, but we must complete the chase," Beetle answered happily.

I was happy too, even happier to see Steady get the better of Dillen for once.

"We need to step up our game. We have given him too much time. Split up. I'll take the New. Dillen stay here. John, hit the Old again. If you find him, yell out loud and bring him back to camp at the New. If you don't find him, meet back at the Old in half an hour anyway," Beetle ordered.

I was happy to be able to run off some nervous energy. I rushed through some woods and into an open field. Several cows glanced up at me as I raced by. I was free at the creek. The field was the land of possibilities. I ran toward the white rock. I looked to my left and saw a dog sniffing something about forty yards away from me. I didn't care. I came to a fence, carefully climbed it, and headed down the path to the creek. The creek was running on this sunny morning. I even saw a fish swimming downstream with the current. I turned right and walked the fifty yards or so to the Old. As I looked around, I determined that I would camp here more. I was ready for a solo mission, which meant camping with kids my own age, without my brothers or any of their friends. My parents still didn't think I was ready, but I would convince them.

I looked around the site, but Steady was nowhere to be found. There were no obvious messages here either. I sat down and just dreamed with the rush of the creek. It was truly beautiful. After fifteen minutes or so, I heard some movement in the brush above me.

"Hey, up here, John!"

I looked up, and there was Steady. What a spot!

"How long have you been there?" I asked.

"Longer than you've been here," Steady answered.

"Wow, that's a great spot. I had no idea you were up there. I guess we should head back now."

"Not on your life," Steady refused.

"Okay then, what's the plan?"

As Steady told me the plan, a smile formed on my face. I moved into my position to keep watch. About twenty minutes later, I carefully climbed a tree and focused my breathing. I was covered almost completely by branches and brush. Steady was within a couple of feet of me. He put his finger to his mouth as he spoke, "Shhh." He didn't even need to say it.

Beetle and Dillen approached from the field between the New and the Old. I heard the fence rattle as someone crossed it.

Then another rattle. They walked into the campsite. Dillen was pacing around in a panic.

"Where are they, man? What the hell? Don't they know the rules?" Dillen asked.

"It's been over an hour. I'm starting to worry a little. What if something's happened to one of them? Or both of them?" Beetle asked.

"We need to leave. They must have gone home. Something doesn't feel right," Dillen declared.

"I can't leave John, he's just in sixth grade, dude," Beetle replied.

"Screw him. Joel can come back for him," Dillen answered. He was really nervous. I had never seen him that nervous. He was usually cool and collected.

Steady slowly turned his head to me. He put up three fingers and began the countdown.

3 ... 2 ... 1

We jumped from our hiding spots and landed right behind Dillen.

"The fox has landed!" Steady yelled in triumph.

"Shit! Oh my God! Damn it!" Dillen screamed in surprise.

Steady and I roared with laughter. Dillen was breathing heavily, and Beetle was catching his breath as well. I had never felt such a rush. Dillen was so flustered. He sat down on the ground and held his head between his knees. He was really upset. Beetle held up a hand to me to high-five. I returned it with glee. It may have been my finest moment of elementary school. Beetle was clearly impressed with our ability to remain still and quiet.

"Great plan, Steady. Excellent work," I told him.

"It was nothing," he mused.

Steady shook Beetle's hand. Beetle was pretty happy for somebody who had just been played like this.

Steady walked over to Dillen and bent down in front of him. He spoke loudly so we all could hear, "That's for your mom."

Steady then crossed the fence and headed back to camp. I followed, as he was clearly in a zone. We gathered our stuff and began to march back toward civilization. It was now past noon, and Beetle and Dillen were just starting to gather their things for the return trip. I stayed with Steady because he needed a companion to share in his victory. Beetle understood this.

We made it home by 1:00 that afternoon. Steady never camped with us all night at the creek again, but I have the memories.

✳ ✳ ✳

CHAPTER 6

GRADE SIX ANALYSIS: ONE CRAZY YEAR

Midway through the first half of my second-grade year, Alex Bields Elementary first opened its doors to students. I spent almost five years at the new school, which was as long as anybody up to that point. It was much cleaner and closer to my house than Possum Fields Elementary, which was across the railroad tracks. Waynesville was a smaller town, but there were more than enough kids to fill up the new school. As I mentioned in the previous chapters, I loved my creek camping experiences, but at that age they were still few and far between. Besides camping, there was of course school and soccer. School was okay, and soccer was fun because I was on a good team.

One Saturday morning everything changed. I remember feeling like the anchor of the "doomsday defense" as the center fullback of my squad. Sometimes, I played center halfback (or "rover," as my coach liked to call it). My team had locked up first place earlier that fall, a full two weeks before this game. I had made it through the season with only a few yellow cards. I guess the refs were getting used to my rougher style of play, since I had been able for the first time to avoid suspensions.

This particular Saturday was cold for Texas, hovering somewhere in the forties at game time. My team won the game six-nothing, but at high cost. Our main forward, Harry Lee, broke his foot in a weird collision with a rival defender. In addition to this bad news, I could barely walk by the end of the game. I remember the coach telling me I must have twisted my knee and that it would feel better after a little rest. As this was the second-to-last game of the season and we had already clinched the division, all would be fine. I hopped off the field, and my dad helped me to the car. We stopped at Mickey D's, which is what we called McDonald's.

By Wednesday of the following week, the knee was no better. In fact, my right knee was also hurting now. My mom made an appointment for me to see the doctor. The doctor gave me bad news. I would miss the next season due to some cartilage problem. Basically, he said, bone was hitting bone and if it didn't get better with ten weeks of no running and limited walking, I would need surgery of some kind. Needless to say, I was bummed by this news. It meant no PE and no recess, but the worst part was missing my last season of soccer with the team I had been with for the past three years. I remember sitting in the classroom on the new computer playing Oregon Trail while the other kids ran free outside. This sucked, but the knee did get better.

The soccer injury wasn't the only memorable part of my sixth-grade year. I had the luck of getting Ms. Gowry for a teacher. This woman was the one radical lefty in a sea of moderates and conservatives. This was my first experience with a real liberal. She was nice and competent, but the woman believed the opposite of what I had been taught on virtually everything. For example, at Christmastime she told us that Jesus was a man who lived a good life, but he was not God. She also told us there was no Heaven, but that our dead loved ones lived on in our hearts as long as we remembered them. I wondered what that meant for our loved ones after they died. Did they just disappear from existence? Anyway, we still learned a lot that year from Ms. Gowry, and I never felt threatened by her ideas. Of all my grade school teachers, I remember her the best. There was perhaps one main reason for this.

Sometime during my sixth-grade school year, Ms. Gowry read a cool book to us. The book was a murder mystery without the solution. I can't remember the title, but the publisher offered ten thousand dollars to the first person to submit the correct solution. They wanted the name of the killer for each murder, the motive, and the means. Ms. Gowry read this fascinating story to us each day for a couple of weeks until we got to the end. We then came up with a class response to the mystery. That was by far the most fun I had ever had in a classroom. In many years of education after, I never equaled that experience. It turned out we were wrong on a few of the answers. We got something like four out of six – not bad for a bunch of twelve-year-olds.

Because I didn't get to play a lot of sports that year, I remember the academic stuff more keenly. If my mom had known the politics and ideology of my teacher, the following situation might have turned out even worse for me. I guess I brought it all on myself, but because of it I learned a vital lesson that I still follow to this day: Don't bring shit home with you!

You've probably guessed by now that I come from a pretty conservative, Christian background. Clearly not all of it stuck, but we each forge our own path in the world. I can honestly say that my parents were and still are very sincere in their beliefs. However, the results of our upbringing (my brothers, sister, and me) are still being tabulated. Out of five marriages, we are batting three for five, sporting a 40 percent divorce rate. I guess that is probably a little better than the national average. Although this divorce percentage is not attributable to me, I have done things in life much more reckless and stupid than screw up a relationship. My life could have turned out a lot different if I had just followed the advice of my parents. But all things considered, I'm glad I didn't always do what they wanted. The basis for this policy (or even strategy) goes all the way back to sixth grade, when I made the serious mistake of bringing the "shit" home.

The problem I speak of took the form of a simple Judy Blume book. I remember it was called *Then Again, Maybe I Won't*. I can't really remember much about the book, mainly because it was ripped from my hands in a display of moral outrage. I was excited to read a book other than *The Three Questions Marks* or *Encyclopedia Brown* for once, but I made the mistake of telling my mom about one scene in the book in which the main character had just received a set of binoculars and discovered the beauty of the older high school girl living across the street. I don't know what happened in the book, but

I know the trouble this fictional character caused me. My mom talked to my dad about the book that night after our dinner, and she decided to go and speak with the librarian the next day. What had I done?

The librarian spoke with my mom. The situation remained unresolved after this conversation. In other words, the librarian had not yielded to the hurricane known as P.J. Decker. My mom had talked about how the book was too mature for elementary students, saying that the content would open our impressionable eyes to situations we weren't ready for. I don't know if she actually read the book before making this statement or if she had gotten the opinion from *Guideposts* or some other Christian magazine. Regardless of why or what, she was on a mission. She met with the principal the next day, who agreed with the library staff that the book was appropriate and would remain in the library. Most people would have let it go at this point, but my mom was certainly not "most people."

After hearing another denial from the superintendent, my mom somehow had the clout to get the topic on the agenda of the next school board meeting. By then, word had traveled around the school that I was a punk who wasn't allowed to read anything but the Bible. It wasn't worth arguing with people, so I just sucked it up. Mom arranged to have a number of local parents accompany her to the meeting for backup. (She worked in the local community theater, so she knew a whole lot of people.) They all spoke at the meeting, and the librarian didn't even show up. End result: Book banned from Alex Bields Elementary library. I took a lot of shit at school about that, but it wasn't too bad, because I missed much of recess that year due to my knee issues, which gave the kids less opportunity to jack with me about the book and my mom.

Even though I was embarrassed by what my mom had done, I was proud of the fact that she had triumphed over the school on this issue. I learned that if she believed enough in a mission, she simply could not be stopped. She could, and did, accomplish any goal she set her mind to. More importantly, I learned that I would never again give her fodder for a crusade. She was easily triggered and loved to exercise influence whenever possible. I closed up and did my own thing. Music, books, movies, and basically life were all filtered before I let them get in front of my mom. The craziest part is that she reads stuff that would make Judy Blume blush and Agatha Christie hide under the covers. Still, she obviously wanted better for her kid, for me.

That was a long school year, and I felt like I had finally earned the right to go on a solo mission to the creek. By that, I mean without my brothers or any of the older kids. I wanted a trip with just dudes my age. I had recently met Jerry Kiplin on the bus. He was Brett's buddy Mike's little brother. He also heard the call of the creek, and together we talked the parents into letting us camp alone at the creek.

On the evening of the last day of school that year, we loaded up our stuff and headed to the creek. This time we didn't go through the Shermans' yard; we just walked across the street from Jerry's house. We went through the backyard of the Smitters. There was a well-worn path to the white rock of the creek I had never seen before. The trip there was easy and accident free. The path even led across the creek and up the other side to a field that would start us on our journey. As I stepped into the field, I nearly fell backward as I gawked in amazement. What was I looking at? The only description that has stood the test of time is the best answer: the Structures.

CHAPTER 7

* * *

THE STRUCTURES

The end of my sixth-grade year was both fun and scary. The fun part was completing my time at Alex Bields Elementary. The scary part was knowing that in three months I would be going to Possum Fields Junior High. I remember Ms. Gowry giving me a form asking for electives and if I would be in the honors program. I chose band as my elective and left the honors choices alone, even though I was qualified to take them all. I look back on that choice now and wonder if it was the right one. I mean, would things have turned out differently if I had hung closer to the smarter kids? My reason at the time was that I just wanted to be normal. Ms. Gowry picked up my form and frowned at me.

"Why don't I see honors on here?"

She was clearly displeased with my selections, which probably shouldn't have been left up to a twelve-year-old.

"I am ready to try the middle road. I already know all the Talented and Gifted kids," I said.

"Whatever floats your boat. If that's how you feel, I'll sign and send it," she answered with a disappointed tone.

The bus ride home went smoothly, like it had the past few weeks. I was finally able to run and play outside again, so I had struck up a new friendship with Jerry Kiplin, who was the little brother of my brother Brett's friend Mike. Although we had ridden the same bus for the past three years, we had never really hung out. We were in the same grade, but we had never been in the same class. One day we had to share a seat on the bus and I realized he was actually pretty cool, and now I went to his house after school a few days a week. His room was a converted attic, and it felt segregated from the rest of the house. He liked rock music and girls, so we were on the same page. When he realized I loved the creek as much as he did, he asked when we could camp together. We hatched the plan that we would go on our first mission together on the night of the last day of school. This would be the first time I went without an older brother–type figure. I'm not sure if Jerry had been without his big brother.

My bus stop came first, and I grabbed my stuff.

"I'll be there at six if that's cool," I said.

"I'll be ready," Jerry replied.

I ran home and got my stuff ready, although I had about two-and-a-half hours until I was set to be there. I still had to get Mom to take me to the store for supplies, so I got my new sleeping bag and mini-backpack ready to roll. The only thing I needed now was the cooler.

"Mom, can we go get a six of DP and some Pop-Tarts?" I asked.

"Sure thing. Let's go," she said.

The store was only about a mile or so away, so it was a quick trip. We bought six cans of Dr Pepper and a box of strawberry Pop-Tarts. I got a bag of Doritos and a can of Wolf Brand Chili (with no beans). We grabbed a bag of ice on the way out the door. I was set. We got home, I put the food in the small backpack, and I put the ice and drinks in the cooler. At 5:45 I said bye to the parents and headed out to Jerry's house.

The walk took about ten minutes on a good day, so I was there with all the stuff in about twelve minutes. The walk would have been over a mile if I had taken the road, but about 200 yards down the street from my house was a field we cut through that led straight to Jerry's house. I must have traveled through that field at least a thousand times over the years. We used it that much. It was a pretty simple choice: No bike, take field. Jerry was already waiting outside with all his stuff.

"You got the lighter fluid?" I asked.

"Two bottles of it," Jerry answered.

"What about the jam box?" I inquired.

"Shit, I forgot. Hang on while I get it," Jerry ordered.

I set my stuff down and waited for him to grab the music, which was as essential to a creek mission as the food and drinks. Only fire ranked higher on our list than a working jam box. Jerry was back with the box within two minutes, and we were on our way.

I started to head out toward the Shermans' house. Jerry stopped me.

"Where are you going?"

"To the Shermans' so we can get to the creek," I explained.

"No. Follow me across the street. I know a shortcut," Jerry stated.

I did as he asked and moved forward into the Smitters' yard. We went around back and hit some white rock on the creek. This would have made a great site itself if it hadn't been so close to all the houses. We rambled up the other side with all of our stuff. I remember feeling like I was heading away from our actual campsites. We weren't, but I had never tried this route before.

Jerry got to the top of the other side and said, "You're gonna love this."

I made it up the other side and followed him through a small patch of brush and trees. The instant we emerged, I saw the weirdest items I have ever beheld. Right in front of my eyes were several large red metal structures. Some were twenty feet high, if not more.

"What the hell are those?" I asked.

"We call them the Structures," Jerry replied.

"Wow," I said.

This was all I could say. What were these? How did they get here? Were they alien in nature? I had no idea, and Jerry had no answers to my many questions. If I had had a cell phone, those things would have gone viral in minutes. They looked almost like red farm equipment that had been broken up and reshaped. I counted eight spread out in random fashion in a field of about twenty-five acres. I grabbed on to one of them and began to climb. It held me.

I must have stood there staring at these artifacts for at least fifteen minutes. They were so cool looking, but they were also really weird and seemed oddly out of place in the field.

We eventually had to move on to our campsite. We chose the Old site on the white rock, and our mission began (with visions of red robot war machines filling up my head – I really couldn't get them out of my mind).

Jerry looked pretty satisfied with his position, since I had never experienced the Structures. He began to work on the fire as I organized the rest of our stuff and got the jam box playing. The radio station of choice was Eagle 97. It played a mix of pop and pop rock. If we wanted straight mainstream, we would go for Kiss 106.1. Tonight was a rock night, and we moved quickly to ready ourselves for the evening's events, which we made up as we went along. After the fire was rolling, we went down about twenty yards from camp to the white rock below. We could see a few small fish swimming in what was left of the water. There were also a number of anthills on the dirt next to the rock. I made a note to be careful where I stepped. We got in the water and walked along the creek bed about a half-mile further than I had ever gone. There were plenty of spots that would have made excellent campsites. After we had explored enough, we got hungry and worked our way back to camp.

We had been stupid and left the small fire going while we were gone, mainly because I think we had expected to be down at the creek bed only for a few minutes and you could see our fire from where we thought we would be. The fire had died down to virtually nothing, but it was easy enough to bring it back to life. I pulled out my Wolf Chili and put it in a pot close to the fire. Jerry whipped out a foil pack and put it in the fire. I later found out it contained hamburger, onions, and potatoes. The cooking chili and the contents of the foil pack smelled delicious. After a little time, they were ready to eat. I handed Jerry a DP to drink, and we ate dinner. We sat on two big stumps close to the fire. This campsite could have accommodated ten to twelve people comfortably, so we felt like kings commanding such space.

The sun went down, and the campsite grew still. There was a barbed wire fence behind us and fifty acres of field (give or take) between us and the New campsite. There were fifteen or so cows enjoying the night air in this field, and the sight of them made us feel really good for some reason. Dinner went fast, and I remember thinking that we had the radio up too loud. Jerry was up dancing around to Quiet Riot's "Cum on Feel the Noize." That was such a great tune. However, I couldn't get my mind off of the structures we had passed earlier. I had watched a lot of TV over the years and had never seen anything that crazy looking. Each of the eight landmarks I noticed was somehow different from the others, but they were all red and they were all large. After Jerry's dance ended, he sat down on the stump across the fire from me.

"Dude, what do you think those structures are?" I asked.

"My brother thinks they are assembly points for some weird cult or group, like worship points," Jerry answered.

"But what do you think they are?" I countered.

"Shit, I don't know. I've known about them for two years. I've never seen anyone out there before. Me and Trina went out there and scoped the place out for a few hours one night, hoping someone might show up. No one did," Jerry said.

Trina was his older sister. She was a few grades ahead of us but never hung out when I was around.

"I want to see them again. Is it possible they are some kind of alien markers? I mean, I know that sounds nuts, but that shit is weird," I wondered out loud.

"Who knows?" Jerry responded.

We speculated about the structures for another hour or so. It was fun to discuss this mystery around the fire. I determined that I would go back there soon on my own and maybe show Beetle.

We took turns getting wood, and we never seemed to argue. We got along really well. After a few more minutes, Jerry got up and went to his bag. He pulled out something I had been curious about but had never tried. Now that I was headed to junior high, it seemed time to grow up a bit, so I figured I should try. He threw me a full pack of Marlboro Reds. He had a pack of Winston's. I had a lighter on me to help with the fire. Jerry began to pack his cigarettes. I mimicked what he was doing but didn't know why. He muttered something about doing it to keep from losing the smoke's cherry. I got mine lit and there was a lot of smoke. I didn't inhale much at first because I wasn't sure about it. I smoked the cigarette and it was good. I felt really guilty and knew my parents would be severely disappointed in me for doing this, but I wanted more. Thanks to Jerry, I had nineteen more on hand.

"Where did you get the smokes?" I asked.

"Jensen's Market," Jerry replied.

I should have known. The old man there was well known in the community, and almost every kid knew he would sell anything to anybody. I knew guys that went there to get Skoal, but it was still kind of crazy to think he sold Marlboros to twelve-year-olds. I liked smoking so much I had already planned my first purchase. Jensen's was only a six-minute bike ride from my house. It was an older store without gas pumps. It sold basic grocery items and snacks, and that was about it. The convenience store a quarter of a mile down the road from Jensen's was the better store. It had gas, groceries, hot food, and even a small arcade. However, if Jerry could buy smokes at Jensen's, I figured I could as well.

It must have been around 10:30 that night when we got a little restless. We had already gotten the fire to epic size with lots of wood and lighter fluid. I was starting to get tired and figured if I didn't move soon, I would have to hit the sleeping bag. Neither of us wanted the adventure to end, which is usually what sleep means to a mission.

"Hey, man, remember what I told you about my trip to the New-New campsite earlier this year?" I asked.

"The one with the dudes chasing you guys out here?" he asked.

"Yes. That night was really fun before we got mixed up with those jokers. We should go out and hit the neighborhood. We just need to be more careful than I was last time," I noted.

"Hell, yeah. Let's do it," Jerry excitedly agreed.

We smothered the fire, grabbed our smokes, and headed down to the white rock to begin the trek back to society. It would be hours before we got back.

This time we took my route, the one that went through the field, the ravine, the Kirks, and the Shermans' yard. After the long walk, we hid in a cedar tree close to the road and lit up a smoke. It was just after 11:00 p.m. and there was little movement in the neighborhood at this point. We could see Jerry's house down the street, and his brother's light was on. We finished our smokes and put them out on the road. We began to walk toward Beetle's section of the neighborhood. We crossed the field and ended up on my street. We took a right and soon reached the wooded portion of the street by Beetle's. I thought about knocking on his window and asking him to come, but I figured that was just me craving some supervision. Nope, we were doing fine. We walked about another mile and ended up at the baseball field. We saw no cars during the journey, so it went pretty quickly. We had already determined that if we noticed any cars, we would hide, as it was unusual for boys our age to be out this late unsupervised. We sat down on a bench and lit another couple of smokes. This was my third, and I still felt fine – really good actually.

"Pretty calm out tonight," Jerry said.

"Right. I guess nobody stays up late on weeknights," I answered. "You wanna go to Bields? I think it's about four more miles."

"Why not?" Jerry replied.

Looking back, it seems weird that we would want to go back to a place we had just achieved independence from earlier that day, but we both felt it was what we needed to do. We finished the smokes and headed out to the main road that led past the church and to the school. There were large ditches and fields along the road for most of the journey, so we walked as far off the road as we could. It may have been dead in the neighborhood, but this road had its share of cars. We had to hide many times on the way to Alex Bields.

Once we had passed the local Baptist church, we saw multiple headlights down the road heading toward us. We ran a little ahead and dropped face down in the large ditch on the roadside. We hoped the drivers would not look over and notice us. We tried to remain as still as possible. In my mind, each car was a cop or my parents out looking for us, or members of the "secret structure society" trying to find us to keep our mouths shut. I was having a hard time controlling my breathing. Jerry was too. This was intense. The cars got close, and the ditch lit up like a Friday night football game. We were facedown and as still as two young dudes could be. The cars passed by and did not stop. We kept still another minute to make sure they were gone.

After what seemed like a minute, I whispered, "Hey, dude, you think it's safe yet?"

"I don't know," he answered.

"What happens if we get caught?" I asked.

"We're in deep shit if we do," Jerry replied.

After a few more minutes, we slowly got to our feet and carried on toward the school. This process repeated several times before we reached the school. I tell myself that we just hid so well that no one saw us. I mean, as an adult now, I have to think some parent would have called the police on us or tried to confront us about being out so late. It comes down to this: they either saw us and didn't care or they didn't see us at all.

We finally made it to the school at 12:30 a.m. or so. We worked our way out back to the empty playground that I had missed out on so much that year due to my knee injury. I sat on the big swing and lit up a smoke. This was number four. I guess I thought I was being cool smoking so much. I didn't realize I was initiating a battle that would plague me for the next thirty years of my life.

"Jerry, are you excited about junior high?" I asked.

"No, but we don't have a choice. I will miss this place," Jerry said.

We sat there another thirty minutes. It felt like we were losing part of our childhood. Leaving the school that had been so good to us the last five years was hard. We both wanted to grow up but also wanted to stay children. We stood up in silence and started the long walk back to camp. I knew I couldn't take the cigarettes home with me, so I decided to smoke most of them on the journey back to the creek. This turned out to be a big mistake.

As it was even later now, the traffic had slowed down significantly on the road home. We only had one dive into the ditch between the school and the church, and then two more hiding sessions between the church and the creek. Because it was a straight walk with few interruptions, I must have logged another twelve Marlboros or so. I needed some water, and I was getting nauseous. I could also barely keep my eyes open. When we got to the white rock a little ways down from our campsite, I threw up all over the ground. I stumbled around trying to get my bearings.

"You need help, man?" Jerry asked.

"Just grab me some water, please," I answered.

I moved down the rock into the water to wash off. I hurled again. It was bad, but better than the first time. Jerry arrived with the water, and I took a few sips. I was dry heaving at this point, with hardly anything coming out. I stayed that way for a few minutes and then washed my face off in the creek. Jerry helped me to my sleeping bag. It was too hot to get in, so I lay on top. I tried to shut my eyes, but my head was spinning. I was flat-out dizzy, and it was miserable. Bugs kept buzzing close to me, and the OFF I sprayed on myself did not help my upset stomach any. I sipped water and suffered until I was so exhausted, I fell asleep.

"Hey, John. John. Wake up, dude. It's about nine o'clock," Jerry said.

I opened my eyes to bright sunlight coming through one of the small gaps in the tree cover arching over me. As if to add insult to injury, smoke from the fire was targeting me for some reason. I couldn't get away from it. I had automatically climbed into my bag sometime during the night. My head was pounding, so I reached for Jerry's canteen and took a sip.

"Here, dude. Take a Coke. It'll help," Jerry offered.

"Okay. Thanks," I replied.

The Coke did help. Also, the untouched bag of Doritos made for good medicine. I reached over and grabbed my shoes. They slipped on easier than I expected, and I was feeling a little better. I sat up on the stump close to the fire. The heat felt good. I looked across at Jerry. He was smoking another cigarette. I certainly didn't want another. I had made up my mind on that while heaving in the creek five or six hours ago! However, I looked in my pants and found the pack from the previous night. I had four left. I grabbed one and lit up. By now, my headache was manageable, and we were discussing the events of the trip and the coming school year.

"You playing football in the fall? I asked.

"Yep. I figure I will go out for defensive back," Jerry answered.

"All of our brothers played for those coaches, so I figure we'll at least make the squad," I added.

"Everyone makes the squad. In fact, I've heard our incoming seventh grade class is so big they may have an A and a B team," Jerry informed me.

"Shit, that's a lot of people. I wonder if I'll be good enough to make the A team," I said.

We sat there for a moment contemplating life and the fact that we had just camped on our own.

"This is fun. We should do this again in a few weeks," Jerry said.

"Right. Just call me whenever you're ready. I got baseball three nights a week, but that's usually over by nine or ten. I am game for the creek after that. I want to try camping in the dunes one night. You got time to scout out a potential campsite on our way out of here today?" I asked.

"Hell, yeah," Jerry replied.

We cleaned up around camp and gathered our stuff. We burned our trash and put out the fire. We grabbed our stuff and headed down into the white rock area. We climbed up and over the other side into some woods. There was a slight trail heading southeast. It led to a field, so we followed it. We then traveled through the field toward the dunes. I had been to this area for the first time with Beetle when we were fleeing the drunks earlier in the year.

The dunes were basically small to medium dirt hills grown over with grass and weeds. In between some of them were mini-valleys that made excellent spots to camp. In fact, there were so many it was hard to choose one. I figured they might be harder to find coming from the other direction, because I only knew how to get here from within the realm of the creek.

I came to the top of a dune. This was the highest point around, as far as I could tell. I looked down between this hill and the next, and there was a sweet spot to camp. However, someone else had already thought of this. Jerry and I went down the hill into the valley below us. There were five stumps and a fire that had been put out recently. It still had embers. Two trees stood at the bottom of the hill. There were some empty beer bottles on the ground. A blue igloo cooler sat next to a rolled-up sleeping bag. Someone was still around. Jerry found a crumpled-up piece of paper on the ground next to the stuff. He read what was on the paper to me.

We know who you are and where all of your spots are. It is only a matter of time before we get you.

Was this letter for us or for the people camping here? I did not want to find out at that moment.

"Jerry, grab your shit, we need to get out of here now," I said.

"You don't have to tell me twice," Jerry agreed.

We grabbed our stuff and headed up the other side. From the top of this dune we could see the end of the dunes about a hundred yards east of us. We quickly wound our way through the maze of dunes to the end. We then walked through a brief stretch of woods and came to another field. Full circle complete. We had found the red structures from the other direction.

As we left the woods for the field to take a final look at the structures, I heard a buzzing noise to the right of me, coming from further up in the field. From this angle, I could also see a well-traveled dirt road that started about twenty yards from me and headed south into another set of woods. The buzzing got closer, and I realized it was a motor. We moved back into the woods and ditched our stuff. I lay flat on my stomach and Jerry followed suit. The motor noise was coming from a blue tractor with large wheels. It wasn't pulling anything, so I couldn't figure out what it was doing in the field. The driver wore a white motorcycle helmet with the visor pulled down to cover the face. The tractor went by us and stopped at the first structure. The driver got off, touched the monument, and then got back on the tractor. The driver eerily repeated the process with each structure. After the last structure, the driver turned right and went south, away from us, on the road into the woods. I knew we might not get another chance.

"Get your shit together and let's run for it," I ordered.

Jerry didn't reply. He was already thinking the same thing, and he took off like a jackrabbit through the field ahead of me. I picked up my sleeping bag, rucksack, and empty cooler and sprinted through the field at top speed. It must have been eighty yards across to the other side, and I was breathing heavily by the time I made it to the end of the field. I hoped we hadn't been seen. Jerry had already blazed a trail through the woods to the white rock below. I followed him, and we were soon in the relative safety of the Smitters' backyard. I took a deep breath and made my way back to Jerry's house.

I put my stuff on Jerry's driveway and lit a smoke. I didn't care if anyone saw me at that moment. (Also, I knew his parents were at work, and mine never came this way, so I guess I did care but acted confident due to the lack of parents around!)

"Have you ever seen that tractor before?" I asked.

"No. This is the first time I've seen any evidence of anybody out there. What the hell did that note mean? Was it written for you?" Jerry inquired.

"I don't know, but it's scary to think they were camping less than a half-mile away from us last night, whoever it was," I replied.

We finished up and said goodbye. I couldn't wait to tell Beetle about the night's events. I took a slow fifteen minutes to get home and jumped in the shower. I washed off the burden of the previous school year and any remainder of my heaving incident the night before. My first camping trip without an older kid was complete, and the new summer had begun!

CHAPTER 8

✳ ✳ ✳

SUMMER

had plans of camping and chilling out that summer after sixth grade, but I was so busy with other things I didn't get to go on any additional (full) creek missions during the summer break. I think I saw Jerry twice between July and August, and I could tell he didn't understand the importance of my busy schedule. I guess he thought I was blowing him off and that I didn't want to be friends with him. As far as I know, he never participated in Little League sporting events. After that summer he did play football and run track in junior high, and we quickly began hanging out again. As for me, I was busier in the summer than when school was in session!

First off, I had baseball practice Monday and Wednesday and games every Tuesday and Thursday for basically all of June and July. My team won the division and went to regionals that year. We got crushed there and exited the double elimination tournament too quickly, but that took us into the first week of

August. With school starting right around Labor Day, that left only a few more weeks to do anything else.

I had originally intended to go on camping trips after practice or games, but that clearly didn't work out. One of the main reasons for this was that my dad and my brother Brett ended up being our team coaches. I remember that this wasn't the original plan. Somehow the scheduled coach couldn't get it done, so my dad got drafted. My brother Brett was eighteen and loved baseball, especially pitching. There were other dads that helped out, but my dad was the mainstay. For some reason, I felt like I couldn't leave them to camp on baseball nights after they spent so much time helping my team. In addition, I was a little unnerved at the thought of other people camping out there at the same time as us, the letter we had found about knowing where we were, and the existence of the red structures. This is the best explanation I can give for missing the summer creek season.

As I said, when baseball ended I had only a few weeks left of summer. I was running out of time, but I thought I might put together a creek trip in mid- August. My parents had other ideas; they made plans for me that would consume a whole week's time. I first heard of these plans at one of our after-church potluck lunches. I was hanging with Beetle on the back porch watching one of our "famous" polo matches. It was hot, but we were in the shade.

"Hey, man, you think I can catch a ride each day to OSYS with you and your dad?" Beetle asked.

I answered his question with a question of my own.

"What the hell is OSYS?"

The Organization for Standard Youth Struggles, better

known in those days as OSYS, was the brainchild of a radical Baptist named Bob Goddard. The famous teacher held sold-out conferences around America for several years in the eighties. These conferences were based on radical interpretations and inferences from the Bible. For example, I remember it being taught that women should always wear dresses and that I could never drink alcohol. Another thing I had a problem with was that they taught the practice of "courtship" to guide young relationships. This guy actually taught that the only reason to date was to court for marriage. Last but not least, it was wrong to dance.

Bob Goddard got so popular during this period that a large group of Baptists actually self-identified as Goddardites. Whatever he was selling, my parents, indeed the whole church, seemed to be buying. This shouldn't have surprised me, because we had fallen prey to another radical nut the year before. A holier-than-thou named Bob Larson wrote a few books about rock music. He detailed the evils of rock and the "hidden agenda" of various rocks bands in America. My parents took away all of my rock records and tapes after reading this dude, and it was a year before I was allowed to listen to secular music again. This struck me as odd, since my dad had been in a rock and roll band in high school. Thank God the influence of Larson faded, but now we had Goddard to deal with.

I had never even heard of this guy until Beetle filled me in on the plans for the week. The conference was at the convention center in downtown Dallas from 9:00 a.m. to 5:00 p.m. Monday to Thursday, and 10:00 a.m. to 9:00 p.m. Friday and Saturday. I went ahead and told Beetle he could ride with us if we were going. He confirmed for me that his mom had already told him we were going and he would ride with me. He had never been to one of these conferences and didn't know much more than I did. I guess I felt happy knowing I would be hanging out with Beetle, but for some reason my brothers didn't have to go. This was more than likely due to their summer jobs at the Waynesville Market, the convenience store just down the road from Jensen's Market, which I mentioned earlier. Anyway, we settled on Beetle arriving at the house at 8:00 a.m. so we could drive into the conference. I wasn't happy to lose a week of sleeping in, but I've learned over the years that there's a lot more out there than sleep!

Beetle arrived, we got in the car, and we left the house heading downtown at about 8:15 that first morning. We learned then that traffic required an earlier start, as we ended up being about thirty minutes late to the opening session. My dad usually went to work around 6:00 a.m., and the 8:00 a.m. traffic was much worse than what he was used to. We pulled into the parking garage about 9:15, and my dad was much more enthusiastic than we were. He handed me a twenty-dollar bill and told us to meet him at the car at 5:15. Either he didn't want to be tied down with us all day or he realized the possibilities for us. Either way was fine with me.

Beetle and I walked into the convention center around 9:30 a.m. the first day. The lobby was buzzing with people and merchandise tables. It seemed a few other organizations had programs going today as well. We took a sheet from our event representative in the lobby and started down the long hall toward the main auditorium. We went past several bathrooms and concession stands that already had people in line. I realized we had to go upstairs to get to our general admission seating. We found the doors and went inside. An usher pointed us to several sets of empty seats. We actually had some room. I sat down and prepped myself for a long day.

Bob Goddard was already rolling out his message by the time we got settled in. We had been handed a workbook on the way in. Goddard was talking about different Bible characters and how they would be used as examples in his lessons each day. More people started filling in around us as he spoke. I would guess there were five or six thousand people in all at this part of the conference. It was fairly dark in the room. The houselights were down so people could focus on the stage better. We were up and to the left of the stage. I had no idea where my dad and the other church members were. I was able to pretty much do what I wanted, and I basically just daydreamed. I can't remember much of what was said that day or on any of the others. They gave us a break every hour or so. I remember going out and walking the halls each break, looking at girls. There were a lot of them there. When it got to lunchtime each day, they gave us over an hour. On Saturday, the last day of the conference, they gave us two hours for lunch! I had about fifty-two dollars left from all my lunch money, so I was good to go. Beetle and I left the convention center on foot and headed into downtown Dallas.

Hundreds of others had the same idea, and I saw a group of five girls about my age or maybe a little older. I headed in their direction, and Beetle did not stop me. I wasn't stalking them but figured I might see if they wanted to hang with us during lunch. That idea was crushed within a minute when two giant dudes joined their group. I realized those girls weren't going to hang with Beetle and me with these two dudes as chaperones. They headed into a restaurant and we kept moving toward Commerce Street. We got close to the Federal Building and then crossed the street. The building we were now at looked cool, and several people were heading inside. Beetle thought there must be some food places in there, or a store at least. We headed in the door and followed the crowd to an escalator going down. I asked a woman in front of us where we were headed, and she told us there was an underground section of Dallas! We rode the escalator down and saw a few food joints and shops.

"Hey, man, want to eat at Dickey's?" Beetle asked.

"Isn't it barbecue?" I answered.

"Yep," Beetle replied.

I wasn't really in the mood for BBQ today but would eat it if Beetle wanted to.

"I was hoping for some pizza, but I'm good with whatever," I said.

We walked over to a map that looked like one of the map boards at a mall.

"There's a pizza place a few tunnels over," Beetle informed me. "Let's go!"

We took off down a hall to the left. There were a number of people but not nearly as many shops as I thought there would be. There was a lot of open real estate for rent down here. I remember wondering why there weren't more shops. When I went back twenty years later, it was no different. This place could have been really cool, but I never saw it reach its potential.

We took a right at the next junction and finally arrived at the pizza place about ten minutes later. We had used up about thirty minutes so far, but we still had plenty of time left. I bought four big slices of pizza. I figured I would buy for Beetle since he didn't get his BBQ. He bought two drinks, and we sat down to eat. This was a small eatery that was clearly designed for mostly to-go traffic, because there were only three tables in here. We were at the furthest table from the counter.

"How is it? I asked.

"Delicious. Almost as good as Brother's," Beetle replied with a mouthful.

Brother's Pizza at the Red Bird Mall in the eighties is the standard by which I judge all pizza even to this day. Back then, you could get two slices and a drink for $4.25. They were big slices as well. They made the pizza right in front of you, and there was a sweet arcade just across the mall lobby to top it all off. The pizza they made was New York style, and I have never had better (even counting my three trips to New York). It wasn't thick like that Chicago style some people like. It was thin but with an incredible crust edge. We both got busy eating the pizza that wasn't quite as good as Brother's. There was no talking for the rest of the meal because we were just crushing the pizza. We eventually had some conversation.

"What do you think of the conference so far?" I asked Beetle.

"I think it should be over," Beetle answered seriously.

"No shit, man. How long can this dude talk about character sketches and how to speak to a girl's dad? The conference sucks, but I'm still having a pretty good time hanging out."

Beetle agreed, and I could tell he was becoming anxious to get back or at least move.

"You ready to get back?" Beetle inquired.

"Dude, why do we even have to go back? It's not like any-body's checking on us. We aren't due back at the car until nine-fifteen tonight. Let's do something. I'm tired of OSYS," I ranted.

"Like what?" Beetle sounded intrigued.

"Let's go to West End. It can't be that far. I think it's about a mile's walk from here."

I decided I would let it go if he wasn't interested, but he quickly joined in.

"We got some money and a lot of time. Let's do it. Who needs the conference? I don't," Beetle capitulated.

We threw our trash away and put up our trays. We asked the cashier how to get to the street. There was an escalator about fifty yards down the hall. We made our way to the street and headed to the West End Marketplace. The West End was a mall in downtown next to some bars known as Dallas Alley. There were some unusual shops there to peruse. We didn't know it yet, but there was a cool movie theater as well. It took about twenty minutes to make the trip.

This was my first time in West End, and it was very differ-ent from the mall closer to my house. This place had four or five floors, with a middle space that was open all the way to the top of the building. Each floor formed a square around this empty space. You could look up to the next floor or down to the ones below. Each of the floors had five or six offices or shops. I don't remember any food chains, but I do know we passed a steak-house and a spaghetti restaurant on our way there. Of course, I may not have been paying too much attention to food spots since I had just had some pretty great pizza. I remember see-ing a "gourmet" popcorn store close to the entrance and taking an elevator up to the next floor. We explored the mall floor by floor and killed about an hour. The store I remember best was a candy store. It was a few floors up, but I don't remember which one it was on. The store had a wood-themed design and was just really fun. It had barrels full of hard candy, gummy worms, and flavored taffies of all stripes. I spent ten dollars or so on some flavored tootsie rolls, which they didn't sell at our local Winn-Dixie grocery store. Beetle bought something tasty as well.

After an hour we reached the top floor, where there were only two businesses I remember. The first was some kind of puppet theater for kids. The second and more important was a movie theater. They were showing *Ghostbusters* at 3:00 that day.

"You want to catch a movie?" I asked hopefully.

"We might as well," Beetle answered.

We bought tickets and watched the movie. It took a few hours. We then bought tickets for another movie we had both already seen in early summer when it had come out, *Indiana Jones and the Temple of Doom*. Somehow this movie had hung around Dallas all summer and was still available. The theater was about half full, which I thought was pretty impressive three months after release. I wondered how many people in the audience were avoiding the final crushing day of Bob Goddard!

The movie let out about 7:15 and we headed out of the theater, down the elevator, and into the street. I still had eighteen dollars, and Beetle had about twenty. About halfway back to the convention center, we saw a small burger joint on the left side of the street. We crossed the street right there, not knowing the city well enough to worry about crosswalks. We ordered our burgers at the front and took seats in a small booth toward the back of the mid-sized seating area. I ordered onion rings as well and a Coke. An employee delivered our food a few minutes later. As we still had an hour and a half to burn, we took our time. I figured this was as good a time as ever to tell Beetle of my camping trip on the last night of school.

"Right. We went to Bields and then back to the campsite. I was throwing up all night because I smoked too many cigarettes. Besides that, it was a great night," I told him. "The next morning, we hit the dunes looking for campsites. We found some good ones, but the best one was already in use. We think they may have been out exploring or looking for us when we found their site," I continued. I told Beetle about the cooler and sleeping bag and recently put-out fire. I told him about the threatening note and our hasty exit through the remaining dunes to the field and back through the Smitters' yard. Beetle had a few questions for me.

"The guy in the motorcycle helmet just drove to each structure and touched it?" he asked.

"Yep. And he was moving pretty quickly between them. He then disappeared south down the road into the woods," I told him.

"Do you really think the note was for you, or could it have been for the other campers?" Beetle asked.

"I don't know for certain, but it sure felt like it was for me," I answered truthfully. "Once Jerry read the letter, we hightailed it out of there!"

"It seems the creek god protected you on the journey," Beetle said in a tone a stranger might have taken as serious.

I don't know how many times I heard that same phrase uttered over the years, in one form or another. We spoke of the creek god whenever anything worked out in our favor or when it didn't. It basically meant fate, but it seemed in those days to be much more than that.

After dinner we walked the remaining distance to the convention center. We arrived at the car about twenty minutes early. There was already a stream of people heading into the garage. Most of the parents looked oddly satisfied, while most of the kids I saw had a wide grin of relief on their face. The conference was over! As we stood there waiting on my dad, Beetle returned to the previous conversation regarding my last camping trip.

"What are you doing when we get back?" Beetle asked me.

"I don't know," I answered him.

"Ask your dad if you can come with me to the creek tonight. We won't stay the whole night, but we will explore a bit and then come back to my house to sleep," Beetle said.

"Cool. What's up?" I asked.

"I want to show you some stuff at the house, and then the creek, if you're up to it," Beetle replied.

"That would be sweet," I replied with elementary school–level excitement. My dad then arrived at the car and we drove home. He dropped us off at Beetle's house and told me to come back when I woke up in the morning. The conference week was over, and most of the summer was as well. However, there was still one more adventure to be had.

CHAPTER 9

✳ ✳ ✳

SOME ANSWERS

Beetle told his mom I was staying over and we would be back from the creek in a few hours. She instructed us to be careful and to stay out of trouble. Beetle then asked me to wait for him in the backyard while he went to grab his flashlights and a few other things. It was about 11:00 p.m. when we headed out to the creek. At the end of Beetle's backyard was an old creek bed. We walked down to the creek and up the other side and found ourselves at a construction site at the end of my friend Jerry's street. We walked through the building materials on the foundation and realized this was going to be one hell of a house. The dad of a kid I knew at school was building it. He was contracting it himself because he was in the air conditioning business, so he knew a lot of construction guys. We got to the street and took a right. We didn't go all the way to the Smitters' yard; instead, we went through the yard of a kid Beetle knew named Danny. Danny's family had a few wooded acres that also led down to the white rock, about a few hundred yards before the entrance to the field containing the structures.

We walked along the white rock on the way to the field. This was a great area to fish: there was a lot of rock on the bank, and it looked like there were still some deep pockets of water that could have some fish in them. Beetle handed me a flashlight and then shined his own light on a snake swimming on top of the creek water to my left. The snake made its way to the rock about twenty yards to my left and disappeared into the weeds on the other side.

"Was that a water moccasin?" I asked.

"Pretty sure it was, but they have never messed with me before. I think they keep to themselves," Beetle answered.

"I worry about stepping on them in the water and getting bit," I said.

"I've heard they stay away from people in the water. We've been in this water for years and no one I know has been bit yet," Beetle assured me.

"I don't want to be the first!" I exclaimed.

We walked a while further, and I recognized the light in the backyard of the Smitters' house coming up on my right. We reached there, crossed the creek, and went up the left side of the bank to the field with the structures. Beetle led the way. We stopped to take them all in. In the dark, they looked really creepy. On a full-moon night they might have looked cheerier, but tonight they looked like dark, uneven masses in the middle of a field. I hadn't even seen them at night the first time, but I remembered why I had avoided coming back here. These things were flat-out scary!

"Follow me and don't make any noise," Beetle commanded.

I obeyed, following a few steps behind him as quietly as I could. He walked between the edge of the field and the structures. He was heading south toward the first structure in the field. I hadn't come down this far, but I remembered seeing the tractor driver coming to this one last. We got close to the structure. Beetle took a right and walked about twenty yards. He was now standing next to the red object. I knew it was red only because I had seen it during the day; tonight it looked gray and even more menacing than the last time I saw it.

"Come over here. I want to show you something," Beetle whispered loudly.

"Okay."

Beetle shined his light about halfway up the side of the structure toward the center of a connection joint that led to a weird branch or arm-like piece. In the angle produced by this junction was a carved-out signature:

McMinner 77

I shined my light on the signature. McMinner wasn't a common name in the area, but it seemed familiar. Beetle said the name appeared on all but two of the metal structures. He sat down next to it and reached into his pocket to pull out a *Dallas Morning News* article from 1981. The article consisted of a blurb next to a picture. The picture showed an aerial view of the very field we were in now. The article read as follows:

World-famous artist Brenan McMinner just announced his latest masterpiece in a field in Ellis

County. He worked ten years on these items at an undisclosed location in Europe and shipped them here in 1977. The pieces have appeared in seven art magazines so far, including national publications *Metal Art Quarterly* and *Statues of Steel*. McMinner is hosting a tour of the art this weekend for selected guests and patrons. After that, the work will be closed to the general public and only available upon approved request of the artist.

Wow. I had spent the last two months wondering what the hell these things were, when a rational explanation was down the street at Beetle's the whole time. I mean, I had actually thought this might be the meeting place or worship grounds for some weird cult out of Dallas or something. Aliens had also seemed a real possibility. Beetle was giggling while I used the flashlight to peer at the article.

"Man, you never mentioned these before. Has Joel or Brett seen these?" I asked.

"Joel has, not Brett. Joel and I came here a few years ago and discovered them. We saw the name and decided to do some research at the Indian Lake library. It was all there," Beetle answered.

"Why would he hide this in an empty field in the middle of nowhere? I mean, who sees these?"

"I think that is part of their mystique. McMinner is known for being a hermit who keeps to himself. It stands to reason he would want the same for his artwork," Beetle suggested.

As we discussed the art, relief set in. Just having an explanation made the place so much less intimidating. I could now let Jerry know what the structures actually were and who had made them. I resolved to do this the next time I saw him.

As Beetle put the article away and we got ready to move, I heard music to the southwest. The entry to the road I'd found last time I had been here was about a hundred yards away from us. The music was clearly coming from that direction, but we couldn't make out what it was. It must have been past midnight at this point.

"Do you hear rock music?" I asked Beetle.

"Yes, I do. Not sure what song," Beetle answered.

"Let's go take a look," I said as I started in that direction.

"Sounds like a plan," Beetle played along and followed.

I think Beetle loved adventure as much as I did, and he allowed me to do some stupid things over the years because of that love. He was a reasonable dude, but when adventure knocked, he almost always answered.

I picked up speed to a light jog as I headed toward the entrance to the road. The music grew louder as I got closer. There was no doubt I was moving in the right direction. Beetle caught up and was now jogging beside me. We came to the edge of the field and stopped. The music was loud and recognizable at this point. As if providing me with a warning, the creek god amplified the music in the dark with terrifying clarity. The song shattering the tranquility of the night was now "Shout at the Devil," by Mötley Crüe.

At this point my blood was pumping and the adrenaline was in full effect. Beetle and I just looked at each other while the song blasted through the night.

"Whoever that is must not be worried about anything," I said.

"This is McMinner's property, but maybe somebody has permission," Beetle suggested.

"Let's take a closer look. Another *Three Question Mark* adventure, minus Steady," I proposed.

"All right, but I'm in the lead," Beetle declared.

Beetle began moving slowly south down the road, and I followed. The road left the field and entered some woods. There were trees now on both sides of the road, but the woods weren't that thick, so you could see space between them. The trail was pretty dark, but the music continued to grow louder. The song had changed to one I didn't recognize. It was some kind of heavy metal. The road grew a little narrower, but there was still plenty of room for a vehicle. As we moved slowly down the road, we could see a light in the distance, presumably at the end of the road. I wondered at this point if adventure was a good excuse for being stupid. I knew inside that it wasn't, but somehow I kept trekking down the road toward the light.

I sped up a little to catch up with Beetle. We had turned off our flashlights and were moving cautiously down the dirt road. As we continued, the noise increased and the light grew brighter. It seemed like we had traveled maybe 200 yards up the road, but the darkness may have thrown off my judgment.

I grabbed Beetle by the shoulder and whispered to him with urgency, "Dude, is that a barn up there? Am I seeing a bunch of trucks and motorcycles?"

Beetle stopped moving forward and hurried to the side of

the road, into some trees. He motioned for me to follow, and I did. I settled into the woods about six feet off the road.

"What is this? I had a hard time believing your motorcycle-helmet tractor driver story, but now I'm not so sure," Beetle said quietly as he lay down next to me in the woods. "Let's get out to the road, sprint up closer to the barn, and then take cover. No talking until I say so, okay?"

"I'm in. Lead the way," I quietly responded.

Beetle slowly got to his feet, and I followed suit. He stepped as stealthily as he could through the woods to the road and then took off at a mad dash toward the vehicles and the barn we had seen. I made my way to the road and started sprinting too, but I was falling behind. My heart was pumping furiously as I neared the vehicles. The barn came closer into my view, and through a semi-opened door I could see people milling around inside. A big floodlight on the front of the barn illuminated the area where the trucks and cycles were parked. Inside, from what I could see, the barn had soft lighting to create more of a mysterious party atmosphere than a bright, functioning workplace. The road ended at the field outside the barn, where the vehicles were. I saw Beetle jump left into the last patch of woods at the end of the road. I got there a few seconds later and tripped when I hit the woods. I felt a thorn rip into my left arm, close to my biceps. We both got settled into the woods lying flat on our stomachs. It was hard not to make noise, but we were trying our best. I touched my biceps and there was blood, but it was not flowing. We both knew it wasn't the time for talking. We waited to make sure no one had seen us.

After about five minutes of silence I dared to whisper, barely audibly, "There are fourteen bikes and eight trucks. You think this is just a college party or something different?"

Beetle waited a minute before responding even more softly. "I don't know. Something seems off. I hate to think that they are so close to where we camp. I mean, if there were no woods in between it would be about a fifteen-minute walk from here to the Old campsite on the white rock."

"Right. I need to know what they are doing. This is a good place to party I guess, but it is so out of the way it's hard to believe this many people would know about it," I whispered.

"We could sneak up through the trucks and try to get a closer look," Beetle suggested.

"Okay," I agreed.

"If they see us, get the hell out of here as fast as possible. If we get split up, meet at the white rock behind the Smitters' place," Beetle instructed.

"Got it," I whispered.

We crawled single file out of the woods and into the vehicle area by the first truck. We'd made it.

I could hear myself breathing as Beetle looked back at me with his finger to his lips. I got the message and tried to quiet myself with large controlled breaths. I managed to turn down my volume. Beetle then launched into a bear crawl from truck to truck. I remember thinking these were some redneck trucks – not your typical Chevy work trucks, more like monster trucks. I felt my left arm and there was more blood than before. I could feel the cut pulsing as blood rushed to the area. At this point I actually thought about turning around and running back to the structures. Instead, I got into bear-crawl position and crawled my way up to the side of the barn. There was a small toolshed attached to the barn, and I tried to hide myself in the shadow between the two buildings. I was now about twenty-five feet from the barn door. I had passed by Beetle because I knew I was about to lose my nerve, and I always wanted to complete my missions. I figured I could get to the door, take a quick peek inside, and then get the hell out of there. Beetle made his way to my new spot and settled in as well. The light was not directly on us at this point. In fact, we were in pure shadow.

"Let's get a quick look and then jet," Beetle whispered.

"My sentiments exactly," I responded.

Just as I was readying myself to sneak up to the door for a peek, it slid wide open! People started filing out into the vehicle area. Most had bottled beer in their hands, and some even had motorcycle helmets on. I thought that was strange at this time of night. The music roared even louder with the door wide open. It was less menacing now, as I recognized Journey's hit song "Who's Crying Now?" The strangest part I remember was that I didn't see any girls.

Beetle and I clung to the decreasing shadow of the shed as people continued to pour out of the barn. I counted just over thirty dudes. What kind of party was this? The stream of testosterone came to a stop a minute or so later, and I saw the group had congregated out by the entrance to the dirt road leading back toward the structures. It was a good thing we had moved, because there was no way someone wouldn't have seen us at our previous spot. A motorcycle fired up its engine and revved a few times, and then we heard the shout:

"Go!"

The motorcycle and its rider bolted down the road toward the structures to the cheers of excited, drunk spectators.

We sat there in silence for a minute, lost in wonder and speculation. Was this some kind of race? The group was now well away from us, and they seemed really excited. People started chanting in the darkness:

"Nick! Nick! Nick! Nick!"

This chant went on for more than a minute. I could hear the motorcycle working its way through the structures, speeding up then slowing down. Was it the same routine I had seen at the beginning of summer, where the rider had to get off the tractor, touch the structure, get back on, and proceed to the next? That seemed the most logical assumption based on what I was hearing.

I looked over at Beetle and whispered, "There's nobody left in there. Let's check it out really quick."

"Only one of us should go in case he gets caught. Then the other can go for help," Beetle reasoned.

"Got it. I'll go. If I'm not out in five minutes, head to the white rock and wait for me there. I promise I'll make it as quick as possible," I whispered.

"Good luck, John."

I crept to the front door and looked inside. I could see long card tables lining the walls on all sides. There were stacks of papers on some of the tables and beer bottles on others. I couldn't see anyone in there. I entered slowly, taking the place in. I crept over to one of the tables and grabbed a piece of paper. Nothing was on it. Nothing was on any of the papers that I saw. About fifteen feet to my right was a stairway leading up, with a wall to the left. About ten feet up the wall was a white banner with neon green lettering that read:

Nick!

This was really weird. I heard another motorcycle rev up outside and begin the course. The loud music, engines, and chanting from the audience made for an eerie setting. I had an uneasy feeling but wanted to know more. I crept up the stairs slowly and methodically. I knew this was stupid, but I was propelled by an uncontrollable curiosity that would get me into all kinds of trouble later in life. Tonight was no exception.

I reached the top of the stairs and turned the corner into a room. I suddenly felt myself being shoved to the floor, and the door to the room slammed shut right behind me. I looked up and saw another card table with a man sitting in a chair right behind it, directly facing me. There was no one else there. I was sure I had been shoved, but whoever it was must have left with the slamming of the door. The man wore a motorcycle helmet with the visor down. He stood up, and I got a better look at him. He was wearing jeans, motorcycle boots up to his knees, and a green jacket with some letters I couldn't make out.

He began to speak to me in a monotone voice, "Who are you? Do you have an invitation to my party? I'm waiting," he said impatiently.

"Uh, my name is Eric Biggles," I responded.

This was the only name I could think of. I didn't want to use anyone else's real name and certainly not my own. He laughed at my response.

"Eric Biggles, right? Well, Eric, you are not on my guest list for this evening. What should we do about that?" the man asked.

"Sir, why not add me to the guest list? I don't mean any harm. I was out at the Structures and heard music and was just trying to see if I could come party with you guys," I answered.

"Bold. 'The Structures.' I like it. I've never heard them called that," he said.

He went on talking as I sat there in terror, not knowing what would become of me. I hoped Beetle had already taken off but wasn't sure.

"I was told this was far enough out that no one would hear us. That we could do what we wanted – and we do. You're Screwing that up for me right now," the man declared.

"Well, if I hadn't heard the music, I never would have known you were out here. I am really sorry, and I promise I'll forget everything I've seen out here," I said as calmly as I could.

"You've seen nothing, and your friend outside hasn't either," said my captor.

Now I was about to lose it. He knew about Beetle. I had to do something, but what? The man walked around the table and toward me. He reached down and pulled me up off the ground and onto my knees.

"Ah shit, I ain't going out like this," I thought.

"My name is Nick, if you haven't already guessed. My friends outside will do anything for me. I don't believe you, Eric.

However, I am in a good mood tonight. So, I issue you an invitation after the fact, but since young lads like you can't participate in some of our more fun activities, you will have to perform a different role."

He grabbed me under my left arm by the biceps that was cut and pulled me to my feet.

"All right, down the stairs, jackass! If you run, I won't be so nice. So, move now," Nick ordered.

I opened the door and walked down the stairs. I had no doubt this guy could destroy me, so I did what he said. When we got into the barn proper, there were now a few guys there with helmets on. I could not make out anyone's face because the visors were down.

"Fellas, we got a new element to our game," Nick announced.

"Cool," said one of the helmeted men.

The next thing I knew I was being hustled along to the start of the road. There were twenty or so guys milling around. I didn't see Beetle anywhere, and I prayed he had gotten away somehow. The music still filled up the night in the background.

"Hello, players! There is a new element tonight. The first rider to catch and bring me Mr. Biggles here will win triple portion," Nick yelled to the group.

They began cheering:

"Nick! Nick! Nick! Nick!"

"All right, all right. Calm down. The rules are simple. Biggles here gets a two-minute head start, and then it's a free-for-all. Got it?" Nick asked.

He looked at me, and I could almost see him grinning through his visor. I could see the bottom of his face, but not the nose and above. I wondered what I could do with two minutes, but I was too scared to ask what would happen to me after I was caught. I began to think I had pushed my luck one too many times at the creek.

"Go! Time's ticking!"

The crowd roared. I hit the road at a dead sprint. I figured I needed to cover as much ground as possible in the first ninety seconds. Then I would either hit the field with the structures and try to hide, or if I hadn't gotten that far, I would try the woods. My heart raced. The music and chanting back at the barn started to fade out due to the overwhelming sound of my own heart in my head. As I ran, I remember wondering why I had told Beetle all of this today, and what I would be doing right now if I hadn't. It's funny how crazy moments in life can spur our most rational strings of thoughts. I kept running. I heard some motorcycles start revving their engines. I knew it wasn't two minutes yet, and if they came now, I was done. This thought got me moving at a speed previously unseen by any of my sports coaches.

I was nearing the end of the road when I heard the cycles take off in hot pursuit of me. At least he had given me my two minutes! I wasn't quite to the field yet, so I hooked a right into the woods. The woods were only twenty yards deep, and I would come out the other side into field containing the structures, about a football field away from where I needed to be to hit the Smitters' white rock area. I made it through the woods quickly and launched into the field at a full sprint. Ahead of me,

I saw a light flashing on two seconds and off two seconds. Beetle had made it.

I was passing one structure on my right when I noticed two cycles storm their way into the field. They were about forty yards from me to the south. The riders quickly scanned the structures and found me in their headlights. They both turned toward me as another cycle entered the field. I saw the flashing light east of me on the other side of the field. Beetle was the lighthouse that gave me hope. I decided it was now or never when I heard the riders yelling my fake name as they rode through the field in my direction.

"Biggles, give up, Biggles! It won't hurt that bad," the fiends cried into the night air.

I didn't want to begin to contemplate what they meant by that, so I sped faster toward Beetle's light. From my right, a motorcycle quickly caught up to me. The rider hit me on the back with some kind of strap as he passed by. It stung and knocked me down, but I was able to quickly get up and keep moving toward the light. The rider turned his bike for another pass. I noticed Beetle's light had gone off. Smart. Now that the riders were close, he couldn't risk them finding our way out. I was twenty yards away now and breathing so heavily I thought I might have a heart attack. The rider came at me again at high speed. As I braced for the impact of the strap, I heard a yell and a thud as the rider was knocked from his cycle by a large branch swung by my friend. Beetle!

"Over here! Run," Beetle screamed at me.

I ran toward the woods with Beetle close behind. The other riders were nowhere near us, and we made it into the woods.

I didn't stop running until I made it down to the creek bed, up into the Smitters' backyard, and out to the street by Jerry's house. I was doubled over, desperate to catch my breath, when I noticed Beetle next to me doing the same. My back stung, and my left arm had a pretty good amount of dried blood from the thorn that had nicked it in the woods.

Beetle and I instinctively turned right on the road and started jogging back to the end of the street, where the construction site led to his backyard. It took maybe five minutes. We made it into his yard and inside his house with no further challenges. I had never felt happier to be indoors in my life. We sat in his room in silence for a few minutes before we spoke.

"How did you get away?" I asked.

"I waited five minutes like we agreed, and then I wound my way through the maze of trucks to the woods. I went slow and was easily able to find the white rock to wait for you. I started worrying when I heard multiple motorcycles hit the road at once. What the hell happened?" Beetle asked.

I relayed every detail of the story to Beetle while he sat there dumbfounded. He gave me some hydrogen peroxide to put on the strap wound on my back and the cut on my left arm. They both looked much better in the light than I thought they would. After discussing the terror of the night about thirty minutes longer, I passed out from sheer exhaustion. I was so tired I didn't even dream. Thank God.

I woke up the next day to sunshine. This was a welcome sight after the previous night's events. I have learned through the years that daylight usually cures night fears. Beetle was still asleep, and I needed to get home. I left a note saying I was going home, then hit the street and took a left for the five- minute walk up Brightwood Street to my house.

I figured last night hadn't been a total loss, because I had found out the structures were simply art projects created by a recluse. That took some of the fun out of it, but the uneasy fear of not knowing their true purpose was gone as well. As far as the crazy cycle rider dudes and Nick were concerned, what could I do? I was trespassing on someone else's property in the middle of the night. Did they have permission to be there? I somehow doubted it. However, I was completely willing to let it go and never encroach on their part of the creek again. The creek was a big place, and those motorcycles would not be able to make it up to the areas we camped in without a lot of help, time, and noise. My main concern now was wondering if Nick and his crew had left the note we'd found at the dune campsite on my last trip. If it was them, then maybe they had left it for another group of campers who had encroached much more on their ter- ritory by being in the dunes.

I shook these thoughts off and headed into my house to shower and change. Junior high was starting soon, and I didn't want to waste my last ten days of freedom. I grabbed a glass of Coke from the fridge, sat down at the Atari, and inserted *Raiders of the Lost Ark,* the game. Like I said, I didn't want to waste any time!

CHAPTER 10

✳ ✳ ✳

JUNIOR HIGH BLUES

'd been at Possum Fields Junior High about a month now and wasn't impressed. The building was just old, and it brought together kids from two different cities and elementary schools. The seventh-grade building was on one side, and the eighth was on the other. The cafeteria and the gym sat between the two buildings. All these buildings were connected in front by a small covered walkway we could use to travel between them. The majority of my classes were in the seventh-grade building, with the exception of my Life Science class on the eighth-grade side. There was probably an acre of space between the seventh-grade building and the cafeteria, and another acre between the cafeteria and eighth. I'd just spent the majority of the past five years at Alex Bields, which had been brand new when I got there. This was the polar opposite of that situation.

PFJH (as we sometimes called the junior high) was falling apart. It resembled those grim inner-city school buildings in any number of movies about kids growing up in rough areas. Except that this area wasn't rough. Most of the people weren't rich by any means, but the vast majority were middle class. The school buildings just didn't really fit the community. As if to add insult to injury, the field behind the junior high was already being cleared for the new Possum Fields Junior High, which would be ready a few weeks after I left eighth grade. Too little too late, but at least I knew this place would be history after I left. The current school was slated to be used as administration buildings for the school district.

A new school meant change and new responsibilities. For one, I had never had to change classes every fifty minutes in the past. Second, I'd never had to stay after school before to participate in sports, as I was doing now for football. Third, I had always had a group of friends at my disposal in elementary. This was an entirely different place, and my random cluster of classes had me paired with an entirely different group of kids. Don't get me wrong, some kids from Bields were also in some of my classes, but none of the kids I hung with were in any of my class periods except Athletics. That was football practice, so there wasn't much time for socializing.

Beetle had told me how the environment was different at PFJH. I just wasn't expecting it to be this different. For the entire first semester, I saw Jerry at football practice and at lunch, and that was about it. He was on the B team, so we didn't really practice or go to games together. Other than him, I essentially had no other friends. Everyone seemed to want a new identity, so I determined it was time to start over myself. My second and third-period classes were English and Reading, taught by the same teacher, and my new school (and maybe life) journey began there.

Ms. Oglethorpe's Reading and English combo course turned out to be the best part of seventh grade. Ms. Oglethorpe was nice but clueless, and she let us sit wherever we wanted to. The first few weeks of class I tried different areas, hoping to strike up conversations with people over the almost two-hour stretch each day. I finally got into a set of people who didn't talk to each other at all. There was a shy kid named Chip Edwards, who wore Snoopy shirts all the time. He and I got to talking one day about music, and we realized we both liked some of the same Christian rock bands, like Petra and Whiteheart. There weren't many people who talked about this genre of music, so I figured this dude and I could be friends. Another kid, named Brenden Frost, was a gentle loner but a killer artist. His parents shared values with mine, so we got along. Last in this seat group was Terry Belthrop. He lived on my side of town, in the richer area called Herkwood Estates. This guy was nothing like the other two. He wore extremely preppy clothes and read Stephen King. In fact, this acquaintance began my descent into fun literature. He loaned me a copy of *Pet Cemetery* that year, which led to the removal of *Choose Your Own Adventure* and *The Three Investigators* from my favorites list. These three people couldn't have been more different from each other, but it worked. Once I had relationships with all of them, they actually started speaking to each other.

Besides our quartet of friends, there was another reason this was my favorite class. Right in the middle of our four-seat group was a fifth seat, which was held every day by the lovely, spunky

Brandy Fremond. She chimed in on our conversations almost every day, and as the class rules said you could sit anywhere, she must have liked us or she would have just moved! This was my first foray into real flirtatious banter with a member of the opposite sex.

We five students got closer as the semester wore on. I remember one day in class after football season was over, sometime in November, the teacher introduced a poem by William Henley called "Invictus." Not only did she introduce it, she made the class memorize and recite it. I also remember thinking that Ms. Olgethorpe made my radical sixth grade teacher Ms. Gowry look like a church nun. Anyway, Henley's poem flowed so well that it opened itself up to tampering from twelve and thirteen-year-old minds. We created the foulest poem out of the base Henley had given us. The name "Invictus" changed perfectly to fit our purposes. Our version was so funny we got kicked out of class during our recitation because we couldn't stop laughing.

Even Brandy participated in our frivolity. Nowadays you could get in serious trouble just mentioning this stuff in front of a girl if she chose to take offense, but we five messed with this poem for a week, and Brandy Fremond led the charge on some of those days. This humor brought the group closer together, and I soon noticed that Brandy was talking to me more and more. She was cute and funny, which made her very attractive to an average thirteen-year-old boy. After class was out one day, I walked with her to the cafeteria. We walked slowly.

"Hey, Brandy, you did a good job on your poem," I complimented her.

"Thanks. I can't believe I made it through without breaking up," she said.

"I think Ms. Oglethorpe heard what we were saying and just didn't care. My mom would wash my mouth out with soap if she even heard our new title," I stated.

"Not mine. My mom is cool with it," said Brandy.

"What? You told your mom about our new poem?" I asked.

"Yep, and she laughed almost as hard as we did," Brandy answered.

"Wow. I need to hang out at your place. Your mom sounds really cool," I said.

"Or we can hang out right now," Brandy offered.

"You can always sit with me at lunch. You know that," I told her.

"I'm not talking about lunch. Follow me," she said.

I followed her to the six-foot hedges that lined the side of the gym and the cafeteria. There were two areas that had cut-out walkways to go back behind the hedges for maintenance purposes. One of these areas had no windows overlooking it. Brandy led me to that area.

Once I was out of sight behind the hedge, she wrapped her arms around me and launched into a long kiss I still remember to this day. I hadn't kissed a girl since second grade on the bus, and that was just playtime compared with this. The next thing I knew her tongue was in my mouth, and I ran with the ball. She basically taught me how to kiss that day, and there was no doubt she had more experience than me (since I effectively had none). After a few minutes we came up for air. She seemed to be having a good time, so we continued for about fifteen minutes. I finally let go of our embrace.

"You might miss lunch. Don't you want to eat?" I asked.

"I'm good," she said.

"Well, we've got about ten minutes before the next class," I told her.

"I've got PE, so I'm already here," she declared.

I looked at her, and she moved in for another kiss. We stayed that way until the five-minute bell rang to tell us to go to the next class.

"Lunch was fun today," Brandy said.

"Yes, it was. Does this mean you're my girlfriend now?" I asked.

"Nope, it just means we can make out sometimes," she answered.

"Okay. See ya in class," I said in amazement.

"Back at ya," Brandy replied as she walked to her next class.

That same scene played out maybe four more times during the rest of my seventh-grade year. After the last time it just ended. I saw Brandy from time to time in the halls over the next several school years, and we always said "Hi" to each other, but that was it. However, the guys from our five-seat group were a different story.

Chip Edwards, or Snoopy as we later called him, became a full-fledged creeker. Sometime shortly after spring break, Jerry and I took him camping with us to the New-New campsite. This was the site furthest away from the dunes and the Structures. He went camping with me several times in our junior high years, until his parents decided he no longer needed the bad influence of the public-school system.

The entire first three hours of his first creek mission were filled with tales of Farmer Brown and of us being chased off the land in the past. I made the fictitious landowner sound like a monster who ate trespassing campers. I told Snoopy we had never seen Farmer Brown this far north out here before. Around 10:00 p.m., as if on cue, Farmer Brown showed up, announcing his presence loudly for about fifteen minutes while he traveled toward us. We freaked Snoopy out pretty bad, but because he didn't know where to go, he at least ran with us as we fled the "crazy landowner." After several minutes of terror, we let him in on the prank that Farmer Brown was my brother and told him he had just gone through his initiation. He was a good sport, and Jerry and I welcomed him into the creeker family. During the rest of junior high, Jerry went with me on almost every creek trip. I made it clear to him that I was open to any of his friends coming with us anytime he wanted. I never knew that I was his only real friend.

We also got Brenden and Terry to come to the creek. The same initiation scene played out. Brenden took it okay and came back a few times over the years. Terry, however, did not. After we had introduced Beetle, who was playing the role of Farmer Brown, Terry Belthrop wanted to fight. I did not indulge him, mainly because he was a good bit smaller and weaker, and we had pulled a prank on him. I talked him into calming down, but he was adamant about going home. It was after 10:00 at night, but he would not shut up about it. I walked him back to Jerry's house, where we called his mom to pick him up. We never spoke again. I said I was sorry, but he did not accept the apology. Brenden had passed the initiation, and Terry had failed.

The rest of my junior high years were pretty uneventful. Jerry and I played football on different squads, so we didn't get to hang out much there, but in the spring, we ran track together. These meets were fun, and our friendship grew. We both loved to camp at the creek, and we both loved the band Oingo Boingo. This made us good friends in a select group, because I knew only two or three other Boingo fans the rest of my school years. We camped mainly at the New and the New-New. We avoided the Old white rock site in junior high because it was so close to the dunes and I was seriously freaked out by the Nick Motorcycle Gang (as I had named them) incident. Jerry was relieved to hear that there was a rational explanation for the structures, so he let his investigation into them die. I am sure my story of the crazy night with the motorcycle gang played a role in his decision as well.

Almost as quickly as junior high began (or so it seemed at least) we graduated eighth grade and were off to high school. Junior high was a rough time for me because the school was so enclosed, it was full of bullies and fights, and it just had an overall bad atmosphere. I couldn't simply let bullies do their thing, and that got me in a lot of trouble. It also made me some friends. I was happy to see that things were much better at the new junior high building that opened the year after we left. We got to marvel at its construction over almost two years, but we never got to take classes there. I went back for a drama tournament a few years later, and it was really nice.

As time passed, the sting of the motorcycle gang attack on me wore off significantly, so as a celebration for completing eighth grade, Jerry and I planned our greatest creek mission ever. Snoopy, Brenden, Jerry, and I, as well as two more kids I knew from summer baseball, planned a trip a few weeks into the summer before high school began. We knew that with so many people we needed to go to the Old site to be comfortable. We all met at Jerry's house on a summer evening in June. That night went on to become one of our more memorable creek missions. The creek god made sure of it.

CHAPTER 11

✳ ✳ ✳

THE FIRE

Jerry's front yard often served as the staging area for our larger creek missions. It was easier to have parents drop kids off there than at my house. This saved the half-mile walk from my house to his or having to pack stuff into my mom's station wagon and getting a ride. Usually, I would grab my cooler and sleeping bag and walk over to join the group at Jerry's. Jerry's front yard was about a half-acre by itself, so there was plenty of room to spread out. In fact, most of the houses on his street had a few acres. On Jerry's side of the street, the houses had large backyards, but there were houses behind them (also with large backyards). Houses on the other side of Cedarwood Street had even larger yards, with the average yard being three acres. All of these houses had backyards that led up to the creek, so there was nothing but land and water within seeing distance behind them. I always thought it would be cool to live on the creek, but I was happy enough to live within walking distance of it.

On that summer evening in June after eighth grade, Brenden's dad had just dropped him off for our camping trip. We now only needed Snoopy to arrive for the real fun to begin. While we were waiting for Snoopy, I introduced Bobby Mavis and Dustin Merrik to Brenden. Jerry already knew them from the neighborhood. He wasn't really friends with them, but he was okay with them coming along, if only so we could initiate them. Jerry and I had worked out a new initiation plan with my brother Joel and Beetle. Since most of our friend set had heard about our last few initiation attempts taking place at night, we decided to spice it up a bit and do it the next morning. They would never expect it to happen in daylight.

Bobby was the son of Mr. Mavis, who had believed us when the yellow Camaro dudes had destroyed the stop sign outside of his house that night a few years back. Bobby was on my ball team, and he and I had hung out here and there over the years when neither of us had anything better to do. He was a year younger than us and was one of the lucky ones who would get to leave PFJH for the new and improved PFJH. I won't lie, the new junior high was huge and looked really cool. I was glad Bobby would get to rule the halls there.

Dustin Merrik was also a year younger and lived a few doors down from me on Brightwood Street. He had been raised by his dad and was a loner. Every now and then, he would come out and play. I didn't really expect him to accept the camping invitation, but it seemed a few weeks of summer had him ready for some activity. I had already gone to his house twice that summer to swim, but only when I was out of options. He was a nice guy, but Dustin was one of those kids that had to have everything his way when he was at his house, so he didn't have a lot of friends. After the loss of his mother to cancer, his father had spoiled him massively. I didn't understand that then, but I do now.

Snoopy arrived about thirty minutes late. Nobody blamed him, since none of us had a car yet. We quickly introduced him to Bobby and Dustin, grabbed our gear, and headed off to the entrance to the Shermans' place down the street to our right. Bobby and Dustin had never been to this part of the creek before, so we knew they were in for a treat. I hoped they might enjoy it enough – and respect it enough – to become full-fledged creekers. The initiation usually separated creekers from casual friends who had just come along because they had nothing better to do that week. It was pretty simple: If you took the initiation for what it was and embraced it, you would be given a chance to be a creeker. If you were overly offended and failed to see the fun in the initiation, you would never be invited back. This logic may have been cruel, but we took our camping club very seriously. We didn't want someone who couldn't handle our ways in the group. It didn't mean we couldn't be friends with someone who missed the mark; it just meant they wouldn't be in this part of our lives.

We did not travel the traditional path to the Old campsite, which involved getting into the creek and traversing a combination of water and white rock until you got to the camp. This year, there was still too much water, and we didn't feel like getting wet so early in the trip. Instead, we went through the cedar trees on the Shermans' property and through the Kirks' passage to the ravine. It was a dry day, so the ravine crossing was fairly uneventful, except that Dustin dropped his bag on the way down and threw a mini-tantrum while picking up his stuff before heading up the other side. We then traveled through the long field toward the forest that led to the New campsite. We came to the end of the field and stopped at the platform. Instead of heading into the forest and following the tree marks to the New campsite, we took a sharp left and walked about seventy-five yards to the fence line. We climbed over a large metal gate and walked down the path to the white rock. This gave us a straight 150-foot walk (give or take) on white rock to the Old campsite. I saw everyone's eyes light up when we walked into the site. It was the perfect location to camp for sure. Everyone found a spot to place their gear and by doing so had marked their sleeping areas as well.

Jerry and I started working on the fire, while Snoopy and Brenden got the tunes cranking. Bobby and Dustin had walked down to the white rock to get a look at the creek. It was a magnificent spot, and usually everyone did this several times each trip. While they were gone, Jerry and I filled the others in on the next morning's initiation plans. They were as psyched about the initiation as we were. Jerry pulled out the Marlboros and offered them to the fellas. I took one and lit up, but Snoopy and Brenden declined. The creek god allowed no harsh peer pressure, so their "no" was considered final according to our code.

Bobby and Dustin came back up from the white rock. Bobby was a happy-go-lucky kind of guy with a lot of charisma. Both he and Dustin looked impressed by the glory of the creek setup outside of our camp.

"This place rocks. Who found this place?" Bobby asked.

Jerry blew out a puff of smoke and answered him. "My brother Mike and John's brother Brett found it several years ago. Someone actually told them about another spot further down the creek that they never found. On their trek to locate it, their flashlights ran out in the dark. They finally gave up hope out of exhaustion and went to sleep here. When they woke up the next morning, they realized they had found an awesome, much closer campsite."

I had heard this story before and decided to chime in to give more creek history to the newbies.

"Right, and my brother Joel and his friend Beetle Batson were looking for this site and had similar troubles. They found the New campsite across that field there," I said as I pointed in the direction of the other campsite.

Bobby was taking in the scene, obviously considering all the possibilities the creek had to offer. I remember thinking he would make a good addition to the creeker roster. Dustin was sitting on his newly unrolled sleeping bag eating a stick of beef jerky and listening to some personal music on his Walkman. Snoopy and Brenden stood around the fire enjoying its beauty in the late evening air. Jerry and I sat on some old stumps close to the fire and went through a couple of smokes each before suggesting dinner to the troop.

"Who wants chili?" Jerry asked.

"I'll take some," I answered.

Brenden, Snoopy, and Bobby all voiced acceptance of the dinner invite. Dustin pulled off his headphones and spoke to us.

"I have some Vienna sausages, so I'm good," he said.

Jerry pulled a large pot out of his bag. I used the can opener to open three cans of Wolf Brand Chili with no beans. Jerry poured the chili into the pot and set the pot on two big rocks close to the fire. He stirred it every few minutes, and in ten minutes we were passing the chili around, taking turns to eat. It was delicious. We cranked up Oingo Boingo's "Dead Man's Party" and danced around the fire as darkness set in for the night. Dustin lay down on his bag in true loner style, but he seemed to be enjoying himself, so we were cool with it. Snoopy and Jerry went to the creek to wash out the chili pot and goof around. Bobby and Brenden were discussing some artwork Brenden had brought with him to work on if he had time. I sat there tending to the fire and the radio, feeling like this was shaping up to be the best night ever. I lit another smoke and dreamed of high school possibilities in the fire's glow.

Many conversations took place that night and the next day. We were basically a group of kids who didn't hang out much stuck together for at least the next fifteen hours. The talk got interesting. Brenden spoke of his art and his plans for the future. Snoopy talked about his church, his four horses, and the barn on his property. Dustin didn't speak much, but when he did it was normally about the time he hit a home run in the regional baseball finals (after hitting less than a 150 average that season). Jerry and I pretty much just smoked a few and listened carefully. We loved watching these non-friends interact in a positive way. It gave us hope that our creeker ranks might grow. The conversation really got going when Brenden asked Bobby about one of his seventh-grade "conquests."

Before I relay the details of this conversation, I need to describe Bobby in a little more detail. He wasn't exactly a handsome guy, but he was what many girls considered cute. Even then, he was not the cutest, or even the tenth cutest, guy in his grade. However, he had something that most other guys didn't: confidence. He had a natural calm that broadcast coolness to the world. He wasn't arrogant, and I had never to this point in our time together seen him angry or flustered. These characteristics all worked together to give him the charisma of a Kevin Bacon, or even a young Denzel Washington. With that kind of swagger, he had many girlfriends.

Brenden and Bobby were now sitting on the stumps around the fire. Brenden would move his stump every few minutes when the smoke found him. Out of nowhere, Brenden asked an uncharacteristically gossipy question.

"So, did you get in Sherri Mason's pants?"

My mouth dropped open and Jerry's eyes widened as we pondered the question. However, Bobby must have fielded a ton of questions like this, as he took it in stride. Later in life I saw hardened war vets squirming at this kind of conversation, but Bobby answered as if he was a well-traveled sailor with a girl in every port. He had just finished seventh grade, so I now question how much experience the guy could have actually had, but at the time I didn't.

"Yep, a few times in the choir room, and once in the field house."

Brenden kept the questions coming.

"How does it feel?" he clumsily asked.

"What do you mean? You just finished eighth grade. Don't you know?"

Although not trying to, Bobby shamed him (and by extension all the rest of us who didn't know how it felt).

"No, I've never even kissed a girl," Brenden replied.

Bobby looked amazed. He was honestly shocked that Brenden had never kissed a girl – like he thought every guy was as lucky with the ladies as he was. That's how clueless he was about the ease with which he could impress girls. Brenden didn't realize how uncomfortable this conversation was; he looked as if he was about to launch into a hundred more questions of a similar nature. Out of nowhere, Dustin spoke up.

"Tell them about Jenny and Shannon, and the homecoming party. You gotta tell 'em, dude," Dustin loudly insisted.

"All right. I met these eighth graders at the pep rally, and they asked me to come to their house after the homecoming party. I am not sure whose house it was, but I think it was Shannon's, close to PFJH," Bobby began.

Out of nowhere Jerry jumped into the conversation.

"Enough. Creekers don't kiss and tell, jackasses. We know these girls. Have some respect," Jerry demanded.

"Okay, dude, we're just having some fun, man," Bobby responded.

I wondered why it had taken Jerry so long to interject. I knew he hated love life–type talk, and I agreed. No more girls would have their reputations tarnished here tonight.

"Jerry's right. Let's change the subject," I chimed in. "Besides, it's about time to hit the town, right?"

The group agreed to hit the neighborhood with us. We smothered the flames and moved the wood away from the firepit. We left some good red coals so we could get it cranked up easily upon our return. I figured we would be away no more than an hour or two, due to the large number in our group. People in our neighborhood might let two or three of us slide out late at night, but certainly not a gang of six. And besides, I wanted us all back and in bed asleep a good couple of hours before the next morning's initiation activity with Beetle and Joel.

We liked to walk the streets at night, and to ring a few doorbells and run when we needed some thrills. It all seemed innocent at the time. It also gave us a chance to smoke and talk, and to feel older than we really were. I had never managed such a large group before, so our chances of getting caught were dramatically increased, but so was the thrill. We certainly didn't want to get caught; we just liked the *chance* of getting caught. Our town had only one cop, Marshal Bill. He was a rough Vietnam vet who looked like he had seen his share of action. There were even rumors he had caught one of those creepy white van kidnappers a few years back and tried to drown them in the creek. Suburbs have their legends too, I guess.

We all merrily made our way back the way we had come. We took a left at the white rock and then another left at the trail leading to the field. Next, we took a right at the field and then traveled down the ravine, through the Kirks, and over the cement drain back to the Shermans' backyard. From there the possibilities were endless. We could take a right down Cedarwood and work those houses, or we could travel through the yards of these houses to the wooded portion of Brightwood Street, close to Beetle's neck of the woods. Beetle's area had three or four girls our age living there, and we figured we might try knocking on a few windows to see if they wanted to hang out with us. I thought we might as well take advantage of having Bobby along, since I knew that after his girl stories earlier Jerry would never agree to him becoming an official creeker.

If I remember correctly, it was already past midnight when we knocked on Kelly Garnett's window. She talked to us a few minutes but said her dad would kick our asses if he even saw us, so we moved on to another house. We tried the homes of a few more girls we knew. We had some good conversations but no luck adding them to our ranks. We rang a few doorbells, hung out for about an hour at the playground by the ball field, and then headed back toward Cedarwood Street. We had been gone close to two-and-a-half hours, so I figured it was time to get back.

This next part of the chapter comes from extensive talks with Beetle and Joel, and a few talks with our old friend Steady. The rest of this chapter just won't make sense without switching gears for a few minutes.

Around 11:45 that same night, my brother Joel heard a knock on his window. He thought this was weird, since Beetle wasn't set to meet him until 6:00 a.m. or so to start the initiation. He looked out, and sure enough it was Beetle and Steady.

"What's up, dudes? Aren't you a little early?" Joel asked.

"Yep, and they won't be expecting it. We can get John and Jerry as well! Steady's got the cannon," Beetle answered.

Joel was cool with getting it over with, as he had just graduated high school and was set to start Dallas Baptist University in the fall. He had made it clear that this would more than likely be his last initiation acting job at the creek.

"Sounds good. Man, they're gonna freak at the cannon. Let's get it done," Joel agreed.

Joel got dressed, grabbed a flashlight, and headed out the front door to meet the guys. They walked all the way to the creek.

At 12:15, they entered the land of "Oh Shit" through the Shermans' yard and traveled through the field to the platform.

"They're at the Old, right?" Joel asked.

"Yep. I figured we'd hit the New, cross the fence on the other side of the mini-pond, and come at them from the field behind the campsite," Beetle answered.

"Good plan. I'm actually excited. We're gonna scare the shit out of these boys," Joel declared. "How long does it take to set up the cannon?" Joel asked Steady.

"I can launch in less than a minute," Steady methodically replied.

"Cool. Follow me," Joel instructed.

Joel turned his light back on and began scanning the forest trees for the axe marks leading to the New. Beetle and Steady followed behind, making as little noise as possible.

They reached the New campsite and took a breather before going down the steep walkway to the mini-pond below. Joel rested on the long, bent tree that served as the main anchor for the New site. This tree had been stripped of all its usable branches over the years to provide various creekers and others with warmth. Joel thought about building a quick fire, more out of nostalgia than anything else. He knew this might be the last time he would ever come down here, with college starting just a few months from now.

"What time is it?" he asked Beetle.

"Twelve forty-five," Beetle answered.

"Beetle, how many times have we camped here over the years? Ten? Twenty?" Joel inquired sentimentally.

"So many times. This is our best site," Beetle said.

"Even I find this place appealing. I hardly ever come, but even I've camped here at least five times," Steady added.

"Guys, this is probably my last chance to come down here, what with my summer job and all that. Let's make this the best initiation acting job ever," Joel said enthusiastically.

"Aye, aye, Captain," said Steady.

"We'll make it great, but I bet it's not your last," Beetle commented.

However, they all instinctively knew it was Joel's last mission here.

A few minutes after this they were already down the creek, up the other side, across the fence, and into the field that led to the Old campsite. The Old was a more attractive site than any of the others, but it was also the most vulnerable. Besides our group of friends, other people had clearly camped there over the years. The fact we were technically trespassing made it a more dangerous place to camp. We were pretty sure the other two sites had somehow remained undetected up to this point.

Joel had the lead, with Beetle bringing up the rear. When they got within 150 yards or so of the Old campsite, Joel took a knee in the middle of the field. He turned his flashlight off and motioned the other two to follow his lead.

"Hey. I don't see any activity yet. Let's do one cannon launch to get things rolling," Joel whispered.

"Okay. Let me prep and then give me the countdown," Steady responded as quietly as possible.

Steady turned on a small pen-sized flashlight and illuminated the hole in the top of the PVC pipe. He then handed the light to Beetle.

"Please shine it on this spot," he instructed.

Beetle pointed the light at the hole while Steady poured in a few ounces of water. The moon above was lighting up the field pretty well, but this hole was small and the team only had enough water for three firings of the cannon, so the flashlight pen was essential.

"Okay, give the countdown when ready," Steady whispered.

He pointed the end of the cannon toward the Old campsite. Nothing was being fired this time; it was the noise of the awesome explosion they were after! Joel and Beetle crawled a few feet away to the side and to the left of Steady. Steady took a knee and held the device.

"Five, four, three, two, one," Joel whispered.

Steady dropped a small black rock into the PVC pipe, and the water started to sizzle. Five seconds later an explosion rocked the late-night air!

Boom!

"Shit! Wow! That's always so great," Joel said without remembering to whisper.

"Hell, yeah! Awesome, but keep it down," Beetle whispered insistently.

"Yes, I sometimes amaze even myself," Steady whispered.

"Let's see if that gets any movement," Joel instructed the crew.

They sat in the field looking in the direction of camp for a few minutes. They didn't see any movement and couldn't yet make out the light from the campfire.

"All right. Let's move in closer and then launch it again," Joel whispered.

Beetle and Steady agreed, and they slowly got up and walked toward the Old campsite.

They crept through the moonlight to within fifty yards or so of the Old campsite. Beetle dropped to his knee and motioned the others to do the same.

"Hey. See there? There's the campfire," he whispered.

"Right. It looks pretty tame compared with most of John's work. Maybe they're getting ready for bed," Joel answered.

"I hear no music. They must be bunking down for the night," Steady observed.

The fire did look tame. It would have been normal for people who were just drinking a few beers and telling ghost stories around a fire; however, for this group of campers, it was a little early to not be cranking music loud and rocking a bonfire-size inferno.

"They must be trying to get out early so they can be sure to be up for our planned morning initiation. That must be it. Let's shoot the cannon off again and get this going," Joel said.

"Your wish is my command," Steady said as he prepped the cannon once again for launch.

Boom!

"Damn! That was even louder than before," Joel whispered a little too aggressively.

"Yes, it was. I believe that is due to our proximity to the white rock. There must be some kind of echo," Steady stated.

"Shhh. Shut up. This is the pivotal moment," Beetle whispered.

Beetle got down on his belly in the field, and the others followed suit. They waited another five minutes for movement. It finally came.

"Look there. The fire just shot up. Somebody heard us and they're juicing the fire with lighter fluid," Beetle spoke in a low tone.

The flame did rise really high, as if somebody had piled a bunch of wood on the fire and doused it for several seconds with what we used to call "boy scout juice." You could now see a little bit of the camp as the fire got bigger.

"You want to start Farmer Brown now?" Steady asked.

"No. Let's wait a few minutes and see if the fire goes down a bit. I want to catch them during a lull," Joel answered. "Follow me," he whispered as he took off at a slow bear crawl.

Beetle and Steady followed as closely as they could. Joel stopped and got on his stomach about twenty yards away from camp.

"Dude, those idiots are playing with the fucking lighter fluid too much," Joel whispered as a second large campfire grew on the other side of the campsite, closer to the white rock.

"Is anybody even there? I can't see anybody, and the place is lit up like Christmas," Beetle asked.

Just at this moment a third fire shot up in the camp. Joel was sure they were being screwed with.

Beetle was starting to get concerned at this point, and he spoke up. "Joel, look. There's only one person there."

Now that the campsite was so lit up, a figure became visible to them just as the fourth fire shot up into the night.

"Hey. Stop that shit! You're gonna burn the place down," Joel yelled as he got up and started running toward the campsite.

Beetle and Steady followed behind him yelling similar statements.

"Stop. Hey, bitch, stop!"

The figure was now more visible, but all they saw was his back as he ran out the camp entrance toward the white rock. Joel got to the barbed wire fence that separated the field from the campsite and was forced to slow down to climb over it. Beetle and Steady crossed over as well into an outright fire frenzy! There were four fires going simultaneously, and one was now moving up a tree. If not for the fence, they might have caught the culprit.

"Grab a cooler. Dump it and head to the creek," Joel yelled.

Beetle grabbed a blue cooler and flipped it over. He then carried it down to the creek, where he joined Joel in filling them up. The trip back to the campsite was much slower, because a cooler full of water is damn heavy. Steady had caught up and was now heading to the creek with a cooler of his own. Joel and Beetle hit camp about the same time and began putting out the two large trees that were burning at their base. If these trees had gone up, it could have been the start of a full-on forest fire. Steady got there as they were heading back to the creek for more water.

"This tree here," Beetle demanded.

"Got it," Steady replied.

Besides these two trees, every sleeping bag, backpack, and

piece of clothing lying out was ablaze. They made several more trips down to the creek over the next twenty minutes. They were exhausted and out of breath, but they had put out the fire.

"What the hell was that?" Joel asked while surveying the fallout from the arson job.

"If we hadn't been here, the woods would be on fire right now," Beetle answered. "All I caught was a black jacket with some green lettering, but I couldn't make anything out. It just happened so fast," he continued.

They shined their lights over the campsite after making sure every fire was out. The damage was bad, but nothing like it could have been.

"Shit. This is what's left of John's birthday Members Only jacket. He loved this thing," Joel lamented.

"It wasn't smart to bring a jacket to the creek in the middle of summer," Steady declared.

Besides the jacket, there were three sleeping bags that would never be slept in again. Two backpacks were torched, and whatever had been inside of them was trashed. Other damaged goods were scattered all over the campsite. Last but not least, Dustin's Walkman was nothing but a melted piece of plastic.

"I've warned John time and time again not to leave the creek at night. Bad shit happens when you do," Joel stated.

"Right," Beetle said, "but who knows what would have happened if they had been here tonight."

"Good point," Joel acknowledged.

After resting for ten minutes or so after their firefighting efforts, the three older guys grabbed the cannon and their flashlights and headed out to find John and the other campers. They walked slowly during the long journey back to the road by the Shermans' house. They looked and felt like they had just been through a war zone. At about 2:15 a.m. they sat down behind a large cedar tree just off the street at the edge of the Shermans' vast property. They were far enough off the road to be hidden from cars passing by, but with a good enough view to catch John and the others on their way back to the creek.

My firsthand knowledge of the story picks up again here.

The boys and I were passing Jerry's house on our way back to camp. This was less than a minute from the Shermans', so we were getting close. I was tired and ready to catch a few hours' sleep. Dustin, Bobby, and Brenden were unusually quiet, which told me all I needed to know. They were flat-out spent and needed some sleep. I wanted to make sure they got a few hours at least before Beetle and Joel stormed into their lives as the infamous Farmer Brown.

"Hey, Jerry," I whispered while walking next to him. "Let's try to bed down fast."

"You're preaching to the choir, John. Preaching to the choir," Jerry responded.

Snoopy was up ahead, already making his way left into the cedar trees at the entrance to the Shermans' place. He turned his head toward us and waved us into some trees to our left. He jogged back to us and ushered us into hiding.

"Dude, I walked around the trees up there, and there were some people sitting behind the trees talking."

"Were they adults?" I asked.

"Not sure. We should bolt," Snoopy answered.

"Jerry, we should make a mad dash to your backyard," I said.

Just at that moment, a figure came walking out of the darkness directly toward the tree we were behind.

"John. Jerry," someone whisper-shouted.

Thank God: it was Beetle. I got up and walked to meet him. The others stayed put, unsure what to do or who I was talking to.

"Dude, you're early," I said.

"Initiation's off," Beetle said in a serious tone.

I wondered what that meant.

"Dude, your shit was on fire! All on fire. Someone torched the camp," Beetle declared.

I stood there dumbfounded as Jerry walked up. What Beetle had said suddenly sank in, and I took off running toward the site. At that moment I saw Joel and Steady by the tree north of me.

"It's out, dumbass. You think we would have left it to burn?" Joel asked.

I turned in their direction and stopped. Joel and Steady looked tired and dirty.

"What happened?" I asked.

By that time the others had all joined us, and we were now a group of nine.

"Let's go back to camp. We'll catch ya'll up on the way," Joel instructed.

We slowly walked the long hike back to the camp. Beetle told the story of them coming to do the initiation early and launching the cannon twice. Joel added the part about seeing fires spring up at random places around camp. Then Beetle finished with the mysterious arsonist and them using the coolers to put out the fire. We made it back to camp sometime around 3:00 a.m. I remember thinking it looked worse than they had described. We now had six or seven flashlights illuminating the camp. The crew began rummaging through all their stuff, hoping something had made it through. It didn't feel right to be there this late without a fire, so Jerry cranked a small one up in the pit.

Joel and Beetle spoke to each other while we looked around the scorched debris of the site. Dustin was almost crying.

"Man, this was the Walkman my mom bought me her last Christmas," Dustin said sadly as he held up a charred, flat piece of plastic that had once been a radio cassette player.

"I'm really sorry, Dustin. I know you loved that thing," I said.

Joel picked up a piece of black fabric and walked toward me.

"No one escaped unharmed. Everyone knows you don't bring nice shit to the creek," Joel said.

I realized he was holding what was left of my black Members Only jacket. I'd got that last February and loved it, but he was right: I had been stupid to bring it. Snoopy and Brenden had some clothes that had made it through the flames, but their backpacks and sleeping bags were history. Jerry's jam box was smashed and black from fire. I noticed some drink cans on the ground in multiple places around camp, where Joel and company had emptied the coolers before using them as fire buckets. I grabbed a Dr Pepper and popped the top. I drank it down quickly and grabbed another. Jerry grabbed a drink, and so did Brenden.

As I lamented the damage and tried to straighten things up a bit, I noticed Bobby sitting at the back of the camp by the barbed wire fence. He was crying, holding the remaining half of his backpack. I walked over with a drink and handed it to him.

"I'm sorry this happened. It was a nice bag," I said.

"This was my dad's stuff. I had to beg him to bring it, and I swore it would come back fine," Bobby whimpered.

"It's not your fault, dude. Shit happens," I said.

He wasn't happy, but there was nothing I could do. I looked over at Beetle.

"Thanks for putting the fire out. Who knows what would have happened if we had been here when the dude got here?" I pondered. (We never thought or asked the obvious question: What do we do if he comes back?)

Steady finished a drink and then motioned to Beetle that he was ready to leave. Joel took the cue and got ready himself.

"Well, keep your eyes open. I doubt anybody will come with so many of you here now. Just keep the fire going and keep watch," Joel ordered.

"See ya at home," I answered.

As they headed out the front of camp to the white rock, Steady's flashlight caught something shiny about ten feet up one of the trees. Snoopy saw it.

"Hold up! What's that?" he asked.

"What's what?" Joel answered his question with a question of his own.

"Shine the light up there," Snoopy said, pointing up into a tree to the left of the camp exit.

"There, I see it," I confirmed.

Beetle and I gave Snoopy a boost, and he just managed to grab the item.

"Shit! It's a knife, and a piece of paper," Snoopy advised us cautiously.

He moved into the light, close to the fire. Brenden and Dustin were out cold, and Bobby was still sniffling in the corner. The rest of us moved in to get a closer look.

"Read it," Steady demanded.

Snoopy shined a light on the paper and looked up with a dreadful frown on his face.

> *Don't think we've forgotten!*
> *Nick*

"Get your shit together now," Joel ordered. "Nobody's staying here tonight with this nut hanging around."

Nobody argued. We woke Brenden and Dustin up and filled them in. Bobby had heard and was now sniveling hard, but he was clearly on board with vacating the camp. We gathered what remained of our stuff. We drank most of the sodas and burned the cans in the fire. The damaged bags and clothes were stuffed into our three coolers, and we burned the items that wouldn't fit. I made sure to put the knife in the bottom of my cooler so I could get a closer look in the light. We burned the note, because we never wanted to see that handwriting or threat again. When we were sure we had picked up all the trash and burnt stuff, we put out the fire, grabbed what was left of our gear, and headed out to Jerry's house.

It was about 5:30 a.m. when we lay down under the covered porch in Jerry's backyard. It felt good to be back in civilization after seeing the devastation caused by the fire. Jerry had snuck inside, and his sister Trina had given him some blankets for us to lie down on. Joel, Beetle, and Steady had gone back to their various homes to sleep. I had to stay with the crew to make sure everyone made it home okay. I don't think anyone slept well, but we all seemed to get a couple of hours of rough sleep anyway. By noon the next day it was just me and Jerry sitting there having a smoke on the swing in his backyard. Everyone else had made it back home uneventfully. I could tell that Brenden, Bobby, and Dustin were pretty shaken and would probably never want to camp with us again. I put my smoke out on the ground with my shoe and picked up the remaining filter. That's one thing we always did. I looked at Jerry and made up my mind I would walk home soon.

"I hadn't thought of Nick and his crew for almost a year. I guess they are still out there," I told Jerry.

"Obviously they are still pissed about that night. I wonder who they are," Jerry mused.

"All I know is they were older and I didn't recognize his voice, but that doesn't mean anything," I said. "I'm starting to think I may avoid the Old campsite altogether. That's the only place we have ever run into them," I said with hesitation.

"Well, we got all summer to think on it," Jerry declared.

"All right, man. Maybe we can hit the New-New in a few weeks," I said unenthusiastically.

"Sounds good. See ya later," Jerry said while walking inside.

I grabbed my cooler and started the journey home. I was pretty shaken up by Nick's note. Why would some group of older dudes be worried about a couple of kids? As I walked home, I wondered if I had seen something I wasn't supposed to and just didn't know what it was at the time. I pondered the memory in my head but couldn't remember anything inside the barn or outside that would merit this fierce level of animosity toward me. I guess there was always a chance they just screwed with everyone they saw in the area. Like a Magic 8-Ball, the note telling us they hadn't forgotten could be applied to just about anybody camping down there. I made up my mind I would eventually make my way back to the barn in the daytime to check it out. However, I was in no hurry to do so. The mystery would remain for now. I finally hit the driveway of my house and was ready to sleep the rest of the day. I dreamed of fire and high school.

CHAPTER 12

* * *

CAM

Jerry and I actually camped several more times that summer. We took a few random dudes from church and baseball, and some community theater contacts I met while working that summer with my mom. We switched up the initiation to feature Jerry as Farmer Brown; Beetle was getting older, and trivial things like that were starting to be beneath him. My brother Joel had one foot out the door to Dallas Baptist, so he was also out of the question. However, most of our trips were just the two of us. We stayed at the New or the New-New. We pretty much avoided the southern portions of our campgrounds altogether. This kept us well away from the dunes and the Structures. We had no other negative run-ins the rest of that summer. I was determined to investigate the barn from the crazy motorcycle night, but I wasn't yet ready to take the risk.

The summer gave way to fall, and we began our freshman year at Possum Fields High School. The school was about a fifteen-minute drive from Waynesville. The area was growing, and the school district moved up from 3A to 4A for competition purposes. This meant we would compete against larger suburban areas, but still not the 5A groups in and around Dallas. Our district played football and all the major sports. We still didn't have a swim team, but we did have small tennis and golf squads. In addition to sports, we competed in scholastic activities. These included debate, science, and drama competitions. The school itself had about 750 students. Jerry and I played football that year, which meant the dreaded "two-a-days": two weeks before school started, we had two football practices a day in the Texas heat. This was a level of dedication to sports none of us were used to, but most everyone got through it.

Besides football, Jerry wasn't in any of my other classes. Snoopy had transferred to a private Christian school in Indian Lakes. I knew almost everyone in most of my classes, but none of my friend group were with me. Life at PFHS (Possum Fields High School, and we were lazy and used the abbreviation a lot) was not easy for the first few months. Back in the eighty's initiations were a big part of public-school life. Freshmen were forced to carry upper-classmen trays in the lunchroom and to participate in the penny races on the sidewalk outside the lunchroom. These races involved bear crawling on the ground pushing a penny with your nose, competing against another unlucky freshman. The winner would be free to leave, while the loser had to score a win to get free. Most of this hazing was ended by the bell to class. Of course, there were head flushings, towel spankings, and wedgies to contend with as well. It was best to avoid the lunchroom and bathrooms at all costs. Overall, I got off pretty easy because people knew my brother Joel and liked him. He had been senior class president the year before, so I got off with a few penny races and a couple of lunch trays.

The football year came and went. I started every game and played both sides of the ball, but the game was no longer fun for me. I came to the realization I just wasn't big enough or fast enough to ever make it beyond high school ball. Both Jerry and I ran track that year as well, and that was fun. I won district in the 800 meters and placed third in the 1,600 meters. After track I was approached by the cross-country coach, who asked if I would consider running cross-country my sophomore year instead of football. I told her I would let her know. Jerry had already decided he would avoid football next year and just do track. Sports was a diminishing part of my life now as it became less and less important to me. Since I had no real friends in my classes, I decided to strike out as I had in junior high and make new ones.

Although I stayed friends with Jerry the remainder of my high school career, we primarily were just camping partners. We both loved the creek and worked well together on our missions. It was by sheer accident that I ended up hanging out with the dude who would become my best friend for the next eight years of my life.

I mentioned earlier how I decided to make new friends to replace the junior high friends I had lost. By now I was in tenth grade, and I had joined the cross-country team instead of playing football. In addition, I had fifth-period drama class. We basically did improvisation and two-person scenes, and quirky feel-good exercises the drama teacher had learned in her acting career. My brother had been Ms. Kertel's favorite student over his four years of high school. He had always been in the one-act play competitions and had won a number of awards for her.

One Thursday in late October, Ms. Kertel came to me with a request. She asked me to go to the drama tournament in Longview, Texas, on the Saturday that same week. Cross-country had ended the week before, and I didn't really have much else to do, so I agreed without so much as asking why or what I'd be doing. Once I said yes, she handed me a ten-page script and told me to memorize the part of the preacher. The script was from *Inherit the Wind*. I was teaming up with a guy named Cameron for the duet scene competition, and I was put into an improv group as well.

To tell you the truth, I hadn't had any action with a girl since the summer before high school, when I had made out with Bendy Pearson during rehearsals for my mom's community the-ater play. I was on a dry streak of over a year now, so I had hoped the scene would be with a girl, any girl. My partner Cameron was a nice guy and was in my drama period, but for some reason I didn't seem to click with him. He dressed a little differently and hadn't been in our district long. He also acted a little dif-ferently than most kids because he had grown up on military bases with his dad. This, at least, was my impression of him from afar. Anyway, it didn't matter who my partner was at this point, because I had told the teacher I would do it. The rest of the pe-riod found Cameron and me working on the scene in the small practice room to the right of the stage. The guy at least took his work seriously, so that was something in his favor.

"Dude, how long have you been doing this scene?" I asked.

Cameron had a concerned look on his face as he answered. "Since last year. My partner Lonnie failed English the last six weeks, so we just found out he is ineligible to compete."

"Well, you know your part well. I will learn the lines tonight so we can have a better practice run tomorrow," I said.

"Okay, but why don't you stay at my house the night before the trip so we can practice?" Cameron asked.

I knew this guy was serious about drama, and although I thought this might be a little much, he was trying to reach out, so why not?

"Okay. I'll have my mom drop me off about six and we can do some run-throughs. Can your mom take us to the school Saturday morning?" I inquired.

"Sure thing," Cameron said.

I went home Thursday night and learned the lines for the part. I also worked on my blocking, which was basically me sitting on the witness stand being harassed by a pro-evolution attorney. The script was really powerful, so it was easy to embrace the scene.

Everything worked out as Cameron and I had planned. I stayed with him Friday night, and we got pretty decent on the scene. His lived in a small but cozy house on the far side of Possum Fields. His dad got off work and took us to Blockbuster to rent a movie. I can't remember what it was, so it couldn't have been all that impressive. His parents were weird but nice, and I could tell they were putting on a show to impress me. I thought maybe it was because Cameron didn't have many friends. I turned out to be right. As the night wore on, I realized he was a good guy. He seemed pretty nervous around me, but so what? He had worked hard on his scene and wanted to succeed. He had a stepbrother in our grade, whom I remembered from one of my classes. I hadn't put it together until I saw the family pictures on the mantel. Cameron's stepbrother wasn't there that night, but I didn't bring him up and neither did they. We had a pretty fun night at his house, went to sleep, and were dropped off at PFHS by his mom the next morning at 6:00 a.m. – really early for a Saturday. We got on the bus for the three-hour drive to Longview for the drama tournament.

We made it to the competition in time for our 10:00 a.m. first-round duet scene match. There must have been fifty different teams total, because there were five rooms and ten teams in my room. We did our scene, and it went really well. However, I remember thinking we would never make it out of this room to the second round, because I felt at least three of the other teams were better than us. Two teams from each room would make the second round, and they told us they would post the results and schedule in the lunchroom, which served as the hub for all the schools to hang out in while waiting for their next events. It was about 11:30 a.m. when we left the room, and Cameron and I didn't have improv until 1:00 p.m. I grabbed some nachos in the lunchroom and sat down at a table with some others from our school.

"How did you guys do this morning?" Ms. Kertel asked.

"I thought we did really well, but I'm not thinking we'll make it to the next round," I answered.

"Oh, why not?" she asked.

"There were at least three I thought were better than us, and only two teams move on," I said.

She smiled and tried to look like she thought we had a chance. I appreciated the support.

"One team did a scene from *To Kill a Mockingbird,* and another pair did *Of Mice and Men,*" I offered.

"Those are powerful pieces, but *Inherit the Wind* is something they haven't seen very much of recently," Ms. Kertel instructed.

"I'm hoping we make it. I always make it past the first round," Cameron said.

At this point I felt bad because I was sure we weren't moving on.

Cameron could tell I thought I had brought him down, but he patted me on the back and said, "Don't worry, John. We either make it or we don't. It's fine either way."

Some official-looking teenage helper came into the lunchroom and headed to the bulletin board where the results were posted.

"Looks like we're about to find out," Ms. Kertel said and headed to the front to take a look.

We made the second round and then the finals. We eventually took second place for our scene. This was the highest any team from Possum Fields had placed in years. Ms. Kertel, as quirky and different as she was, clearly was extremely happy with our performance. She told me that even if Lonnie came back, I could have the scene at other events if I wanted it. I knew Cameron and Lonnie were friends, and I didn't want to get in between that, so I just let her know that I would fill in anywhere she needed me to.

Our improvisation team made the finals and finished in

third place. This also pleased the teacher. By now it was 4:00 p.m., and we were still waiting on some competitions before we could start the long drive home to Possum Fields. The next couple of hours laid the groundwork for an unlikely, powerful friendship of the future.

It was 4:15 in the afternoon, and my part of the battle was over. I sat in the lunchroom with LaShonda Andrews. Like almost every drama guy there, I was jockeying for position to sit with a pretty girl on the bus for the drive home. With her light brown hair and brown eyes, LaShonda was the prettiest girl ever to talk to me. I thought she might like me but wasn't sure. I knew I would have to be really lucky to sit with this girl for three hours, but I figured I'd aim high. High school had been all about rejection so far, but I still hadn't lost hope. After I had been sitting with LaShonda for about fifteen minutes, Cameron came up and asked if he could speak to me. I excused myself and joined him by the vending machines on the opposite side of the cafeteria.

"John, I need your help, man," Cameron said.

"What's up? I thought we were done for the day?" I asked.

"It's not about drama. I need you to come to the four-person ensemble finals with me," he said.

"Why is that? Didn't you see me talking to LaShonda?" I inquired.

"Yes, I'm sorry. I wouldn't ask if it wasn't important. I met a girl from Longview, and she will be there," Cameron offered as an explanation.

"I'm trying to work on a girl much closer to home," I countered.

"John, you meet girls all the time. You're good with girls.

I suck at it, and a pretty girl is actually talking to me for the first time," Cameron explained.

"Dude, you don't want me to close the deal for you. That won't end well for you," I joked.

"I'm serious, dude. Please. She came with a friend, and she won't leave her. I need you to run interference. Will you come, please?" Cameron said desperately.

"What's the girl's name?" I asked.

"Nicole," he answered.

"No, dude. What's the name of the girl I'm talking with? If you want a wingman, I at least need to know her name," I acquiesced.

"Sweet. Her name's Bridgett. There's one other thing," he added.

I knew there was always "one other thing" in these situations between guys.

"What is it?" I asked.

"She's not pretty at all, dude," Cameron stated apologetically.

"Beauty is in the eye of the beholder. Let's do this!" I said as I grabbed him by the shoulder and headed out the door to the hall that led to the rest of the school.

We ended up leaving the main school and walking through a few acres of parking lot and field to get to a gym. As we walked in, I saw a really pretty blonde girl waving at Cameron. The girl next to her didn't appear happy. I remember thinking I would try to change that for her.

I slowed him down before we went up the steps and gave him a word of encouragement: "Dude, you pull this off and you're no longer Cameron, you're Cam!"

Cameron quickly sat next to Nicole and starting chatting. He was overplaying his hand big time. I whispered some advice to him when she was saying something to Bridgett.

"Cameron, don't try so hard. Let her do most of the talking. Just give cues here and there to keep her talking about herself and stuff she likes," I said.

"Got it," he said.

I sat down next to Bridgett and introduced myself. It never crossed my mind she might not like me, until I sat down at least.

"Hello, I'm John," I said.

"I'm Bridgett," she responded and shook my hand.

I held a few seconds longer than normal to help me gauge the situation. She was nice, but I could tell she was really nervous.

"I hear you two are from Longview. Do you like it here?" I asked.

That was all the priming she needed. She talked to me the next hour straight. We actually had a great conversation. I forgot all about Cameron for that time. When the competition was over, I asked if we could walk with them back to the school.

"Nope," said Bridgett. "We're taking off, but you can walk us to our car!"

"Cool," I said.

Cameron looked relieved that we had at least three more minutes with the girls. I slow played it to give him as much time as possible. We got to the car, and I heard him asking Nicole for her number.

Bridgett and I were talking about the virtues of Sonic and Jack in the Box. It was dark now, and her green eyes looked pretty under the glow of the parking lot lights. I could tell

Cameron had got Nicole's number, and the girls were still not in the car. I decided to take the lead again. The worst that could happen was rejection and striking out. I knew Cameron needed a confidence boost. I gently took hold of Bridgett's hand, and she didn't pull away.

"I enjoyed meeting you," I said.

"Me too. I hope you'll come back next year, and we're coming to beat Possum Fields in volley ball in three weeks," Bridgett joked.

"I'll be there!"

I pulled her in close and kissed her. She responded as hoped, and we shared a nice kiss. When we finished up, I opened the car door for her. She got in and smiled. I looked over and saw Cameron had taken the hint. He and Nicole were in a full embrace and deep kiss for at least a minute! He was now Cam!

We walked back to the lunchroom to meet up with the rest of our group. They were already moving in the direction of the bus to head home. Cam and I stood in line and joked around a bit about how much fun this trip had been. I had never seen a kid so happy, and I couldn't blame him. Nicole was the kind of girl you meet in a dream, almost like a pixie or even a Disney princess.

"John, you're the best wingman ever," Cam announced loudly so anyone still in line could hear.

"Glad to be of service, my good sir," I responded.

We finally made it to the bus. It had filled up fast. Cam was on cloud nine and he made his way to a seat in the back. He was in la-la land. I looked down the center aisle and there she was. LaShonda had saved me a seat. Best school trip ever …

CHAPTER 13

* * *

THE BELL AND DUSTIN PUNCH

After our drama success in Longview, Cam and I started hanging out more and more. However, he wasn't able to come to the creek all that often, because his mom was massively controlling. His first trip with me was on Thanksgiving night that same year. After all the eating, Cam and his buddy Lonnie met me at my place for the trip. Lonnie had already turned sixteen and had his license to drive, so I threw my stuff in his beat-up Pontiac Bonneville and we drove to Jerry's place. Jerry's parents were cool with us parking there, and this became our normal parking spot for future missions. Jerry came later that night, and we pulled the Farmer Brown initiation scam. They fell for it, and we had a good laugh. Jerry and I agreed that both Cam and Lonnie had passed the test and were now official creekers. We had a few more outings that year, and Snoopy joined us from his private school on occasion. Lonnie was a regular, as was Cam when his mom could be convinced. We had a pretty good, full group of creekers now.

Besides our camping trips, Cam and I made the drama tournament rounds. Lonnie was never academically eligible that year, so it was Cam and I on the duet scene circuit. We always placed in the top three, and we actually won first at the Dallas Baptist University competition. We were also in group-of-four improvisation team that won several awards. The group was Cam, Michelle Jones, Nickie Benton, and myself. For some reason, this combination in the field of improv created a lot of synergy. We took most competitions by storm and then began winning the readers theater ribbons as well. The most impressive part of this was that our play was written by Nickie, and it was hilarious. I felt like her eight-minute script was as good as any of the professional plays we saw. The fact that we won first at three tournaments was enough proof for me. All this drama work helped Cam and me to form a real bond.

In March of that year, Cam asked me to drive him to Longview on a Sunday afternoon to see his girlfriend, Nicole. I had just got my license, and my dad had given me his Toyota Corolla. It was brown, and we called it the "turbo machine." The name was a joke, because I never was able to push the thing above ninety. Anyway, I drove Cam to see Nicole that day, and she proceeded to break his heart. I guess she had the guts to do it in person, so that was something. The boy was seriously messed up. We smoked Marlboro Reds and listened to George Michael the whole way home. Those three hours gave him a chance to unload, and we actually ended up having a good time. The next day at school he was a different guy. He was more confident and had taken more care with his appearance. As I told him on the drive, he had already dated a girl better looking than anyone in our school, so what was there to be nervous about? We both grew in confidence and developed our own identities. I no longer cared what people thought of me; as long as Cam was good, I was. In that way, we really helped each other. Anyone who's been to high school knows it can be a brutal game, but we walked the halls like we had already won! I had decided I would do drama the rest of high school and also continue cross-country. This left April and May open for all kinds of fun.

One night in April, we planned another creek event. I was still seeing Jerry at his house at least a few times a month. He had a job at the Waynesville Market that took up a lot of his free time. He grew to be even more of a loner in high school but was always cool with me. This trip was creekers only, with the exception of Dustin, who had not camped or hung out with me since the fire. My dad and his were in the Lions Club together, so my dad had agreed to watch Dustin that weekend while his dad went out of town on business. Dustin and I walked from my house to Jerry's that Thursday night. I remember we had a teacher in-service day that Friday, which meant we didn't go to school. We met Snoopy, Lonnie, and Cam there as well. Jerry was waiting, and we started the journey to the New-New campsite. Instead of going into the woods once we hit the platform, we turned right and followed the edge of the woods all the way up and around to the left, where there was another field and a clump of trees. The New-New was the furthest site, but it was becoming more popular as there was still a lot of wood available and good cover, so we had plenty of privacy there. Outside the New-New was a big field where we often played football in the mornings when we woke up. The camp was nestled inside a group of cedar trees. The only drawback was that it was a long way from water, so we had to be a lot more vigilant with the fire. It was a little before dark when we reached the camp and got settled.

Jerry got the tunes playing, cranking Oingo Boingo's "Who Do You Want to Be?" while I got a nice fire going. We lit up our traditional smokes and settled down for dinner. Jerry seemed a little distant that night, and I wasn't sure why. It didn't take long to understand.

"Hey, who's getting wood?" Jerry asked.

"Why don't you?" answered Lonnie.

I hadn't thought that these guys knew each other too well, but it seemed they had a few classes together and a rough dynamic.

"Because I'm cooking the steak and chili, dumbass," Jerry answered.

"Cam and I will get it, only because we want to eat," Lonnie responded.

"Good call," Jerry replied as he flipped a piece of meat on a large rock in the middle of the fire. (Jerry cooked the meat on the end of a sharp stick. He set it down on a rock whenever he needed to tend to it or switch stuff around.)

Snoopy also got up and went to fetch wood. While they were all busy getting wood, I quietly asked Jerry what his deal was.

"Hey, dude, what's wrong?"

"That dude's a douche. He tried to bang my sister and was a jackass to her when she told him no," Jerry explained.

"Well, did he get the message, and does he leave her alone now?" I inquired.

"Yeah, but he broke creek code," Jerry answered.

Jerry had a way of taking commonsense things and acting as if we had actual rules in place – or even attributing the rules to the creek god.

"Well, man, I agree he should have left Trina alone, but she looks pretty good, man. Can you blame him?" I joked.

Jerry laughed and punched me in the shoulder. He seemed to lighten up a little after this.

We now had wood for the entire night piled up inside the camp. Everyone was seated near the fire, and we were just sipping drinks and telling school stories. Snoopy had many more than us to tell because he went to a different school. The situations he described were all new and exciting. I remember thinking I would probably meet more girls if I went to his school. I was actually friends with a girl down the street that went to school with Snoopy. There were a lot of them there, and their parents had money – at least we assumed they did.

After a little while, Jerry busted out a bottle of Jim Beam whiskey. I knew his parents kept a lot of booze around, but I'd had no idea he was going to bring a bottle of the hard stuff. We stupidly passed it around and all took a swig. I had had some margaritas and beer in the past but never straight shots of liquor. It burned but gave me a warm feeling. Dustin then went to his bag and brought out a big jug of something that looked like tropical punch. This did not surprise me: we used to have margaritas at his house during the summer when his dad was out.

"What's that?" I asked.

"It's my special drink: Cherry Kool-Aid with tequila and Ever clear, and a lot of sugar to make it drinkable," Dustin said.

"Pass it over here and let me try it," I ordered.

Dustin reached over the fire and handed me the clear jug. I took a drink. It was sweet and yet burned my throat at the same time. I had to blow out, take a breath, and shake my head as if I was trying to deal with brain freeze.

"Wow. That is some good shit! Dustin Punch!"

The name caught on as Jerry, Dustin, Lonnie, and I took turns. Cam and Snoopy wisely laid off this concoction. I'd had one shot of the Jim Beam and three swigs of Dustin Punch and was already feeling pretty good. I decided I had had enough for now. Jerry and Lonnie kept drinking.

We hung out a while longer around the fire. The group got along pretty well, although I could tell Jerry just didn't like Lonnie and never would. The dude wore his heart on his sleeve. I remember thinking this guy would suck at poker. However, he played along for the night so we could all have a good time. I appreciated that. But he was drinking more than I thought was smart, and I remember worrying that something was wrong with him tonight. He must have slammed a third of the bottle by himself, and at 140 pounds it had to be having an effect. I had no idea just how much. I decided to ask him about it while Cam, Snoopy, and Lonnie were wrapped up in a conversation about hitting Snoopy's high school football games next school year to meet girls.

"Hey, Jerry, what's up with the whiskey tonight?"

He smirked at me and replied, "Nothing, just off work and wanted to chill."

"You may want to slow down, man. You drank a shitload already," I warned.

"Screw that," Jerry replied in a defiant tone.

I dropped the subject and lit a smoke. Jerry lit one as well.

Cam then told the group the story of Nicole and how she had broken his heart. He had a picture that proved how hot she was, and of course I backed up the story. Really, she was an awesome physical specimen, and I was still shocked that Cam had held onto her as a girlfriend as long as he did. I guess it is always easier to be the mysterious boyfriend from another school than a stooge walking the halls of the same school. Without a boyfriend there, she could be herself and not have to deal with the pressure of multiple guys hitting on her all the time. Or maybe she just liked Cam. It didn't matter, because any guy I knew would gladly have played either role. After Cam's story, I retold the story of the fire and of all our shit getting burned to a crisp for the benefit of Lonnie and Cam. I also showed them the knife that had held the message, which gave a little more meaning to the story. The knife itself was a big item in the eighties due to the *Rambo* movies. It had a jagged edge and a compass on top. I loved this knife, and it was now part of my standard camping gear.

Lonnie had a little liquid courage running through his veins at this point.

"Who the hell does this Nick guy think he is? I'll kick his ass if he shows up."

This was funny to think of. Lonnie was an average-height, lean guy with glasses. He wore Rec Specs with a headband at most sporting events, so I pictured him fighting Nick in a basketball uniform and Rec Specs. We all laughed a bit, but those of us who had been there that night were still unsettled by the fire and the other incident with the motorcycle riders.

"Give me a smoke, Jerry," I said.

"Sure." He handed me a cigarette and asked, "Do you want to show them the bell?"

"Why not? Let's chill another thirty minutes and head out," I suggested.

Jerry grabbed the Jim Beam and took a large gulp. I didn't know he could handle so much. There was clearly stuff about him I didn't know.

The bell is an important landmark for all creekers. However, the tradition of "ringing the bell" began with my generation, so my brothers and Jerry's brother knew nothing about it. Beetle only knew about it from our stories and his own curiosity, which led him to go with me one night to prove my story. No other single prank was so satisfying and yet so nerve-racking.

Basically, the bell was a large Liberty Bell replica that stood a few feet from someone's back porch. I don't remember how we found it, or what led to the first instance of this prank, but the bell was now a creek institution. Very few camping trips took place without at least one ringing of the bell – and, believe me, this was no small feat. The sound the bell made when rung was like the old church bells that rang to let the town know it was noon or that church was starting. The whole neighborhood heard this thing, which made it a thrill to ring the bell in the middle of the night. We normally made it our last event before disappearing into the land of the creek for the remainder of our camping trip.

We made our way out into the world. We got to where the Shermans' place hit the road, and instead of taking a right to get back to Jerry's, we took a left. The road had a lot of cedar trees, so there was easy cover to dip into if cars came by. It was about 11:30, which was early to be hitting the bell by our standards. The house we wanted was about 250 yards up Cedarwood Street. The road went up a gradual hill to get there, but this made for a quick run downhill to get back to the Shermans' place. Jerry had his bottle of Jim Beam, which was more than half empty by this point, and Dustin had his punch jug with him. When we got within visual range of the house on the left-hand side of the street, I made a suggestion to the crew.

"Hey, boys, why don't we take a few laps around the neighborhood first and ring the bell on our way back to the creek? I think it's a little early to do this."

Jerry was pretty lit at this point and was having none of it.

"To hell with that. I'm ringing the bitch right now!"

He handed me his whiskey and took off running toward the house. Lonnie and Snoopy followed behind him.

"Shit. Come on, follow me," I said to Dustin and Cam.

I didn't want to go back to the creek yet, so I ran past the front of the house and took a right into a cul-de-sac close by. This section of the road went past the house of some other people I knew with the last name of Bellamy, and the field behind their house led to Brightwood Street, very close to my house. I looked back and saw Jerry and the boys go into slow motion, moving stealthily around the house to the backyard. I knew that someone in the house stayed up late on weekends, because I would see them sitting in a chair when I rang the bell at 2:00

a.m. or so on weekend nights. I only hoped that the people in most houses were already sleeping so we could get away. They rounded the left corner of the house and were now out of view. I knew the crash would come any second now!

Dong!!!!!!!!

It always surprised me how damn loud the bell was. Lights were shooting on all over the street. I knew it had been too early to do this. I saw Snoopy and Lonnie round the corner, with Jerry on their heels. I stood waving my light boldly so Jerry could see where we were waiting. Once I knew they were on the right path, I took off down the cul-de-sac toward the Jonssons' house. I heard somebody yelling at us from near the bell. I didn't look back; instead, I made my way past the houses to the field and took a left into a "field alley" behind two wooden fences. The others joined me there. We put out all our lights and lay flat on our stomachs. We were breathing hard and trying to limit our noise, as dogs were now barking all over the neighborhood. To make matters worse, it started to rain. Maybe this was a blessing, because anyone planning on looking for us now had an added problem to deal with.

We sat there maybe ten minutes, while things seemed to calm down. The rain intensified, but lights were being turned off and dogs were slowly starting to shut up and get resettled. My plan was to hit my house if things got too hairy and act like we had been there the whole time. That was always one of my fall-back plans, which I never had to use. I had given Jerry back his bottle, and he took another drink. Lonnie took one as well. Half of Dustin's punch had spilled as we were running, but I took a drink of it anyway. The rain was getting cold, but the punch made me warm inside. We got up and started walking back to the main field. We took a left through some houses and ended up on Brightwood Street, close to my house. No more lights than usual were on here, so I knew we had made it. After a few minutes, we reached the pass-through field that led back to Jerry's street. We got about twenty-five yards in and were forced to shelter under a clump of cedar trees to wait out the rain. We were away from most houses at this point, but it was muddy and getting miserable.

Snoopy sat down in a corner and was clearly wishing for a warm bed. Cam and I were talking about plans for eleventh grade drama tournaments. Dustin was sleeping flat out in the mud, with his empty jug of punch close to his side. The rain would not stop. Lonnie started a conversation.

"Man, that bell was even louder than I expected it would be," he whispered.

"The volume is always a surprise, no matter how many times I hear it," I answered softly.

I heard a thud and saw the Jim Beam bottle lying empty in the mud about four feet from where I was sitting.

"I haven't had to run that fast in a long time," Cam quietly added.

Snoopy stood up and got into the conversation.

"Man, if we're going to be miserable, we might as well be back at camp with our food and shit," he declared.

"I agree. You ready, Jerry?" I asked.

I looked behind me. Jerry was lying face down in the dirt, close to the back of the tree cover. I walked over to him.

"Jerry. Wake up, man. We gotta get back to the creek," I said. He didn't move.

"What's up, dude? Can't hold your liquor?" Lonnie asked.

Jerry gave no response. I got down on one knee and shook him gently.

"Come on, man. We ain't got time for this shit. Quit jacking around!"

I shook him harder this time. He shrugged a little but gave no real response. I was starting to get really worried. Cam came over.

"Jerry, dude. The rain isn't stopping. Let's get you back to camp to sleep this shit off. We're too close to houses here," Cam informed him.

Jerry was basically passed out at this point. Not knowing what to do, I turned him over and was shocked to my core. His eyes were shut, but his mouth was moving and his arm was shaking.

"What the hell, dude? Wake up," I said, louder than I had intended.

I figured he was drunk and was shaking due to the cold rain. Dustin spoke up, which was a rarity, so everyone listened.

"Leave his ass. He's been a dick anyway."

"Shut up, Dustin. He's obviously sick," Cam demanded.

I'd seen drunks before, but I was scared this might be something else. His body was moving in a weird way. At this point I made a decision. We would have to risk the wrath of our parents, and his, and get him help.

"That's it! I'm getting his ass home," I said.

Lonnie and I each took a side and picked Jerry up. For a

moment it seemed like he was walking, but he wasn't. His head and arms were still jerking back and forth. He started dry heaving. I put him into a fireman's carry position up on my shoulder and began to walk toward his house. The others followed. Lonnie and I took turns carrying him until we got to his front yard. By the time we reached there, we were soaking wet, miserable, and tired, but the rain had finally stopped.

I knew where Jerry's mom kept the spare key outside, buried close to a cedar tree. I grabbed the key and quietly opened his front door. No lights were on inside the house. The stairs leading up to his room were a straight shot from the front door. Lonnie grabbed Jerry's legs, and I grabbed his arms. I told the others to wait by the cedar tree out of sight. They said they would meet me in a clump of trees in the Smitters' yard across the street. We worked our way up the stairs as quietly as possible. When we reached the top, we took a left into Jerry's room. His bed was right inside the doorway of this attic converted to a bedroom. We gently laid him down in bed and put a cover over him. We turned on the light, which was a lamp that gave an unobtrusive soft light.

Jerry was still dry heaving, and I asked Lonnie to wait with him while I got some water and a bowl. I had spent the night here enough times to know where stuff was, so I grabbed a glass and poured him some water. I also grabbed a large stainless-steel salad bowl to put by his bed in case he needed to throw up. I took the glass and bowl back up the stairs and tried to get him to sip some water. He didn't.

After a few minutes he wasn't getting better. I knew we couldn't sit here all night, but I also knew he would be in deep shit if his parents found out he had been drinking. I crept out of his room to the other side of the hallway. I quietly knocked on his sister Trina's door until I heard a groggy invitation to come in.

"Hey, Trina, it's me, John," I whispered.

She reached up from the bed and touched my arm.

"What are you doing here?" she whispered in response.

"Jerry got drunk and is acting really weird, so I put him in his bed. I am trying to keep your parents out of this so he doesn't get in trouble," I explained.

She got out of bed wearing nothing but panties and a T-shirt.

"Shit, he's not supposed to be drinking anymore," she said as she moved toward his room.

When we arrived, she noticed Lonnie sitting there with his eyes shut but paid him no concern. Jerry's arm was still jerking erratically, and he was dry heaving again.

"He's having a seizure. Didn't you know he has epilepsy?"

I had never heard this before.

"No, he never told me that," I answered.

"Just get out of here. I know what to do. You two weren't ever here. Get it?" Trina commanded.

"Okay, sorry," I whispered.

"Just go, damn it," she said.

Lonnie and I slowly walked down the stairs and out the door. We buried the key out by the tree and went to meet up with our friends in some excellent brush cover across the street.

We sat there in shock for over an hour. Not one car came by. We were out of sight of the street anyway. Dustin was out cold, and Snoopy sat there with his eyes closed. Lonnie was still juiced, and Cam was keeping him quiet.

"John, did you just say Jerry has epilepsy?" Cam asked me.

"That's what his sister Trina said," I answered.

"That idiot was just drunk, dude," Lonnie declared. "I've seen drunk people dry heaving when there's nothing left to come out. He must have hurled earlier, when we were talking, but those were drunk dry heaves."

"Dude, she said it was a seizure and told us to leave. She said that he wasn't supposed to be drinking," I told Lonnie to get him to chill.

"No shit, dude. We're sixteen. None of us are supposed to be drinking," said Lonnie.

I thought that was a pretty good point, but I still felt responsible for Jerry. Why hadn't he told me about his epilepsy, or even that he had been drinking on his own? I didn't know much, if anything, about epilepsy, and this wasn't the time to learn. I vowed I would learn more about it in the coming weeks.

"Did you see the ass on her under that shirt?" Lonnie jerkishly asked.

I had seen it but wasn't going to mention it.

"All right. Time to go back to camp. You need to sleep this off," Cam said to Lonnie.

I agreed that Trina looked good – and that it was time for Lonnie to sleep it off.

We woke up Dustin and got Snoopy ready. As we were getting up, the front door of Jerry's house burst open. Jerry's dad had Jerry over his shoulder, carrying him. He got to their beige Oldsmobile Cutlass Cruiser, opened the back door, and gently laid Jerry inside. He slammed the door shut, started the car, and drove off quickly into the night. It was now close to 3:00 a.m.

We watched all this in fear and amazement. We sat motionless for a moment collecting our thoughts. Lonnie broke the tension a few minutes later.

"Bitch can't hold his liquor."

"Shut up, jackass," I warned him.

Cam was also whispering something to Lonnie. I never found out what he said. I was nervous as hell now and wanted to get back to camp quickly. I hoped Jerry was going to be okay.

"I'm heading back now. If you're with me, let's go," I instructed and left without waiting for a response.

The group all followed, and we worked our way cautiously back to camp. Snoopy, Lonnie, and Dustin were asleep quickly. Cam and I got the fire going again and smoked Reds the rest of the night. We couldn't have slept if we'd wanted to. This was the first time I really questioned if our creek time had gone too far. I mean, most of our big trips had some kind of problem, as if the creek god really did have it in for us. Maybe we'd brought too many people – or had the club grown beyond what it was meant to be? I wanted to go talk to Trina to see what was going on, but I knew that wasn't the right call. We left the creek as a group about 9:00 a.m. When we got to Jerry's house, the Oldsmobile wasn't there. In fact, no cars were there besides Lonnie's. Everyone went their separate ways for the weekend, which was the longest weekend of my life.

Jerry wasn't at school Monday. What concerned me even more was that I didn't see Trina anywhere either. I saw Cam in fifth period.

"Hey, brother, have you seen Jerry or Trina today?"

Cam gave me a frown, as if he had managed to put the bad

situation out of his mind over the weekend and I had just ruined all of the hard work it had taken to do this.

"No. I was about to ask you the same thing."

We decided I would try to call Jerry when I got home. This was well before cell phones were big, so it was a waiting game for us. I drove the turbo machine home and ran into my mom on the way to the fridge.

"Hey, John, how was school today?"

"Great, Mom. I got a test in Geometry Thursday, but other than that there's not much going on," I informed her.

If she knew the shit that went on during our creek missions this would have been an entirely different discussion. She went to her room, which was just off of the kitchen, so I grabbed the phone and dialed Jerry's number.

The phone rang twice, and Trina answered.

"Hey, Trina, is Jerry home?"

"He's home, but he can't come to the phone," she said.

"Is he okay?" I asked cautiously.

"He had to go to the hospital that night to get his stomach pumped. He was there most of the next day," Trina informed me.

She didn't sound too upset to be talking with me.

"He's grounded for a month. My parents said he can't hang out with you again until summer starts," Trina told me.

"Let him know I'm sorry, would ya?" I asked.

"Why are you sorry? He was the dumbass drinking so much," Trina countered.

She had a point, but I still felt responsible.

"Well, thanks for the information. Should I take the blame with your parents?"

"You're the last person they want to speak with," Trina said.

"All right. Thanks again."

Trina paused for a second as I prepared to hang up.

"John, he said he had a blast that night, up until his memory faded, and he asked you to keep the epilepsy thing at the creek. Is that okay?" Trina inquired.

"No problem, but the others that were with us know as well. I'll tell them to keep their mouths shut about it," I promised.

"He knows they know, so just nobody else, okay?"

"No problem," I answered.

"And, John, nobody better find out you saw me in my underwear under those circumstances," she joked.

"It's as good as forgotten," I said.

We said bye and hung up. I made a note of the qualifier "under those circumstances." It certainly wasn't ever actually forgotten, and I cursed the creek god at that moment for our stupid code. I have no doubt that Trina and I could have had a relationship of some kind, but Jerry couldn't have handled it. However, I try to never regret the sacrifices made for friends. I was just happy Jerry was home and he was okay.

CHAPTER 14

✳ ✳ ✳

THE BARN

The summer before eleventh grade was a good one. Jerry's parents had finally let him do stuff with me. He told me they actually thought I was a good influence on him. That was not normal for me, so I took pride in it. Still, he worked most of the summer at the Waynesville Market, so we hung out maybe once a week. Cam got a summer job at the Shur Value, which was up Old Waynesville Road a few miles past Alex Bields Elementary. I would pick him up from work and take him home sometimes. We camped twice that summer and had a lot of fun. I was the only one of my friend group that didn't have a job. I am grateful my parents let me enjoy my teenage years. There was one three-week job I had delivering pizza the following summer, which was a result of my dad refusing to buy me a hundred-dollar pair of Adidas Torsions. Other than that, I didn't know what work or struggle was until I hit Basic Training after high school – but that's a story for another time!

Hanging here and there with Jerry or Cam was a good part of that summer, but another good part came by random chance. I happened to be out one July day prepping for cross-country, which started in mid-August. I was running the circuit made up partially of my street, Brightwood, another connection street called Bentwood, and finally Cedarwood. While running, I heard a buzzing noise behind me. A minute or so later, a red scooter ridden by a cute girl came zipping past me. On my three-mile run, this girl passed by me another three times. On the last time she stopped, and so did I. It was Clarise Sherman, of the creek Shermans!

Clarise pulled up and started a conversation. She was two years younger than me and would be starting her freshman year. I had seen her on the bus and around town, but I had never spoken to her.

"Hey, I'm Clarise," she said as she turned off the moped.

"I'm John. Did you just get the cool scooter?" I asked.

"Yep. My brother moved back in last week. He used it in college. Wanna ride?"

Of course, I wanted to ride. She started up the Honda scooter, and I got on the back and put my hands on her waist. We drove all over. It was one of the newer models and handled two people well. We took turns driving and had a really good time. We ended up at her house shooting hoops. Clarise was cute like a girl but cool like a dude. She had sandy blonde hair and light blue eyes, kind of like a young Sharon Stone.

"You're the guy who comes through here all the time to get to the creek. My parents know who you are," Clarise told me.

"We've been coming through here for years. I thought they were cool with it," I said.

"They are. I've seen you go by so many times over the years. One of these days, you'll take me out there with you," she said.

We hung out almost every day that summer. I never felt the need to make a move, and neither did she. This was my first real friendship with a girl where there was no ulterior motive. It wasn't that the spark wasn't there; it was just that the friendship fun was too good to ruin. I ended up violating creeker code and showing her all the campsites. She had been to the Kirks and the big field, but that was as far as she had been on that side of the creek. She had also been on the other side of the creek and knew about the Structures and the dunes.

We had a blast that summer. I filled her in on the high school and the good teachers. I told her I would help her if she needed it. I even told her the story of Nick, the motorcycle gang, and the fire. I'm not sure if she really believed me, but it didn't matter. Besides Clarise, I hung out that summer with an old friend who came back to town.

Beetle Batson returned from East Texas State University that summer. He told me the return was for good as he was sick of college and wanted to join the workforce. He had been there about a year and had a good grade point average. I think he just missed the creek and the fun we had. Anyway, we rode bikes all over town, fished, and talked of the old days. On one bike ride, we ended up going south on Old Waynesville Road out toward Indian Lake. This was in the opposite direction to Alex Bields. We explored a new neighborhood being built called Waynesville Oaks. These homes cost more than $200,000 each, which was really expensive in those days. About half of the houses were built, and the roads were complete. We traveled down one unfinished cul-de-sac and parked our bikes. There was a section of woods that led onto the land of one of Beetle's friends, Ericson. We left the bikes in the vacant lot and took a walk into the woods, wondering where they led.

About five minutes into the woods we came upon a cleared-out section of trees. There were stumps and empty beer cans on the ground. This was clearly a campsite. On three of the trees pentagrams had been painted in red. This freaked us out. We weren't sure whose property this was, but thought it might have been Ericson's land. The site felt dark, and we didn't hang around long. The main reason for this fear was an incident about six months earlier, midway through my sophomore year. An undercover cop had been murdered by students a few towns over from us in the same district. They had been caught, but the news said it was a "tangled mess of drugs and devil worship." Seeing those marks on the trees caused us some real fear, so we took off.

We went back to our bikes and rode to Beetle's house. Beetle called Ericson and warned him that someone might be using their property. Ericson's dad was a fire marshal with a badge, so he did actually check it out, but we never heard if they found out who it was.

Beetle was back, and the summer still had another few weeks. The campsite we'd found in Waynesville Oaks had piqued our investigative interest.

"Hey, man, let's go out to the barn by the Structures again, but this time in daylight," I proposed.

"I'm in, but we need to be more careful this time. We can't get caught, dude," Beetle insisted.

"I told Clarise about the barn, and she wants to come as well, but do you think that's really a good idea?" I asked.

"You know her. I don't. It's up to you. Can she run fast?" Beetle inquired.

"Yeah, she's pretty fast," I answered.

"Tell her about the mission and see if she wants to go late tomorrow morning," Beetle instructed.

"Let me think on it. I don't want to put her in any danger, but I know she'll be pissed if I don't at least give her the chance."

Beetle agreed, and I told him we would meet at his house at 9:30 the next morning.

That night, I went to see Clarise. We rode the scooter for an hour and ended up back at her place sitting by a fire in her vast backyard. The fire always looked great in the dark. Clarise had magical eyes that captured the beauty of the flames. I thought for a minute that I was starting to fall for her, but I beat that idea back quickly. It would be a big risk, because she was quietly becoming my best friend next to Cam. Love would ruin that. In my opinion, the friend romance idea will only work one time, and that's when you marry your best friend. Nope, no romance would be pursued here. There was just too much of high school left, and I wanted her in it with me. I determined that if she ever braved it and made a move, I would run with the ball in a big way, but she never made a move on me in high school.

Clarise got up from her seat and headed to the garage.

"Would you like a Coke?" she asked.

"That'd be great."

I determined that when she sat back down, I would ask her to go with us. She handed me a Coke and moved her chair closer to mine. We had a small radio playing in the background. Eagle 97 was hitting the rock hard and mixing in some pop rock as well.

"Hey, Clarise. Beetle and I are going exploring in the morning. You remember the story I told you about Nick and the motorcycles?"

"And the creepy barn?" she asked.

"That's the one. Beetle and I thought we'd try to check it out in the daylight. You wanna come with us?" I asked her while Van Halen's "Panama" played in the background.

"I can't believe you're asking me on a creek mission with one of your friends. I feel honored," she said half-jokingly.

"Hey. You're really cool, and you're my friend. There's no rule that says girls can't be creekers. Just come with us. It will be fun."

She didn't answer right away, and I was starting to feel like I had read the situation wrong. She confirmed that for me with her answer.

"I love hanging out with you, but Beetle's older. He's gonna think I'm a little kid."

"No, he won't. He already told me you could hang with us," I mentioned.

"I know, but I like things the way they are. You and me, here and at the creek. I haven't been to the Structures since you told me the Nick story. I don't want to go near that barn either. Besides, from what you've told me, Jerry will hate me coming down there without him being on board," she reasoned correctly.

"Well, it's not up to him. He's not even part of this trip. I want you to come if you want," I said, as I was clearly losing this invite.

"John, I appreciate the confidence, but that part of your world isn't my thing. I sit on the sidelines, and you tell me the stories when you get back," she politely declined.

"Okay, but I'll get you out with the boys at some point," I conceded.

"Maybe," she said so I could save face.

We sat there drinking our Cokes and listening to the music. The atmosphere was a little awkward, but we got over it. I had been there a few hours by now and needed to get home. I knew her dad would be nudging me on my way soon, because he also had once been a high school boy, and he knew where my mind would eventually go. I got up and prepared to leave for home.

"Clarise, I gotta go. It was fun, and thanks for the drinks," I said.

"All right. I see my dad watching through the window any-way," Clarise said.

"Let him know he doesn't need to worry about me. I wouldn't risk screwing up our camp entry point," I joked.

"It's not you he's worried about," she said with a twinkle in her eyes.

We finished our goodbyes, and I headed down the driveway toward my car.

"Hey, John," she said.

"What's up?"

"Will you come back tomorrow night? We can build an-other fire, and you can tell me all about your adventures," she inquired.

"It was already the plan," I said as I walked away.

The next morning, I left for Beetle's house about 9:15. I had called Cam the night before to see if he wanted in on the mission. He told me he had to be at work by 1:00 p.m., so he was forced to decline. I had also driven up to the Waynesville Market and shared a few smokes with Jerry. He too had to work that day, from 1:00 to 10:00 p.m. It looked like it was only me and Beetle – just as, it seemed, it was always meant to be. I was excited to be going to the creek with him. He had only been back home a short while at this point, so things still felt a little different. This was maybe due to the fact he was no longer in high school. He was over eighteen and could do what he wanted. If he got caught doing some stupid shit, the stakes were high now, and he could get in real trouble. I began to second-guess my plan. I wondered if I should back out now and go it on my own in a few weeks. I quashed that idea quickly. Beetle was a man and could make his own decisions. I walked the third of a mile down Brightwood Street to his house because I didn't want to worry about my car today. I got there a few minutes early and ended up watching him finish a game of Omega Race on an old Commodore computer. He lost a few minutes later, so we were not delayed long.

Beetle handed me a pocketknife and mini–tear gas gun. This thing looked like a small .22 revolver. It had come from the see-through novelty box at the Waynesville Market. I had been shot in the face with one of these pellets, and it had burned for hours. I had no doubt it would give me a few minutes to get away if I got in some trouble. Somehow, it felt like we were going on an actual combat mission instead of one of our standard recon missions. Beetle had camo pants on and a small backpack with him. I had a few pockets in my full-length camo pants, but that was it. The knife fit nicely in one pocket, and the tear gas gun fit comfortably in one of the others. Beetle walked out the door and beckoned me to follow, but instead of walking out his back door and heading through the backyard to Cedarwood Street, he went out the front door this time.

"Dude, where are you going?" I asked.

"Trust me. I've got a different route that I feel good about," Beetle answered.

He walked out to the street and took a right that led away from my house and toward the ball field. We walked down the street in silence, and I realized we were heading for one of our legendary fishing holes: the Two Ponds.

"Are we heading to the Two Ponds?" I asked.

"Right. We will be in that region," he answered.

I was a little confused. I knew there was eventually a way to get to the dunes from this direction, but it was a lot of extra mileage. However, this was Beetle. I trusted him, so I followed.

We passed the glorious Two Ponds. They were on our left as we walked up the narrow road, with another giant field on our right. If you went far enough through the field on the right, you would come out at the bottom of Brightwood Street, about ten houses down from Beetle's. We were now going up a big hill, and the mood was calm. I broke the silence.

"Beetle, do you remember the time you made me a bamboo fishing pole?"

"Yep, and I remember it was useless," Beetle answered.

Until that point in my life, I had caught maybe two fish. I had no idea what I was doing, but I had gone on many trips with Beetle before he left for college.

"Hey, look, the boat's still there," Beetle said as he pointed to his left across the field to the second pond.

"That was my favorite trip," I answered, remembering the time Beetle and I took a radio out on the boat and fished in the middle of the pond. "All right, man, where to now? If we take this curve to the left, we are heading away from where we want to go," I pointed out.

"We will stop before the curve."

At the top of the hill the road curved sharply to the left. On the right, before the curve, was a mailbox by a gate in front of a dirt road. The mailbox said one word, "McMinner." Beetle stopped by the mailbox and pointed to it.

"Here we are, dude. McMinner's place," Beetle said.

"I never knew this led to the Structures. When did you figure it out?" I asked.

"A couple of years ago, me and Steady were riding bikes out here and we came across it. If you do the map work you can see it is the right place," Beetle explained.

"So, we're just gonna walk up and ask to see the barn?" I inquired.

"Well, I figured we'd just go look at the barn and if we got caught, I'd pull out the news article I have and tell them we were looking for the artwork," Beetle reasoned.

I had to admit, I liked the plan. It would give us another side of the property to view, and another exit route if things got crazy. It had been a few years since I had dared to come out here, but I had been dying to investigate the place after my campsite was burned down. Beetle climbed the gate and entered McMinner's property. I followed.

We found ourselves on a dirt road heading up a small hill. About a quarter of a mile down the road, deeper into the woods, we saw a metal building off to our left. It was no barn; it looked more like one of those metal office buildings owned by an AC company or service business. Such buildings were sturdy but much faster and cheaper to build than a conventional brick office. The building was light yellow. It had sets of garage doors on the left side and an office door on the front right side. I assumed this led to McMinner's office. I didn't see a house anywhere, only this building, which could also have served as living quarters, I guess.

There was no sign of recent life there, so I whispered to Beetle, "Hey, maybe he doesn't even live here. I mean, there's no cars, just that workshop over there."

"Never assume, brother. We don't know anything yet. Just keep walking," Beetle said as he headed deeper into the woods on the path.

Once we were out of visual range of the metal shed-like building, I lit up a smoke. Beetle took one, and we sat down for a rest out of sight. The memories of Nick and the gang were coming back to me in a powerful way. I knew we had to be getting close.

We finished our smokes and got back on the trail.

"This place isn't quite as eerie during the day," I said in a low tone.

"Or maybe time has lessened the fear. I mean, you're four years older than the last time we were this close to the barn," Beetle said.

He had a point, and I hadn't seen any crazy motorcycle dudes riding around either. The woods were full and thick on both sides of us now, blocking out a good portion of the sun-shine. The trail had become basically a car path through the woods. We finally came to a clearing. In the middle of the clear-ing was a five-foot-tall stainless-steel sculpture of a dude on a motorcycle. It was an abstract piece; I mean, you could tell what it was, but it was somehow distorted, like crazy art in a funhouse or something. I walked closer to the art. Beetle followed. We got to the statue and both stared at the black plaque at the base of the metal. The words were written in white and in cursive:

In honor of my only remaining relative,
Nick

On the gas tank of the abstract cycle the artist took credit:

McMinner 87

Beetle and I saw the inscription at the same time. Now that I look back, I miss our modern smartphone technology. It would have been awesome to get a picture of the art to help support our story – an ability we take for granted nowadays. Beetle was clearly captivated by the statue, as was I. We looked at it in si-lence for a few minutes, until I decided it was time to move. I tapped Beetle on the shoulder.

"Nineteen eighty-seven. This has only been here for a year," I said.

"Right. So, it appears Nick wasn't trespassing," Beetle declared.

"Well, we know we were, but I still want to kick his ass.

What kind of dude chases kids around on a motorcycle like we're in some kind of dystopian *Road Warrior* fantasy movie?" I asked.

No answer was needed: we knew the kind of dude who did this, and his name was Nick.

The clearing narrowed back into the path through the woods. After a moment or two, we reached another, larger field. There were a few junky, weathered cars on our right. They were rusted out and filled with trash, including beer bottles and soda cans. To the left was the blackened frame of a building. This was little more than a rock foundation with a few weak boards sticking up and out in various places. There had been a fire some time ago. Nothing of value remained that wasn't reduced to ash. Although I had approached from the opposite direction, I knew right where I was. I would never forget this spot. We were looking at what was left of the barn.

"Man, when do you think this happened?" I asked Beetle.

"Who knows? I'd bet real money that the 'only remaining relative' had a part in this destruction. I mean, his crew did try to burn down your campsite," Beetle reminded me.

"Right. At least one of those jerks had an itch to start fires," I agreed.

We headed up to the rubble and walked around, hoping to find something, anything, that would tell us about Nick and his cronies. I guess no evidence would be as plain as the statue we had seen in the clearing a little way back: Nick was allowed to be here. He was related to the famous artist, and that was the end of it. The barn was no more. I wondered if some wild party had gotten out of hand, or if Nick had lost his mind and taken his rage out on the place. It must have been one hell of a fire.

There was little left to look through, so Beetle and I figured we'd head home via the red structures. It had been a long time, and it was daylight. We took off toward the road where my motorcycle chase had begun four years ago. We figured that route would be faster. We were wrong.

As we walked down the wooded road toward the Structures, something felt off to me. I mean, we had come for answers, and we had some, but I still needed to somehow face my demons. Just because we knew who Nick was didn't mean that this was over. The dude had incited motorcycle riders to chase me and had burned down one of my campsites. He was dangerous and needed to be confronted. What I could do at sixteen remained to be seen, but I felt like we were missing something.

At that moment, we heard an engine behind us. The noise sounded like it was coming from the vicinity of the gutted barn. The vehicle was clearly heading in our direction. I dashed into the woods to my right. I knew if I had to run, I would be at the Structures, within a minute or two of the Smitters' creek entrance. Beetle was on my heels. Once I got deep enough into the woods to have some good cover, I turned back toward the road and dropped down onto my stomach. I wanted to see who this was.

"Every time we come out here there's some bullshit," Beetle whispered.

"I know, but we need to see who this is," I returned the whisper.

"Even if we see who it is, what are we going to do?" Beetle inquired.

"I'm not sure. I just know I've had this shit on my mind for four years now and it's freaking me out," I said as I got up on my elbows to better see through the trees to the road.

An old brown Chevy truck was cruising slowly down the path. It got close to where we had entered the woods and then stopped. The driver got out of the vehicle but left the engine running. The driver walked toward the woods in our direction.

"Hey," he yelled in our direction. "I know you're out here. I just want to talk," the man informed us.

He was everything you'd expect an older abstract metal artist to be. He looked hippie. He looked bohemian. He had long gray hair and a scruffy white beard. The guy was skinny to the point I actually felt bad for him.

"Hello. Just come back. I need to know what you want," he said loudly.

At this point, my courage grew and I stood up.

"What the hell are you doing?" Beetle angrily whispered in my direction.

I walked toward the old man without knowing what my plan was. I guess I figured I would play it by ear and just be honest with the guy. When I made it close to the truck, he saw me. I saw no gun, and I figured I could take the guy in a fight if I had to. Beetle was still in lockdown mode. I made it out of the woods and was now within about twenty feet of the man and his truck.

"Hello, I'm John," I said. "Sorry to run, but I've had some bad luck at this place in the past," I told the stranger.

"Well, you shouldn't be trespassing," he said.

"You're right, but that artwork is killer. We came to check it out one night and heard some music and loud noises.

We decided to investigate and found a barn with a bunch of motorcycle dudes partying. I see the barn is no more," I added.

"You like the artwork, huh?" he asked.

"Who wouldn't? At first, I thought they might be alien artifacts. I mean, who knows what the hell those things are?"

"Well, to start, I know what they are. I made them," he proudly stated.

"You're McMinner? You are really good. I wish these were out so others could see them," I said.

"I have the exposure I need. They are not meant for public consumption, just to satisfy my need to create," McMinner said thoughtfully. "Where's your fiend?" he asked.

"He's out there. Once he knows we're safe he'll come up," I said loudly. "We're looking for Nick. Do you know when he'll be around?" I asked hesitantly.

"What do you want Nick for?" he asked.

"I'll be honest. We had a bad run-in a few years ago, and I need to get some closure. Someone set my campsite on fire, and I think it might have been him," I said with confidence this time.

As if on cue, Beetle joined us. I look back now and think he only came out to make sure I didn't screw anything up.

"Well, why do you think it was Nick? What makes you think that?"

I answered by telling him the motorcycle story and about the campsite fire. He didn't seem surprised and never denied that Nick was capable of these things; he just looked at me and started talking again.

"Nick is my nephew. I'm all he has. If you knew how many times I have had this exact type of conversation, you'd be shocked," McMinner stated. "Both of those stories merit an ass-whooping. Come with me and I'll make sure you get your chance to confront him."

"Beetle, what do you think?" I asked.

"We're here. Let's get it over with," he replied, with obvious reservations.

I jumped into the back of the Chevy. Beetle climbed up onto the tailgate. He shut the tailgate, and before we knew it, we were already turned around and moving again. We passed what was left of the barn and the new stainless-steel statue. We made it quickly to the light-yellow metal building. McMinner pulled up in front of one of the garages. He got out of the truck.

"Jump on out," he said.

I was beginning to wonder if this was a soldier spider delivering me to the black widow for dinner. Beetle got out first, and I followed. McMinner entered a side door to the building. He left it open and was clearly wanting us to come in. We followed.

"Nick is down that hall, through the second door on your left."

The inside of the metal shop had been renovated. It turned out to be a really cool three-bedroom house on the inside. Beetle and I walked through a small, well-done kitchen toward Nick's room. I was really nervous at this point.

"Nick! Nick! Got some visitors. Don't say I didn't warn you," McMinner yelled through the house.

I wasn't sure if the dude knew how bad I wanted to hurt his nephew. This all seemed surreal, and I figured we were both missing something really big that should have been obvious. I decided now that he knew I was coming, so I would just open the door and ask about the fire. This might be my only chance to get some answers. I looked back at Beetle as I moved through the house toward Nick's room. I could tell he had my back. Nick had done a number on both of us.

We made it to the room. I stopped and took a few deep breaths. I knocked on the door. There was no response so I knocked again. With my hand on the doorknob, I looked back over my shoulder at Beetle. He gave me the universal nod that said, "I'm right behind you." I turned the knob, threw open the door, and bounded into the room.

"What the hell?" I yelled.

"Aw shit," Beetle lamented.

In front of us was a dude lying in a medical bed. There were machines hooked up to him, including one that looked like a respirator. The guy had a light-blue hospital gown on. He had light brown hair and a little stubble on his face. I guessed he was six foot tall or so. He lay still with his eyes shut. There were no nurses or doctors, only the patient, who appeared to be in some kind of a coma. I felt a touch on my shoulder and turned around. It was McMinner.

"Sorry to disappoint the both of you. Come back into the living room. We'll grab a beer, and I'll tell you the story of Nick."

McMinner walked out the door and down the hall. Beetle and I hesitated and looked at each other. There would be no confrontation today, so we headed in to meet McMinner. He made good on his promise to give us beer. We sat on the couch, and he began his story.

"Nick moved in with me around nineteen eighty, when my sister passed away. I had seen him just once before, when I flew to South Bend, Indiana, to watch him while my sister had surgery. After the surgery, I returned home to Texas and never saw her again. Little did I know the surgery was just the tip of the iceberg. After that came the chemo and additional surgeries. She never recovered, as the cancer came back over and over again. The last six months of her life were horrible, and I had no idea what she was going through. One day, a professor friend of hers from Notre Dame called and asked me if I wanted to clear out her desk. That was how I learned of her death. The hospital had tried to call me at my last known number in Jefferson City, Missouri. She had never updated the form with my Texas phone number. Anyway, I went and picked up her stuff, and Nick as well. I mean, there was no one else. It had to be me. My sister's life insurance was a couple of million dollars. Half a million went to me, and the rest went into a trust account for Nick. As I had my own money, I figured I'd use my cut to take care of her son. I had no idea what kind of boy Nick was. He was sixteen at the time, and he was upset to leave the Bend.

"In eighty-two, when Nick was eighteen, some of the insurance money was released to him. We got along okay, mostly because I traveled around the world making art. I figured he could handle staying here on his own. However, that was not the case. Nick needed supervision, and I just wasn't the guy to provide it. I had too much going on. Needless to say, I got several calls from local law enforcement at my overseas residence. Once, Nick got pulled over with cocaine in the car. Another time, he got caught with a sheet of acid on him. Somehow, he ended up with only probation for both. He also lost his license a few years back because of a DWI. Nick just didn't care. He kept driving cars, and he gained a new obsession with motorcycles – which you obviously know, based on the story you told me. Although I tried to love the guy, I finally washed my hands of him last year when he was hauled in for questioning after that undercover cop got killed. They ended up charging some other kid, but Nick and his friends were suspects as well. I could never trust him, so I made him leave. I was able to tie up a lot of his money in trust so he wouldn't blow it all. My sister would have hated my decision, but I just couldn't deal with a hooligan.

"You guys want another beer?" McMinner asked.

"Sure," Beetle answered.

"So, it was eighty-five when you made him leave? And where did he go?" I inquired.

He came back to the couch area and handed us each a beer. At that moment, a woman in nurse's scrubs came in the door and walked by us.

"Hi, Janet," McMinner said.

"Hello, sir, I'll just be a minute," the woman answered.

"They check on him three times a day, and he has an alarm straight through to the doctor and nurses. Fortunately, I was able to invest the rest of the insurance money wisely, and his remaining money is taking care of the medical work. All they're doing is keeping him comfortable, and maybe giving him an extra year or two," McMinner said in a matter-of-fact style. "It was early eighty-six when he left. I'm not sure who he stayed with, but he came by to see me a few times when I was in town. The last time I saw him before he got hurt wasn't good. He wanted a hundred thousand dollars of his cash for a drug buy. Pretty bold, but of course I said no.

"Shortly after that things started happening. One day, I came home to find half of the outside walls of my home spray-painted with foul language and tagged 'Nick' all over. That damage was expensive to repair. Then, one of the structures got splashed with green paint that refuses to come off. Next, little fires started popping up all over my property. Finally, he burned down my barn. He literally threw a bitch fit, splashed gasoline all over the place, and lit it on fire. At that point, I pulled the shotgun on him and he left. The fire thankfully didn't spread. I should have reported him, but I just couldn't do that to my sister."

"Okay, so what happened? How did he end up back here in the hospital bed?" I asked.

"I can't believe you didn't call the cops on him," Beetle added.

"Like I said, I knew my sister would have never forgiven me were she alive, so I just didn't. Maybe I should have," McMinner said. "Anyway, one evening I was sitting here reading when I heard a motorcycle rush by the house toward the old barn area. I knew it was him, and he was traveling so fast. I went out and got in the truck to tail him, but he was out of sight by the time I got going. I decided to head out toward the red art area and see where he was. A minute or so later, I heard a crash that sounded like metal on metal. I drove as fast as I could, but it was starting to get dark. When I reached the field, I saw him. He had hit the third structure head on; it hadn't budged, but his motorcycle had.

"I rushed to help him, but he was bleeding from multiple wounds. His left leg was broken in two. I could see the bone breaking through just above his kneecap. He was out cold and barely breathing. I didn't dare move him, so I drove back to the house to call 911. It took about twenty minutes for the ambulance to arrive. By then, I had put tourniquets on his left arm and leg. The paramedics took over. They said he was dying, but they would do all they could. They loaded him in the ambulance and headed off down the wooded path back to the road. He ended up taking a CareFlite to Baylor Hospital in downtown Dallas. He lost both legs and one of his arms. They put cheap prosthetics in for the sake of appearance, but he is paralyzed from the neck down. The feeding tube and breathing machine keep him going. I feel like I could have done more, but it is what it is. So, he got worse than you probably imagined doing to him yourselves."

"Right. We never imagined hurting him like that. I'm very sorry. I can't imagine the stress you are under caring for him every day," I said.

"It's not really stressful. He just lies there, and if the alarm goes off, I hit this beeper and a nurse comes. Very simple. I own the equipment, and the nursing company is a once-a-month payment. The worst part is, I'm reminded of my failure each and every day, and my European friends don't see me near as much," McMinner lamented.

"I'm sorry. If you ever need someone to sit in for a few hours or do some errands let me know," I declared.

"No thanks. I have professionals who can do that. Now, it's probably time for the two of you to get going. No more trespassing! I only told you the story because I know Nick was an ass to many people, so I thought after your story you deserved some closure. Now that you have it, don't come back."

Beetle and I walked down the long driveway back to the road. The walk home was pretty quiet. After about thirty minutes of silence, we reached Beetle's house. He told me to hang out in the backyard for a few minutes while he went and grabbed us some Cokes. We drank them slowly and contemplated the day's events. The barn was gone, and Nick was no longer a threat. This wasn't how we'd imagined the day playing out, but seeing him helpless on the bed had lifted a large weight off my chest. I could tell Beetle was relieved as well.

"Man, that was some story. I wonder if Nick and crew had anything to do with the cop?" Beetle asked with a wide-eyed expression.

"Well, McMinner said he was into drugs, and the murder was drug related. I saw craziness in the motorcycle riders that night. Didn't you?" I asked Beetle bluntly.

"Well, I saw them chasing you on motorcycles and hitting you with a strap, so I'd say there was some craziness there, yes."

"I'm out, dude. I'm gonna go eat and then hit Clarise's house," I notified him.

"But are you gonna kick it with Clarise?" Beetle said playfully.

"She looks really good, so who knows?" I shot back equally playfully.

I thanked him for coming on the mission with me, said bye, and took off up Brightwood Street to my house.

That night I saw Clarise in a new light. She really was pretty, and I decided right then and there I would extinguish the spark I knew was growing. It is hard not to like a good-looking girl when you're a teenager, so I had to force myself to stay in the friend zone. There were many reasons for this decision. However, the main reason was that she had a great innocence about her that I did not want to ruin. Also, I didn't want to have to find another launch point for our missions. I told her about the day's events, and she was absolutely shocked. I chilled with her for a few hours and went home.

We hung out a lot over the next two years, and I made good on my promise to myself to never make a move on her in high school. (Note: there could have been moves made in later years, such as at college, but that is another story.) School would be here before I knew it, and I made sure to enjoy each and every day I had left. I hung with Cam, Beetle, and Jerry a lot as well. Soon, the joy of that summer was cut short by cross-country two-a-days, and then eleventh grade began.

✳ ✳ ✳

CHAPTER 15

FAITH

School cranked up after that glorious summer. Cam and I had four classes together, including French. We were juniors in the class with a bunch of freshman girls. It was pretty great. I also was doing really well in cross-country. By late September, we had already run in four meets, and I had placed in the top ten runners in two of those meets. Cam wasn't in a sport this semester, and his mom made him quit the store because she didn't want him working during school, so we hung out a few times a week. However, his mom was still very controlling, and she didn't let him go camping at the creek much with us. Because of this, Jerry and I grew closer, doing at least one trip every three weeks. Although a few others came with us at various times, the majority of missions were just me and Jerry. These missions were fueled by Marlboros, *Playboys*, and tequila. I always felt weird watching Jerry drink after the crazy night when he had seizures in the rain. We talked about it, and he vowed to keep the drinking under control. After that night, I never saw him super-drunk again. I had a few close calls with drinking myself, but the creek god kept my idiocy contained at the creek.

Jerry worked about twenty-five hours a week at the Waynesville Market, so we basically just hung out at the creek on Saturday nights. I remember listening to Oingo Boingo and smoking our lungs out. Clarise faded into the distance, playing sports and making new friends. We were still cool, but we ran into each other very little. Cam filled the void left by the missing Clarise. Neither of us had a steady girlfriend that year, so we became the best of friends. We got in trouble together in French class almost every day, and at one point I got brought into the office to work off seven unserved detentions. Mr. Ginters in the office would let me trade them in for in-school suspension or "licks." Licks was a slang word for a big spanking with a wooden paddle. I made these types of trades multiple times my junior year. My behavior wasn't violent or anything like that; it was just general goofing off. I look back now and think I must have appeared to be a real dick, but that year was still a blast.

If I was asked to sum up the highlights of my junior year, I could do so easily, without having to put much thought into it. First, the best part of school was the four out-of-district drama tournaments Cam and I went to. We won first place in the duet scene competition at two of them, and we took second at the others. I made out with a girl at three out of four of these locations as well. I think girls liked having a two-hour romance and then getting back to life when the competition was over. Life was pretty safe that way, and I didn't mind playing that role for them. Cam met another gorgeous girl at the Lancaster tournament that year, but the meeting didn't lead to the same type of long relationship he had started in Longview the previous year. No, this one was just a kiss in the gym when the lights went out during the improvisation rounds. That was enough for him. Because of our limited success at these events, we both thought we were real players. (No one had to know we were still both very much virgins!)

The next best thing about junior year was my camping trips. I went camping more that year than in any other year. I was able to maintain scene control pretty well, making sure friends that didn't mix well stayed apart. Lonnie and Jerry still didn't get along, but they kept the peace the two times we all went together, which was all I could ask for. Later that year, I started holding creek competitions that were simply a blast, and by the end of the year, we'd had multiple requests from different teams that wanted to challenge us. We called these outings "War Games."

School was great due to Cam and Drama, and the creek was awesome due to Jerry and the games. However, the best part of the year far exceeded these other highlights. Concerts. Yes, I had already been to multiple Christian concerts during my youth, but this year was the best ever. Now that I had a car, I was able to go to places I had never been. For example, I saw the Cure at Starplex in Fair Park, because some New Wave girls from Computer class talked me into driving them to the show in exchange for a ticket and some clove cigarettes. Besides that show, my group of friends made it to the Arcadia on Greenville Avenue to see Oingo Boingo. Even Jerry and Lonnie came along that night. It was simply awesome watching Danny Elfman sing "Dead Man's Party" and "Weird Science." Later that year, Beetle and I made it to another venue to see Stryper. Man, that was a hell of a show. They rocked like no band I had ever seen, and I still feel that way years later after multiple concerts. However, the best show of the year by far was a trip on a Friday night in October 1988 to Texas Stadium to see the George Michael *Faith* tour.

The idea for this trip was hatched by Cam in August, a week or so before school started. Cam had to work, but he needed a ride to the show, and he wanted good seats. To this end, I woke up early that August Saturday morning and drove out to the mall to visit Ticketmaster, which was attached to the local Sears store. By the time I got there, hundreds of people were already in line. By the time I made it to the front, seats were limited. I got two seats in the lower balcony, which actually turned out to be really great seats. At the time, my parents were still on an anti–secular music kick, so there was no way they would let me go to see the guy who had written in lipstick on a girl's thigh in the "I Want Your Sex" video. The solution was simple: I would tell a half-truth and spend the night at Cam's. This would have to go off perfectly, since the cross-country district meet was also the next morning at 8:00 a.m. Although I had my story ready for go-time, the plans were still up in the air as late in the game as the Friday morning before the show that same night.

I mentioned earlier that Cam's mom could be a real tyrant when it came to his freedom. She knew he wanted to see George, so she used that as an inducement for him to get his Algebra II grade up. It turned out to be an effective, if stressful, way to accomplish her goal. The week of the show, she sent a note to school with Cam for the teacher to sign at the end of each class, giving her the status of his grade. It was this simple: either he had a 70 or above or the concert would not happen. Cam skirted the line every six weeks in this class, just managing to pull out a low C at the end of each grading period. This was the middle of a grade session, so he was on the lower end of the 60s at this point. We had a test the Friday morning of the show. The teacher had agreed to grade his paper after class and let us know if we were going to the concert or not. Cam and I sat at our desks after the test while the other students went on their way at the ringing of the bell. We had determined that he needed an 87 on the test to bring his current grade up to a 70. He had never managed this before, so we were worried.

"Dude, how did you do on the quadratic equation section?" I asked.

"Terrible, I'm sure. The bitch is definitely gonna fail me," he mumbled.

"Man, I say we go anyway. I mean, if we're gonna get in trouble, it might as well be for something awesome like this," I reasoned.

"Shh, she's almost done," Cam said.

The teacher, Ms. Dranning, got up from her desk and handed Cam a piece of paper with two problems on it.

"I forgot to hand you the bonus problems, Cam. Please complete these in the next two minutes and turn them in," Ms. Dranning said.

"Okay."

Cam looked hard down at the sheet and started working the problems. Within thirty seconds, Cam got out of his seat and handed the paper in. Ms. Dranning pulled out her pen and began grading. By this time, both Cam and I were standing right next to her watching and holding our collective breath. Ms. Dranning wrote a large +10 above the bonus problems. She then pulled out his test and wrote the same on top, next to the 77 she had previously written. She totaled up the score and wrote in large red letters:

87! Enjoy the Concert!

Cam handed her his daily sign sheet, and she put "70.3%" along with her signature. This was awesome! As least as far as Cam's mom was concerned, we were now eligible to go to the concert. We walked out of the room with a smile on our faces. When we got to the hall, I asked to see the test and bonus questions. He handed them over to me with a smirk. These were the two bonus problems in an Algebra II course:

$$5a + 1 = 11 \text{ and } 6a + 1 = 13$$

It was now obvious that Ms. Dranning was on our side. A first-week Algebra student could have nailed these two bonus questions. Ms. Dranning understood what the concert meant to us, and she made it happen. Without the bonus, the 77 would have stood, and Cam would have been below the 70 percent he needed. Besides, I think she was actually happy with the 77. Even with that score, it was his best test yet this semester!

"Dude, I'm going to be nicer to her the rest of this year. She saved our night," I said to Cam while heading to our French class.

"I know. I think I want her!" I smiled at the comment.

"You and me both, man. You and me both."

The end of the school day came. Lonnie, Jerry, Cam, and I made our way to the rock parking lot of Possum Fields High.

"Sure you don't want to come with us, Jer? There will be ticket scalpers there," I said.

"Dude, you been in love with that faggot since junior high. Besides, I gotta work," Jerry said laughingly.

"Lonnie, you in?" Cam asked.

"Hell no. Jerry's right. That guy's a peter pumper," Lonnie replied.

"So, no concert, huh?" I asked in jest.

Cam and me jumped into the turbo machine and headed into Dallas. This would be the farthest I had ever taken the 1978 Toyota, and I questioned whether it would make the trip. Getting there was all that mattered. The return trip would take care of itself.

"All right, boys. Take care. We'll light some up for you" I yelled out the window as we drove away.

Cam and I looked at each other and high-fived. Concert day was here, and Lonnie and Jerry had actually agreed on something. Miracles do happen.

I look back on this period with great affection, but that doesn't mean the eighties were all rainbows and unicorns. It's about thirty years later, and much has changed in the way of attitudes, even in Texas. Lonnie has a family now and a successful career, and he would be shocked to read the terms he and Jerry used to describe George Michael. Quite frankly, Cam and I didn't care who he slept with, as long as he pumped out the tunes. This was way before George's infamous LA bathroom incident in the nineties, so many girls still held out hope that he was straight. However, we all kind of knew he played for the other team. This was probably the first time I was in blatant opposition to my parents and the church. They couldn't look past the gay lifestyle to see the great singer that George was. They also couldn't understand that you could disagree with someone's lifestyle choices and still appreciate them as a person. George was widely considered the hottest star out in America during this period. His songs topped the charts for a few years. Looking back now, I should have just told my parents I was going to the concert, but I couldn't run the risk that they would turn me down. I can't help thinking about George's tragic life as I write this. He fought depression and drug abuse for most of his life, and he ended up passing away in bed, in his fifties, a few years ago. His was a sad story, but the man was one hell of an entertainer. I have seen at least a hundred concerts at this point in my life, and George Michael is still my favorite. I now go back to 1988, to Irving, Texas.

Cam and I pulled into the parking lot at Texas Stadium. I had never seen so many cars. The parking lot was full, and an outright party was in full swing when we rolled up at 5:30. The host on the radio told a story about George coming to town a few years earlier with Wham! and playing the Bronco Bowl. George had vowed never to come back to Dallas as the crowd did not receive him warmly. The host had gotten ten thousand fans to invite George back to Dallas through a letter-writing campaign. It had worked!

Cam and I stepped out of the car, and we each lit a smoke.

A group of older girls walked by and handed us each a Miller Lite. Yes, it was like a commercial. We popped the tops and nursed our beers, realizing the night could end really early if a cop came by. However, that didn't seem to be a problem, as I saw two of Irving's finest smoking a joint and chatting up some younger girls.

"Man, I've never seen so many hot girls in one place," Cam said with a huge smile on his face.

"No doubt. Jerry and Lonnie are fools," I replied.

Cam lifted his drink and toasted that comment. We partied in the parking lot until about 6:15. The opening act, the Bangles, were set to start about 7:30. We had time, but we lit up another smoke and started the walk to the stadium. We passed several groups of revelers on our way. Everyone was in great spirits. The girls outnumbered the guys about five to one, which made the night even sweeter. I remember thinking I needed just two or three of these beauties to cheer for me like they did George, while he had thousands wanting him and probably didn't even care. Man, I wanted to be George Michael.

We made it into the stadium and found our seats. They were lower balcony stage left. There was a ramp I had seen George use in a music video that ended with a place for him to stand about four feet from us.

"Wow, we lucked out here," Cam said.

I agreed.

"It's only seven. You want to go into the corridor to try to meet some girls?" Cam asked.

He didn't have to ask me twice.

"Let's do this," I answered as I walked out of seating area and through the doors to the walkway.

We went and grabbed a few Cokes at the concession stands. We didn't need to go any further than this area, as it was packed with tons of girls. Many of these girls were dressed in lovely evening wear. It was almost as if they had secret hopes George would notice them and whisk them away to his flat in London or something. We saw two pretty girls smoking by the wall, and we went to join them. They looked close to our age, so we figured we'd take a chance. I lit up a smoke and pulled out the charm, with the confidence of the creek god.

"Hello, ladies. Are you enjoying yourselves so far?" I asked.

"Yes, thanks. We barely made it out of the parking lot with all that partying going down," the shorter, brown-haired one said.

"I know, people were literally giving away beer. I've never seen anything like it," I said.

By now, Cam had zeroed in on the cute blonde, which was fine by me. I reached out my hand to the girl I was speaking with.

"I'm John. That's Cam. We're from Possum Fields," I said to hopefully start the introductions.

"I'm Zada, and she's Kerry. It's nice to meet you," she replied.

Cam and Kerry seemed to be holding their own in the conversation game, so I focused on Zada.

"I've never heard that name before. It's pretty. So, you're here to see the Bangles, right? Girl Power?" I said, hoping she appreciated humor.

She smiled and laughed.

"Oh yeah, I'm a Susanna Hoffs fan. I can't wait to see her in a miniskirt shaking her ass on stage," Zada jabbed playfully back.

"I get it. When George comes on, we don't exist. That's why I'm talking to you now," I said.

"Now you understand the way of things. Better jump on the train before it leaves," she declared.

We bantered like this for a few more minutes. I felt a spark but knew it would die very soon.

All of a sudden, the lights started flashing and someone started talking through the intercom system:

"Ladies and gentlemen, the Bangles!"

Cam didn't even say bye. He literally started sprinting back toward our seating area.

"Wow. Your friend actually does want to see Susanna," Zada joked.

"It's his first big concert. I've had fun and …"

I was stopped mid-sentence with a mind-blowing kiss from Zada. Before I could gather my wits, Kerry grabbed me and leaned in for a kiss of her own.

"Tell Cam he left way too soon," she said.

I stood there speechless, wondering what I should do now. Should I take the huge win or risk overplaying my hand and go in for more? Zada handed me a piece of paper with an address and phone number on it.

"Give me a call sometime. Fort Worth isn't too far from Possum Fields. I know because we kicked your ass in football a few years ago," Zada said with a smile.

"I remember very well, and it was awesome to meet you," I said as music started to fill the stadium. "I'll call," I yelled as I ran toward the door to my seat.

"Whatever, dude. Have fun!"

I glided through the crowds high on life as "Walk Like an Egyptian" started warming up the Texas Stadium crowd.

When I arrived at the seats, they were all filled, with the exception of my own. Cam was chatting with an older lady, probably somebody's mom. She was smoking, and so was Cam. I lit up and danced a little with the Bangles' tunes. The crowd was moving a bit, but the band was not all that impressive. Within a few songs, it was obvious the group was drunk out of their minds. The guitar player fell down twice, and Susanna tripped and fell as well. I think I even heard some boos. They played about twenty-five minutes and left the stage to a smattering of applause. At that moment, a voice came over the loud speaker again:

"Please be patient while we await the arrival of George Michael," the voice said to thunderous applause.

The crowd counter over the stage reached thirty-nine thousand people.

"Hey, Cam, let's go find the girls again," I said.

He agreed, and we walked out toward the corridor to get a drink. I told him the story, and he was a little pissed at himself for leaving so early.

"I thought the Bangles would be a lot better, man," Cam informed me.

"Well, I got Zada's number, which can lead to you seeing Kerry again as well," I said with hope.

We looked around a few minutes and couldn't see them anywhere. The lights began slowly flashing on and off. We decided to head back to our seats. We didn't want to miss the arrival.

The scene around as we walked back into the stadium is easy to set. Cam and I had seats in the middle of a section of about a hundred girls. There were so many teenage girls there it was hard to concentrate. There were so many gorgeous adult women there as well. The houselights were about halfway up. There was a lot of drinking going on.

"Wow, man. Lonnie and Jer are idiots. This is the best night ever," I pronounced.

Cam heard me, but he was already singing "Monkey" and dancing with the girl in the seat next to him. She was juiced and into Cam, so I let it be. I was chatting with a number of girls while we waited. Everyone was anxious. Concerts are always like that, but turn it up one hundred times for a megastar! I looked down at the floor seats, and there was a lot of milling around. In the center of the crowd were a couple of girls in evening wear holding a large paper sign that they had unscrolled:

George, we want your Sex!!!!!!!!!!!

I saw a lot of smoke and smelled marijuana. I expected that at a Bon Jovi or Mötley Crüe show, but I guess it didn't matter what the concert was. The girl behind me was smoking a clove cigarette, and I asked her for one. She handed me one, and I enjoyed it very much. She also shared her beer with me. I think I was on the verge of making a move on this sexy college-age girl as well. I just can't describe the vibe going on in that place, but it must have been a small glimpse of what Woodstock felt like. I mean, the girls were just free and acting uninhibited. It was incredible. The vibe intensified, but the focus soon changed. Cam was making up for lost time with the girl next to him. They were in make-out mode, and nobody cared. If it had lasted much longer, I would have had to intervene with a fire hose. Before I could tell him to keep his pants on, the houselights went dark and the crowd roared like nothing I had ever heard.

You could see the person next to you, but it was really dark for a stadium of that size. People were talking, but the noise had now dropped significantly. Then, a voice was heard over the loudspeaker:

"Hello, Dallas! Sex, yeah. I see good stuff going on. The party is rolling, and I don't want it to end. Guys, get your last kiss in for the night because I'm about to ruin it for you for the next three hours or so, but don't worry, I'm gonna make sure you all leave here happy!"

The crowd was in a frenzy as the organ at the beginning of "Faith" started up. The spotlight came on and then focused on the ramp box stage four feet from my face. George Michael was four feet from us! Girls rushed the rail and were leaning over to reach George. Cam and I were in the middle of the squad, reaching toward him as enthusiastically as any of the girls! He belted out verse one of the hit number while high-fiving the hotties reaching out to him. He then turned and ran down the ramp toward center stage as the crowd went nuts. We danced with girls and had the time of our lives as he went through multiple hit songs, including songs from his Wham! days. I knew the words to every song and sang along with all of them. George would stop singing at points, yet the songs would continue! The crowd was so into this. The best song of the night created a memory that stayed with me and Cam for the next several years of our lives.

After an awesome slow rendition of "If You Were My Woman," a version of a song originally recorded by Gladys Knight & the Pips, the music for the Wham! original "I'm Your Man" started. George went backstage to change or something, and Deon Estus, the bass player, came to the front of the stage. He led the crowd in a chant that kept the ball rolling while George took care of business in the back.

The crowd sang loudly in unison:

"If you're gonna do it, do it right. Do it with me!"

This went on for about three minutes while anticipation built. Then George re-entered the stage and sang the song. It was one big party. Girls were jumping around like mad, and Cam and I were just soaking up all the goodwill! During the second singing of the chorus, George ran up our ramp. The girls rushed the rail and were all reaching out toward him again. I had a blue Coca Cola hat that I wore most of the time. I grabbed it and held it out toward him to extend my reach. George saw me! He looked me right in the eye as he swatted playfully at my hat and said, "What's up, dude?" He then started singing again and ran back down the ramp. I immediately pulled the hat into my chest as at least twenty girls mobbed me and tried to get at it. Cam held off who he could and eventually got me up and out of the fray. What a night!

The concert lasted about three hours. George gave an awesome show with a lot of energy. He sang every one of his hits from his solo and Wham! days. The crowd worked its way out, and we were able to pick up two concert T-shirts for thirty dollars. We thought that was a deal. By the time we got in the car and got rolling, it must have been midnight. We drove back home in awe of the night we had just had. We made our way south on Loop 12.

"Man, he hit your hat. He hit your freaking hat," Cam screamed at the top of his lungs. "Did you see me getting down with that girl? She was smoking hot, and she could kiss," he bragged understandably.

"Everyone saw you, dude. I was proud and ashamed to know you all at the same time," I replied.

"Let's hit Whataburger," Cam proposed.

"I'm already on my way," I answered.

We got our food and ate it on the drive home. I had two burgers with mustard, ketchup, and pickles only. Cam had a grilled chicken sandwich all the way with mayo and a large fry. We both topped off our food with delicious strawberry shakes.

We pulled into his driveway about 1:30 a.m. This was where things got tricky. There was no way I was going to sleep anytime soon after that show. The adrenaline was still coursing through our veins. Yet, I had to be at the school by 6:00 a.m. to catch the bus to the district cross-country meet in Arlington, Texas. This was the most important race of the year for my sport. Well, I guessed I had to try. Cam made a pallet for me on the floor. He hit the sack hard and was out in minutes. I tossed and turned for at least an hour.

I couldn't get to sleep, mainly because I had to pee so bad. I opened the door quietly and crept to the bathroom at the end of the hall to the right. I did my business and now only had about three hours left before I had to be at school. I turned the light out and opened the door quietly. I didn't want to disturb the normal flow at the house. However, my trip to the bathroom must have woken sleeping giants. As I opened the door, I heard a series of soft moans interspersed with grunts. I couldn't help but look in that direction. I saw a sight that thirty years later is still burned in my mind. I was actually stuck in position and couldn't move. The picture in front of me was horrifying! Cam's 350-pound mom was riding Cam's 140-pound dad. She was full-on naked and enjoying herself. I was trapped, and I couldn't look away. After about twenty seconds of torture she noticed me, kept riding her man, and reached over and slammed the door shut.

"Go to bed," she yelled.

Five-thirty came fast that morning. I made my way to school and eventually ran the race. I had completed my best season ever until that day. Not surprisingly, I finished 85th out of about 110. Seventy-five of the people in front of me were runners I normally beat easily, but I was just too tired to compete. My team were highly disappointed in me. One of them pointed out that we would have won district if I had just finished in the top fifty, which was normally a given. I had no excuse. I had let them down. We drove back to the school knowing the season was over because I had partied too hard the night before. Did I feel bad? A little, but not too much. I had seen George Michael. I had made out with two smoking hot girls and almost a third, and Cam had once again made out with a beauty queen in public. Nope, I wouldn't apologize for losing this for my team and school. It was worth it. It was so worth it.

CHAPTER 16

* * *

WAR GAMES

The following Monday at school was a testament to courage and pride. I saw several girls with George Michael shirts on, but Cam and I were the only two guys wearing them. Remember, this was not 2020; it was 1988. People were generally okay with the gay lifestyle as long as you didn't throw it in their faces. Even though he hadn't yet come out at the time, everyone knew or assumed George Michael was gay. However, after that performance I didn't give a shit if he was gay, straight, or whatever. I would proudly carry his flag. The shirt got a lot of attention, mainly from dudes asking me if I was gay too. Cam and I decided to run with the ball. I proudly told anyone who asked that they could suck it, plain and simple.

Lonnie and Jerry were sad they had missed the concert after we told them stories about all the girls there. Monday lunch was full of party stories and girl stories. My normal group at lunch was about six people, but today it was more than ten. Clarise and a few of her friends had dropped by to hear the stories, which brought the crowd up to fourteen. Everyone loved the story of Cam running off while I made out with two girls. Clarise's eyes sparkled a little bit when she heard this, but I quickly moved to the story of Cam taking off a girl's bra in the stands at Texas Stadium. Everyone loved that one. Jerry was slightly amused but used the opportunity to his advantage. Whatever his motivation was – whether he had been planning the idea for a while or was simply jealous and wanting us to shut up – didn't matter. He came up with an idea that revolutionized our camping trips for the remaining year-and-a-half of high school. This one-minute speech produced enough history to propel Jerry into the creek hall of fame.

"Okay, while I have you all here. You all know about our group, the creekers, right? Well, we have created a new game that you will want to join in on. This is a team sport. We are fielding a team of five. That team will be made up of John, Cam, Lonnie, J.D., and me. We need five guys to oppose us. The game is Creeker Capture the Flag. However, it is not the traditional game. This game has no rules, except no punching in the face, and when you are dead, be a man and admit it. The game will take place on over a hundred acres of land, so if you've got the balls, then step up to the plate and sign up to take us on. Any takers?" Jerry asked.

A few people murmured among themselves. Three guys signed up.

"You guys need to get two more to join your team before five on Friday night, and the game starts at eleven. You need to have your five and meet us at my house at nine. Cool?" Jerry asked.

The guys agreed and said they would get two more dudes. Now that cross-country was over, the sky was the limit. This sounded fun, and it was. We called the sport "War Games"!

Later that afternoon, Clarise caught up with me in the halls. We hadn't talked too much that year, but for no real reason other than a lack of opportunity.

"Sounds like you had fun Friday night. Were they pretty?" she asked.

"They were okay – certainly not as pretty as Possum Fields girls," I replied.

"What class are you heading to?" she asked.

"Study Hall, and you?" I countered.

"Oh, Ms. Johnson's Geometry class," Clarise informed me.

Clarise was a real trooper when it came to math. She had knocked out Algebra I in eighth grade, which enabled her to start Geometry with mostly tenth graders.

"Hey, John. Before I go, I need to warn you about Mason. He signed up to face you guys in the War Games. He is really violent and fights all the time. He hurts people really bad too. I've heard he hates Lonnie for some reason and is planning on attacking him in the dark during the games. I just thought you should know," Clarise said seriously.

"I appreciate it. That's good to know. I can't wait for next summer to get here so we can chill again," I said.

"I know. It can't come soon enough."

Now, I had been hearing about Mason Bell for years – how he was a real tough guy who never knew when to quit. He had literally put a dude in the hospital last year. The year before, he'd broken a guy's eye socket, and we never saw the kid again.

Yet, somehow, he never seemed to get in trouble. I had seen him wail on a kid in the cafeteria once. However, I also knew Lonnie could handle himself. As long as Lonnie knew the dude was coming, he would have a chance of holding his own. I gave Lonnie and Cam the news, and it didn't surprise them.

"Yeah, during summer baseball league I hit on his girlfriend. She said she would have messed around with me but didn't want me to get hurt," Lonnie explained.

"Dude, you hit on Gretta Wilson? Don't you have any standards?" Cam asked.

"I have standards. They can't have a dick, and they can't be bigger than me," Lonnie shot back at Cam.

"Well, anyway, keep your eyes open. We don't want that prick getting the drop on you," I said as I walked away.

Later that night, I met Jerry during his break outside at the Waynesville Market.

"Let's light up," Jerry said while pulling out a Marlboro Red.

"I'm in," I said as I did the same. "Hey, man, why was Mason hanging at our table during your speech?" I asked.

"Oh yeah. He's in my Health class. He's really cool, and I found out he hates Lonnie," Jerry answered.

"So why would we want him down there? It's almost like you want a fight to happen or something," I accused him.

"Well, Lonnie deserves an ass-whoopin', and it might as well happen away from school so nobody gets in trouble," Jerry declared.

"Dude, you know the creek rules. If you want to organize a fight, you do it in the ring of honor, not like a punk. Call it off," I ordered.

"Man, quit being so high strung. I didn't plan anything. Mason honestly was talking shit like his team could beat us at the game. I called him on it, and now we will see," Jerry explained.

"So, there is no plan for a random attack, like he is famous around the school for?" I asked.

"Not at all," Jerry informed me.

"All right, man. Has he found his two missing players?" I asked.

"Yes, it's now Mason, Billy Jones, Jim Dunn, Barry Williams, and Cort Manning," Jerry explained.

"Man, that sounds like his whole gang. I hope this doesn't get out of hand," I said.

The night of the game came, and ten players met at Jerry's house at 9:00 p.m. as planned. There was a little drinking and a whole lot of smoking going on. The cars were parked, and the bags were packed. The band of players walked down the street to the Shermans' entrance, from where we eventually made our way through the field and forest to the New campsite. Everyone put down their stuff, and we built a quick fire. Mason's crew had already downed a lot of booze, so I knew trouble was on the horizon.

"Here's the rules, okay? First, the object of the game is to capture the flag from your opponents' base and get it back to your base with your flag still present as well. Now, how do you stop a player who has the flag or stop one from obtaining the flag? Answer: Any way you can. You can wrestle the person into a submission hold, you can knock them down, or you can outright fight with them. The rules of the fight are simple: No biting and no punching in the face. No using sticks or rocks or any foreign objects. Once a person says they are dead, you must cease the attack. The object is to take out the enemy and get the flag. If there is a death dispute, then the game stops, we form the ring of honor, and there is a fight to submission. Now, we are not seeking real damage here, so the moment somebody gives up, it's over. Get it?" Jerry asked.

"How will we know where the enemy flag is?" Cort Manning, one of Mason's crew, asked.

"Before the game starts, I will show you my team's flag location and then walk all five of you to your location. The game officially starts fifteen minutes after I leave you. Any more questions?" Jerry asked.

"No man, let's do this shit," Mason declared emphatically.

We put out the fire and walked through the forest into the middle of the field. This field was often called the Shit (short for the land of "Oh Shit"). After the ten of us had got our bearings, we turned left and walked about ten minutes northwest until we came to the New-New campsite.

"Hey, fellas, the new team's flag will be on the fence at the back of the Old campsite," Jerry informed us.

We all knew where that was, including J.D., who was a guy we had met in Drama that had come camping a few times with us and was a serious candidate for a creeker tab.

"I will be back here in less than thirty minutes. Then we will begin," Jerry said with excitement.

Jerry and the others disappeared into the night, and we made our plans. The short of it was that I would travel through the forest to the New. Then I would go down into the small pond and up the other side, cross the fence, and travel to the

Old site via the back way. I should be able to grab the flag without them even knowing it. One person was to come with me in case I got grabbed. We decided that would be Cam, who was our fastest. I knew the land the best, but if I got in a pinch, I could fight and slow them down while Cam made a break for it on land they didn't know. J.D., Lonnie, and Jerry would stay and guard our flag and fight to make sure no one grabbed it. We sat and smoked Reds, waiting for Jerry to arrive. In about twenty-five minutes, he did.

"Took you long enough, Jerry," Lonnie said.

"Shut up, dude. It's a long walk," Jerry counter-punched.

"Well, do you think they will even be able to find this place?" I asked.

"I don't know. They seemed a little juiced," Jerry answered.

"Well, is it time?" Cam asked.

"It's time. Let's do it," Jerry answered.

"Get going, John and Cam. Trust me, no one will get our flag," J.D. boasted as he took up a defense position close to it.

Cam and I raced through the woods behind the base and headed back to our original New campsite. It took about ten minutes to get there. I was sure Jerry must have taken the other team the long way to the Old site, as he had walked off in the direction that would take them through the main field. This was good: they probably had no idea that we would be coming through the back field. We looked around and then went down into the creek and up the other side. We crossed the fence and launched the final leg of our flag-capturing journey. With any luck, we would pull the flag and be gone before they even knew it. This was the same field Steady, Joel, and Beetle had traveled through the night of the great fire. Although we were still a good distance away, we could hear a lot of noise. We slowed down and went into stealth mode for the remainder of the journey.

We got within fifty yards of the fence at their base and lay on our bellies. I bet they would never have expected this. Cam crawled up beside me and began to whisper.

"Hey, crawl up there and grab the flag. You can see the outline of it there on the fence line."

I focused hard and scanned the line he spoke of. It was true: you could see something that looked like a shirt hanging on the fence. I crawled slowly through the field, and Cam moved about twenty feet behind me. I was picturing a relay of sorts if they saw me take the flag. In that case, I would be forced to hand it off to the speedster, Cam. I wondered if he could find his way back to our base through the forest without a light, but I didn't dwell on that thought. I made it to within twenty feet of the fence and saw no movement anywhere near the flag. The moon was pretty bright, but nothing was coming into view. I figured now was as good a time as any, so I crawled on my stomach all the way to the flag and reached up. I got my hand on it, and it came to me easily. I had the flag but heard no movement. This was weird. No one was here.

I stood up and began hauling ass as fast as my legs could carry me through the field. Cam was on my heels. I made it to the fence before the New site and stopped. I looked around and saw no one in pursuit. Cam came up beside me.

"Dude, nobody was guarding their flag. That worries me," I stated.

"Me too. Let's get back to base pronto," Cam said as he jumped the fence and headed down the bank toward the creek.

He was up the other side and at the New before I even jumped the fence. He took off through the forest toward our base at the New-New. I jumped the fence and followed him. After ten minutes of feverish sprinting, we won the game as I placed the flag on our flag at home base. However, there was no celebration. No one was there.

"Cam, what's up? Why would the creekers leave the flag unguarded? The only time it's right to leave the post is if someone gets the flag and takes off," I stated.

"No shit, man. Something must be wrong," Cam replied.

"Let's go to the main field. We can get clues and a better idea of what to do from there," I declared as I left the base.

Cam followed, and we walked swiftly through the field toward the platform at the edge of the forest, where people tended to congregate. We could see well that night, and we noticed something in the distance. When we reached the top of the field, it did appear that there were people further ahead of us in the field. About a hundred yards from there, we found J.D.

"J.D., what happened, man?" I asked.

He was lying down holding his knee to his chest.

"I don't know. A few of them made it to our camp for the flag, but we chased them off. I twisted my knee in the chase, but Jerry and Lonnie kept going," J.D. answered.

He was in relatively good spirits for someone who had just blown out his knee. He managed to get up and stand beside us.

"So, it was just game play?" Cam asked.

"Yeah. They got close to the flag, but we handled it, unless that was a misdirection and someone else grabbed our flag while we chased them," J.D. observed.

"That's not it. We just won the game. Both flags are now at our base," I said.

"Then let's go see what's going on," J.D. directed.

We followed his advice and headed down toward what appeared to be either cows or people. It was hard to tell from this distance.

As the shapes came closer into our view, I could see what looked like mayhem going on. Cort and Jim Dunn were holding Jerry back, while Mason appeared to be punching Lonnie vigorously in the face. Lonnie managed to wriggle out of the ground-and-pound position and get up. The fight must have just started, although I did notice that Jerry didn't appear to be fighting too hard to break free. I had already seen enough of this Mason character, and he was ruining the sanctity of the creek.

"Hey, dick, the rules say no punching in the face, jackass," I yelled from thirty yards out.

Lonnie had taken a few more hits from the relentless punching of Mason, but I was proud of him for not curling up into a ball and getting beat like a punk.

"That's it. Game over. We got both flags at our base. We won," I yelled at Mason.

"It ain't about a game. It's about kicking this dude's ass," Mason angrily screamed in reply.

Mason was six feet tall and maybe 180 pounds. He was pretty solid. I never feared guys like this. I had seen him fight, but I had never seen anyone really fight back. The flailing arms intimidated everyone. Even Lonnie seemed petrified at the barrage coming his way. I knew right then and there what I had to do.

I looked at J.D. and Cam and whispered, "Get Jerry free, and be ready to back me if these punks jump in."

They nodded in surprise as I moved in the direction of the battle.

At that moment, I switched from a swagger to a burst of speed straight at Mason. I hadn't ever felt this kind of motivation before. I rammed Mason head on in his chest, knocking him to the ground.

"Lonnie, go help J.D. and Cam. I want this bastard," I ordered.

"Whatever, I had him," Lonnie answered while carrying out my instructions.

"Oh, you think you'll do any better?" Mason yelled as he jumped up and ran at me with arms flailing like a hurricane.

He landed a few while I got my balance. I was able to block most of the storm as I quickly figured out the mistake his other victims made. The crazy rush of punches freaked dudes out so much that they froze and just took them. After five or six you went down and just prayed for it to end. I would not succumb to that temptation. This guy was a one-trick pony, and I was determined to see his bullying days come to an end. He came in for another rush of blows, but his swings were really wild and had little power. I stood my ground and threw an uppercut at his chin when he got close. It stunned him pretty good, but he kept throwing punches. There was no point going toe to toe with this idiot. I knew I had to get him to the ground.

As he landed a few more, I made sure to keep my chin down to protect my throat. My eye was starting to swell a little, but I knew my next move. I just needed him to get closer.

There! "Here he comes," I thought. He moved in closer to try to release the flurry on me, and I saw my opening. I slipped in between his blows and wrapped my hand around the back of his head. I then landed another uppercut directly in his nose area. I heard a crack. He lost balance for a minute, and that was enough. I elbowed him in the forehead and put him in a tight headlock. I launched both of us to the ground, making sure to land on him. He was absolutely stunned. I was able to maneuver around him and get him into a submission sleeper hold. He was flailing his arms backwards at me, trying to land blows, but none were connecting. I had an awesome grip in this position and would not let go until he was out. I had my legs wrapped around his waist and was now in total control.

I could hear little mumbles, so I knew he was still getting air. I just needed him to pass out, which tends to put an end to urgent fury. If the situation had been reversed, this punk would have got on me and ended my life as I knew it, but that was not my intent. I just wanted him to know he couldn't attack my friends and get away with it. He finally stopped swinging after a minute or so, and I felt the fight go out of him. I flipped him over so he was face down in the dirt. I quickly let go and popped him on the right side of his head for good measure. I didn't want to do permanent damage to the guy, so I stopped. The bully had been neutralized. I got off of him. My adrenaline was pumping.

I yelled like a fool in the moonlight:

"Don't bring that shit here! The creek god won't allow it. Shit, I won't allow it. I am the damn creek god! Take your shit back to Possum Fields where it belongs!"

At that point, Jim and Cort came to help Mason, who was holding his head and nose but had at least made it up to a sitting position. Cam walked over and offered him help up as well.

"You got your ass kicked, dude, but it stays at the creek unless you bring it up. We have a code here, and although you broke the rules of the game, we will not make a big deal of the fight at school unless you do," Cam informed him.

"All right, man. We're good. We're cool," Mason said as he spit out some blood. Lonnie made his way forward toward Mason, who had a different presence after his defeat.

"I'm sorry I hit on your girl. Can this be over?" Lonnie asked.

"All right, man. It's over. Man, I never knew Decker could fight," Mason said in a daze.

"He's got two big brothers, dude. Life is a fight," Jerry informed him.

As bad as the fight had been, everyone was getting along now, and J.D. was even rubbing in the defeat at the War Games. I walked to within speaking range of everyone and offered an olive branch.

"Now that the game is over, let's go back to camp and have a beer," I said.

Everyone got up. I lit up a smoke and headed back toward camp. My right eye was swollen shut, but I had defended the honor of the creek and won.

After a few beers, the ten of us were getting along like old friends. Mason and I lit up smokes and laughed about junior high football. We had even dated a few of the same girls. He asked for some fighting tips. I explained to him that his method worked against 85 percent of guys. Most people feared the flailing arms and would curl up because it was pretty scary. I told him he could start like he did on me, but if the guy didn't curl up, he should either slow down to land more effective punches or develop a better ground game. He was actually a good listener, and I could tell he had never even imagined getting beat. He also apologized to Lonnie for his plan. He confirmed he didn't really want to play the game; he just wanted to take out Lonnie. He was surprised that Lonnie didn't curl up like his other victims in the past. If Lonnie had had some wrestling talent and an uppercut, he would have ended Mason's night early. My main thought and question was: What was Jerry's role in this? However, after another beer I drifted off to sleep and lost the idea that Jerry had somehow planned this. It just couldn't be possible, and I never asked him. Everyone slept well that night, and the tradition of the War Games had now been solidified.

At school Monday, there was no talk of the fight. I got made fun of a little because my eye was still pretty bruised and battered. I just smiled and said, "You should see the other guy!" I never talked about the fight, and neither did my crew. As far as I know, Mason's boys didn't mention it either. I did, however, hear through the grapevine about a great new game on weekends over in Waynesville. The War Games were a hit, and before we knew it our next ten weeks were filled with opponents wanting to take us down. We scheduled a session every two weeks. We lost session number four when our boy Snoopy mounted a combo-team from Possum Fields and Indian Lake Christian. So, we ended the season with a really good record of five and one. I made it through the year without having even one official girlfriend, which kind of sucked, but overall, I was okay. Looking back now, my junior year was incredible. The George Michael concert, duo-camping trips with Jerry, and the War Games all combined to make it the best year ever.

✻ ✻ ✻

CHAPTER 17

THE SUDAN WALL AND MARSHAL BILL

When my junior year ended, I thought I had maxed out the fun meter. The year had been so awesome I just knew it couldn't be topped. The summer before my senior year started in early June, and I was already missing hanging with Cam each day at school. He started full-time work the very day school ended for summer. His mom made him pay rent and everything. What a ball buster, but she loved him. Jerry and I were able to make two creek trips during the summer, but he also worked a lot. As I sat at the house lonely and defeated with nothing to do, I thought of the one thing I was missing in eleventh grade: a woman. I could have the best of both worlds right down the street. I grabbed the phone off of the wall mount and dialed Clarise's number. She answered on the second ring and was as bored as I was. An hour later, she picked me up on her scooter and we hit the town, which meant we went to the Waynesville Market. We picked up smokes, courtesy of my boy Jerry, and some Dr Pepper. We then rode back to her place and spent the day lying around in her kiddie pool drinking DP and smoking Marlboros. Her mom saw us and didn't seem to care, so we kept rolling.

I don't know if you've ever been to Texas, but at times it can be hot as hell in the summer. I hung out with Clarise all week, and we always ended up in the pool. One day, I asked if she had any friends with swimming pools. She had none that lived close by. I told her about Steady's pool, but he had been gone to college for two years now, and as far as I knew he didn't come home for the summer. His sister didn't like me anyway, so without Steady there it just wasn't going to happen. Then Clarise mentioned a pool five houses down the street, which was three houses to the left of Jerry's house. The girl that lived there had just graduated, and I thought that both of her parents worked. As far as I knew she had no siblings.

"Hey, Clarise, you know that pool you mentioned a few houses down on the right?" I asked.

"Yeah. Brandy Davis lives there," Clarise said.

"I wonder if she'll be swimming and in a bikini?" I half-joked.

"She may not be, but I could be," Clarise said flirtatiously.

"Well, go put in on. We're going swimming," I said with authority.

"You got it. Be right back," Clarise responded.

She came out in athletic shorts and a bikini top, looking really hot.

"It's a good thing we're friends, because if not, I would have to get a shirt for you. Do you really go out like that in public?" I teased her.

"You know you like it," she shot back, knowing the truth that all good-looking girls know; she had called my bluff.

"Of course you look good, and you know it. Let's go swim," I said as I walked to the street and took a right to head toward the Davis residence.

We made it to the house in about two minutes. There were no cars out front, but Clarise and I walked to the door and rang the bell. No answer. We tried a few more times, with the same result.

"What was your plan? Were you just going to ask her if we could use their pool?" Clarise asked sarcastically.

"That's exactly what I was going to do, and now we know no one is home," I answered.

I walked around the left side of the house to the chain-link fence. The Davises' yard was at least two acres in total. The back portion was fenced in pretty securely. I would have to climb over the fence to swim, as it was a little too tall to jump. Just as I was preparing to jump, I saw the dog. It was a medium-size white mutt. It came to the fence in front of me and started barking loudly. The dog was obviously defending its turf. I stuck my hand out to the dog from the other side of the links, but the dog did not come to investigate, as most friendly dogs do. Instead, it ran off to the other side of the yard barking. I threw my leg up to the top of the fence. It was higher than normal, but I did get it up and over.

Through some excellent leg work I was able to finally make it over the fence. I then walked to the gate, which was easier to climb, and gave Clarise a hand. She made it over with no trouble. I looked at Clarise, and I remember really hoping she would take off the shorts. She did, and revealed a blue bikini bottom most girls would die to have and most guys dream of. I pulled off my shirt and sandals and ran to the pool. Clarise had eased herself in, but I entered cannonball style. We swam and played for the next two hours. Man, I wanted my own pool, but this was still really cool. I was nervous for a little bit, but I almost forgot I was trespassing. At around 4:30 that afternoon, I heard someone honking their car horn. Within a minute, a well-dressed middle-aged woman with brown hair and a nice business dress came into the backyard and confronted us at the pool. It didn't take long to realize that private property is a real thing.

"Who are you, and why are you in my pool?" Mrs. Davis asked, with a flash of anger in her eyes.

"Ah, we're Brandy's friends. She said we could swim here," I lied.

"Well, isn't that interesting. Brandy has two friends I know of, and both of them live in Minnesota, where we came from. I never heard her mention either of you," she said.

I couldn't lie anymore, so I decided to come clean.

"Look, Mrs. Davis, we just wanted to swim. It's so hot. I'm sorry we trespassed," I answered.

"Well, get on out. This will be the one and only bit of grace you two get from me. Now go!"

I got out of the pool and went over and collected my shirt and sandals. I walked out of the gate slowly, in shame. However, I guess Mrs. Davis expected more out of girls.

She stopped Clarise and made a comment as she picked up her shorts, "Don't you want boys to respect you?"

"Well sure, doesn't everyone?" Clarise inquired.

"They'll never respect you until you learn to accentuate your mind and not just your body," Mrs. Davis warned.

"I just wanted to swim, and I'm sorry. We won't come here again," Clarise apologized.

"Good. Bye," Mrs. Davis said as we were walking away.

We took off back to Clarise's house. I felt bad that I had gotten her in trouble. She, however, was laughing about it all the way back to her property. On the way there, an idea came to me. What if we challenged teams to visit certain local sites and swim without permission at night? We could find and mark two groups of pools around the block and set the starting points at equidistant locations. Then, the team that got all its members in the most pools without getting caught would win. The biggest catch was that all the team members would have to stay in each pool for at least one minute. We had never done anything like this. I looked forward to bringing the idea to the creek "board" and getting approval.

Clarise liked the idea but figured it was a guy thing. She just wanted me to tell her about our adventures. I went home, grabbed the car, and drove to the Waynesville Market. Jerry came out, and we had a smoke.

"Hey, man, I've got an idea for a new 'creek' competition. The one caveat is that although it will take place during creek missions, it will not take place at the creek," I said.

"I'm listening," said Jerry.

"Well, we know of more than twenty pools in the local

area, right? What if we create two maps with different mile-long routes that end at the same location, and we mark at least five houses with pools on each route?" I explained.

"Okay, easy enough, but what the hell for?" Jerry asked.

"One team starts at the top of one map, and the other team does the second map. Each member of each team has to be in each pool for at least one minute. The team that makes it to the finish line first without getting caught wins," I stated.

"Sounds cool, but it could get dicey at night," Jerry warned. "Let's make the maps and do a test run with just creekers. You and me versus Cam and Lonnie," Jerry suggested.

"Cool. Since you got a job, I'll do the maps, which we won't need but others will. I'll call the boys and set it up for Thursday night. Sound good?" I said.

"I'll meet you guys at my house at 11:30 when I get off work. See ya then," Jerry said.

I called Cam and Lonnie and set it up. They were intrigued and agreed to be there. I set out to make my map.

At the very top of Brightwood Street was a pool owned by a family called the Greenwell's. If you took a left at the corner down from that house on Cedarwood (which led to Bentwood and also to the cul-de-sac several houses down from Jerry's), you would pass several pools. From the Greenwells' house to the end of the cul-de-sac on Cedarwood was one mile and a little change. This route would make up map number one, with eight pools to choose from. Some of these houses had dogs, so the team would need to choose wisely. I marked the known dogs on the map but made no guarantees.

I then went all the way down to Steady's neck of the woods.

I had a friend up the street from him named Kelly Klimler. I had messed around with her at a baseball game a few years back, and we were still friends. She had an above-ground pool in her backyard. It had a six-foot fence, so it would be tough to get to. I knocked on her door and told her about my game. She thought it sounded fun but that we should make sure not to wake up her dad. While I was there, I swam with her a little. On the large deck beside the pool were some cool travel-type signs. One of them read "Irish Spring," with a picture of water running through green fields. Another sign said "Nile Pyramid," with a picture of the famous river and a few pyramids in the background. The last and most unusual sign read "Sudan Wall," with a picture of a weirdly shaped blue-and-white hotel next to an African river as the backdrop. These three pictures provided great atmosphere for this pool area. Kelly was gracious that day and said I could come back any time.

I left Kelly's house and took the long way on the road back to the cul-de-sac on Jerry's street. There were seven pools on this route, and I marked them all. The distance was just a hair short of one mile, but with Kelly's fence being tall and hard to scale, I figured the distances could be considered equal. Thursday night couldn't come soon enough. After I finished the maps, I went to hang out with Clarise. I told her the plan and showed her my maps. She was impressed. We built a fire and drank Coke and smoked Marlboros for the next few hours. After that I went home to hang out and extend the day.

The summer was starting off okay, and I was in no hurry for it to be over. I mean, this was going to be my senior year, and I still had no idea what my plan was. My grades were fine, and I could get into a lot of colleges, but I didn't have scholarship-worthy grades like both my brothers did. I thought I would go to Texas Tech, like my dad, or DBU, like both my brothers. However, both of those would cost money, and I had none. I was pretty sure I could get my dad to pay somehow, but the guilt of not earning a scholarship when I had the potential to do so weighed heavy on me. Anyway, like I said, I wasn't in any hurry to get back to school for my senior year. I hoped that summer would last forever, and the new pool game I had made up could go a long way toward extending our great teen years. I thought back to the signs on Kelly's pool deck. They were great, but the coolest by far was the Sudan sign. Yep, that was it, the "Sudan Wall" would be a great name for our new stealth swimming competition. The Sudan Wall was born that day, and it ended up rivaling the War Games for teams wanting to come to our neighborhood and take us on.

Thursday night finally arrived, and all of us were sitting out front at Jerry's smoking Reds. I explained the maps and the routes. I flipped a coin, and Lonnie won, which meant he and Cam could choose which map to run. They chose to start at the Greenwells' house.

"Dude, I didn't say Simone would be swimming with you. You know the point of the game, right?" I asked jokingly.

"Sure, but if I got a quick peek at her in a bikini it couldn't hurt," Lonnie answered logically.

"All right. Head up to your starting point, and do not start the stopwatch until 12:30. Got it?" Jerry asked.

"On our way," Cam announced.

Jerry and I took the shortcut through Beetle's backyard to

the starting area close to Kelly's house. We wouldn't be able to travel this same route on the way back, as we would have to stick to the main road areas to meet the mileage requirement.

Jerry and I hit the street close to Kelly's pool around 12:10. We couldn't just hang around that long in the street, so we veered off into a field that ran parallel behind her street of houses. We sat at the entrance to the field because it was away from the main road and no one would notice us there. If you traveled into this field and to the north, you would eventually end up behind my own house on Brightwood. The field was pretty awesome, as it was not being used for anything. Every now and then I would be out in my backyard and see some figure passing through the thirty-five-acre tract of land. Ten acres of that tract were woods, and we'd had a lot of adventures there, mainly when I had been in elementary school. Steady's dad had once owned this field, but he'd sold it to an out-of-towner a few years before this night. The rumor was that the man wanted to build a bunch of apartments there. Oh no, not in this neck of the woods! The mayor, Mrs. Janis, who happened to also be my next-door neighbor, mobilized the city council and had a new ordinance passed that limited any new building on this side of town to a minimum size of two thousand square feet per unit. This effectively killed the apartment idea. When I went back twenty-five years later, the field was still glorious – and yes, there were still no apartments to be found.

We sat down to pass some time. I lit a smoke.

"Hey, Jerry. What are you planning after you graduate? You've never really told me your plans," I asked seriously.

"Who knows? Maybe college, maybe ITT. I'm not really

sure. I may just work at the market for a while and try to figure things out," he answered.

I took a puff on my cigarette and asked another question.

"Have you thought about coming to Texas Tech in Lubbock with Lonnie and me? It's not too late for us to room together," I proposed.

"No, man, you know I don't have the grades for that," Jerry said dismissively.

"Shit, man, you know I got mostly Bs and a 950 on my SAT, and I got in. Sure, I blew off the SAT, and my old man's gonna have to pay, but I made it in. My grandparents live there on a golf course, so we'll always have good food. Your dad has more money than mine, and your mom works. They could afford it," I said.

"I didn't take the damn SAT. I'm just not sure what I want to do yet," Jerry said, clearly wanting to end the conversation.

"All right, I get it. It's 12:25, let's hit the pool," I said.

We got up and headed to the left, up the street to Kelly's house. When we got there, it was 12:31, so we had to get moving. Every light in the house was out except a kitchen light. Kelly had told me that they left that one on and that the garage light was on a motion sensor. It had already lit up when we'd walked into the front yard. We moved to the fence gate on the left of the house. Kelly had told me she would leave it unlocked for me. It was, thank God. I opened the six-foot-tall door. It squeaked a little, but not too bad. The pool was in the middle of the large backyard. Man, this would have been a nice place to just swim the night away, and I could do that in the future with Kelly. She wasn't interested in me romantically, but I was sure she could use a friend. I made a mental note to try to hang with her more. Anyway, Jerry took the lead and walked quietly up to the pool. He took his shoes off and set them close by the pool, then walked up the four wooden steps to the nice deck. I did the same and was now right behind him.

"Dude, nice sign. Sudan Wall. I get it, better than the other two," Jerry said.

He went to the pool ladder and climbed in slowly. I got in as well, with very little noise. I looked at the digital second counter on my watch. So far, so good. Sixty seconds crept by. We climbed back up the ladder onto the deck and went down the steps. We put our shoes on and walked to the gate, opened it, and walked through, closing it behind us. When we hit the front yard, the motion light on the garage freaked us out by popping on again. Jerry took off down the street toward Steady's house. There were some cedar trees a few houses down on the right, and he ducked behind one of those. I was close behind and came to a stop behind the tree. I was breathing heavily, and Jerry had moved so fast he was hunched over grasping his side.

"Dude, why are we running? That was a motion light," I asked.

"I don't know. I saw the light flip on, and I just took off," Jerry exclaimed.

We caught our breath and decided to move on toward the next house: Steady's. I'd swum at Steady's house many times at night with permission. This should be one of our easiest marks, because the pool was about a half-acre back from the house and the lot was covered in cedar trees. I also knew Steady's parents, and they were really nice. They wouldn't freak out if they caught me in the pool as long as his sister wasn't involved.

The easiest way to get in was to go down the right (north) side of the backyard fence line and come in through the back. The wooded lot had great cover, and the fence at the back was just three strands of barbed wire. Jerry pushed down on the wire, and I climbed over one leg at a time. I then grabbed the fence for Jerry to climb over. We crept from cedar tree to cedar tree until we were at the pool. I took the lead this time and just got in with my shoes on. There were large cement steps going down into the pool. I walked down them and found myself standing in four feet of water. Jerry came in, and the timer began. When the minute was up, we methodically walked up the steps and out of the pool. It would have been much easier to just go out the back way through the cover of trees, but the course required that we take the main roads to ensure we traveled the estimated mile back to the finish line. I walked to the right side of the back of the house, where I knew there was a gate.

"Damn it, it's locked," I whispered loudly.

"Climb it," Jerry answered, stating the obvious.

I stuck one leg on the cross-board and was able to swing my other leg over. I was now on the driveway by Steady's basketball goal. Jerry made it over, and we jogged to the street. I felt like we were running behind for some reason, so it was time to pick up the pace. This was a stressful competition, but it had been pretty fun so far. Two down, three to go.

As I was jogging, I looked to my right and saw Bobby Mavis's house next to Steady's. It had slipped my mind when making the map. He had an above-ground pool! I motioned for Jerry to follow me around the left side of Bobby's house. At the end of the driveway, Bobby's dad had a huge barn that was used as an auto workshop. The door was open, and the lights were out. I knew that at the end of the workshop was an entrance to the backyard, about five yards away from the above-ground deck. I made my way through the building in the dark to the wooden deck of a nice four-foot-tall pool. It was older, but I could see floaties and lounge chairs on the water. I climbed up the deck and slipped into the pool as silently as possible. Jerry followed, and we waited the minute out patiently. The more I saw these pools, the more I wanted one. They were awesome. My back-yard would be perfect for one, but I could never talk my parents into getting one. When you're a kid, it all makes sense, but as an adult it still hasn't ever worked out for me.

I made my way out of the pool and back into the work-shop. When I reached the front, I accidentally bumped into a hollowed-out frame in the middle of the shop. Something fell off the fender and rattled on the floor so loudly it might as well have been an alarm sounding.

"Shit," I whispered loudly as Jerry flew by me out the work-shop and onto the street.

Lights clicked on in the main house, but they were too late. I made it to the street and around the corner to the right before I stopped running. Jerry was behind a tree off the road, and I sat down next to him. My breathing was so heavy I was sure the world heard me. After about five minutes, we realized there were still no cars and no humans coming after us, so we rejoined the road and headed toward pool number four!

We walked in silence up the from the very bottom of Brightwood Street toward Beetle's house and the Bentwood turnoff. Two houses before Beetle's was Shelly Prevant's house.

She had a sweet pool I had never been invited to, but I would at least climb into it tonight. It was number four on the list. I have to admit I had been rattled at the Mavises' house, and I was starting to have my doubts about this new game. Was it really worth the risk we were taking for an hour or two of thrills? Well, it didn't matter now, at least on this trip, because we only had two to go. It would be a waste to stop now. I wondered how Cam and Lonnie were faring on their side of the neighborhood. For all we knew they could already be done, smoking Marlboros on Jerry's porch swing by now. We made it to Shelly's. We walked around the left side of the house and jumped a small wooden fence. There were smaller cedar trees all around, so we had a little cover. The fence was more for decoration than anything else. Jerry took the lead, and I could tell he was ready to be done as well. This game was pretty stressful. He got in the pool by grabbing the small diving board and lowering himself over the edge. I chose to use the steps, and the time began. The minute went slowly, as usual, and then we were ready to go. Through the small trees a light suddenly shone directly on us.

"Go, the back way," I whispered loudly.

Jerry seemed thankful he had kept his shoes on and that I had encouraged him to go. He pulled himself out, ran through the backyard, went over the fence into the small creek bed, and was gone. The light was still focused on me as I walked up the steps out of the pool. I suddenly froze. Which way should I go?

"Hey, stop! Who are you?" a concerned, serious voice yelled.

I took off for the left side of the backyard. Lights were popping on everywhere now. Dogs began to bark as I jumped the small, token fence on the back left of the house. I hoped I could make it into Beetle's backyard undetected and then somehow slip into his house. However, I would have to go through two backyards with mean dogs to do so. Another option would be to hit the creek and go toward Jerry's house. I chose neither option as I panicked and hit the main road. I ran the twenty-five yards or so to Beetle's house. I heard a truck engine start, and a spotlight was scanning each person's yard. They had me dead to rights, and I didn't want to involve Beetle and his mom, so I kept running. I then switched to jogging mode. I thought maybe they hadn't actually seen me in the pool, but I was so wrong. A few houses up the road, Marshal Bill pulled up beside me in his brown Chevy truck.

"Hello, son. You didn't notice anyone messing around in the Mavises' shop back there, did you?" the marshal asked.

I knew I was caught and didn't want anyone to think I was a thief, so I decided to come clean.

"Sir, I was swimming in the Mavises' pool and didn't want to wake anyone up, so I came through the workshop to get out and knocked some item on the ground," I answered.

"So, you were trespassing. Dumb shit, kid," he said.

"I know Mr. Mavis, and I figured he'd be cool with me swimming there. Can I go now, sir?"

"Can you go? Boy, we're just getting started," said the rugged marshal. (Imagine a 1980s Sheriff Longmire, just shorter and tougher, and that's all you need to know to picture Marshal Bill.)

Marshal Bill stepped out of the truck.

"Get in the back bed, now," he ordered.

Shit, I may have done some dumb things, but I wasn't stupid. I got in. Marshal Bill was a Vietnam vet. He was as tough as they come. I still wasn't sure if I believed the story about him chasing down the suspected child kidnapper and trying to drown him in the creek, but I didn't *not* believe it either. It was certainly within the realm of possibility. You could look in this guy's eyes and realize he wasn't a typical suburban dad out to make some extra bucks patrolling a peaceful little town. No, this guy was a real badass who could handle crime anywhere. I figured he must have got in trouble for beating up some criminal low-life in the big city, and our little town was his punishment. Anyway, my little diversion was probably the most excitement he ever got here, which meant I was screwed.

Bill turned the truck around and headed back toward the baseball fields. This was also where city hall and his office were, as well as the fire station. We drove the mile or so there in silence. He pulled into the small parking lot and parked the truck in his reserved spot.

"Get out," said the marshal.

I stood up and jumped out of the truck bed.

"Go in there, grab a towel out of the supply room, and dry off the inside of my truck bed," Bill ordered.

I went inside the relatively small building and opened the door marked "Supply Closet." It was a really small room, but there was a stack of about eight towels on a metal shelving unit. I grabbed a few of them, walked out of the room, and headed back outside, using one of the towels to dry off the trail of dripping water I left on the floor as I walked. Marshal Bill lit up a smoke. I climbed back up into the truck bed and began to dry off the back, although it wasn't that wet back there. I got it as dry as I could and then jumped out to the ground. He was just watching me. I reached in my pocket and pulled out my Ziploc bag full of Marlboros. I lit a cigarette and started smoking it.

"Boy, you got a set of balls on you. How old are you?" he asked.

"I'm seventeen, sir."

"So, you're gonna trespass twice and participate in underage smoking right in front of me?"

I felt like an idiot at this point and got ready to put the damn thing out.

"No, don't put it out. You might as well finish it," the officer said.

I finished a minute or so later and put it in the big yellow ash collector out front of city hall.

"All right, come inside and find a seat," he told me.

I took my shoes off, walked inside the building and grabbed a chair, using one towel to sit on and another to dry off. He went into an office and sat down. I started wondering how long I would be here. So far, he hadn't even asked me my name or asked for ID. I wasn't planning on volunteering anything either. By now, it must have been around two in the morning, although I didn't see a clock. After what seemed like an eternity, the city's lone policeman called me into his office.

"Hey, get in here."

I got out of my seat and joined him in his tiny office. It was cluttered, and there were calendars on the wall and files strewn across the desk. I sat down in the chair facing his desk. He was smoking, but I thought twice before lighting up again and didn't push my luck.

"What's your name and address boy?" he asked.

"John Decker. 412 Brightwood Street, Waynesville, Texas," I said.

"I know the town, dumbass. So, what were you trying to accomplish tonight, huh? Stealing shit, vandalism, what?"

"Sir, I was really just swimming in pools for fun. That's it. I didn't take or damage anything," I said.

"Who were you with? The report I got said there were two of you," he informed me.

"Just me," I answered.

"Do you realize that we've had a rash of burglaries over the past three weeks? Do you also realize that somebody could have shot you out there? People are on edge. You can't just screw with anyone's property whenever you want to," he said in an agitated tone.

"I'm sorry, sir. I didn't think about that. I'm just out having fun."

"Well, go sit out in the hall while I think about this," he demanded.

I got up, went to the hall, and sat back in the same chair. I saw a light switch and turned one light off. This reduced the light in the room by half, and I knew I might have trouble staying awake. About thirty minutes later he came out of his office.

"Stay here. I gotta do a few patrol rounds. Don't go anywhere," he said.

"I won't, sir," I responded.

He walked out the door, and I heard the truck pull away soon after that. Now was my chance. I could leave and go home easily now. Of course, he knew my name and address, so what was the point? There wasn't one. I stayed. After a few minutes of cursing myself for getting caught, I must have drifted off to sleep in the chair. What seemed like only a few minutes had passed when I felt somebody shaking my shoulders.

"Get up, boy," said Marshal Bill. "Go outside and wait for me."

I found my bearings and walked outside. I had no idea what time it was. I just knew it was late. He followed me out a few minutes later. He had a cigarette already in his mouth.

"Go ahead. Light up. I don't give a shit," he said.

I pulled out a smoke and got it going. A car passed by on the road, but it was the only one I had heard in a while. It must be the first early bird heading out to work, I thought. After a minute or so, he spoke.

"All right. It's six a.m. Get your ass home. Tell your dad about this. I'll call Monday to make sure you did," he said.

"Yes, sir," I answered respectfully.

"And don't be trespassing anymore. It's not safe, not even in Waynesville. I've seen a lot of crime and criminals in my day. This path you are starting on is a dark one. Don't follow it. Right now, it's pools in the middle of the night, but soon that won't be enough. If I catch you out again, I will kick your ass and arrest you for real," he warned. "Now go!"

"Thank you, sir," I said as I grabbed my shoes and started walking humbly toward the ball field behind the city hall building.

I put my shoes back on and walked the mile back to my house quickly. My car was still at Jerry's, but I was exhausted and needed some sleep before I went back to get it. I went inside and cleaned up, then slipped into bed. It took a while to get to sleep.

I wondered what my dad would say. I felt really bad disappointing him. I mean, he worked hard, and I had a good life. How had I repaid him? I was basically a grade A cock, that's how. I figured I would call him at work when I woke up, which would give him time to digest the information before he got home. My dad was usually very calm, but I knew he held stuff in, and a long drive through Dallas traffic home would give him plenty of chances to release some anger. I drifted off to sleep with these thoughts on my brain. I dreamed of girls, the War Games, and drama tournaments. My subconscious knew these were the things I liked. I actually slept well and woke up about 1:00 in the afternoon. I called my dad at work and told him. He told me not to go anywhere until he got home.

My dad eventually got home. It was a very anticlimactic scene.

"What were you doing?" he asked.

"I was swimming in pools," I answered.

"That's stupid," he said.

"I know," I answered.

The rest of the conversation followed this boring pattern. I was sorry to disappoint him. The final verdict issued was a week of no car. It sucked, but I could live with it. I deserved a lot more than that. Once again, I was given grace. I played Atari that week and talked with Clarise a lot on the phone – and by the way, Marshal Bill never called my dad. I guess he figured I would tell him, and he was right.

The rest of the summer went great. I hadn't learned the right lesson that night with the Marshal. If anything, I got bolder and more daring. I ended up doing the Sudan Wall challenge three more times that summer. We also scraped up enough people to have a summer War Games session one night in August.

Before I knew it, summer was over and I was doing my two-a-day cross-country sessions the week before school. I was excited to be starting my last year of school but was starting to fear it a little as well. I mean, I had no plan and no goals. Most of my friends knew something they wanted to be, or at least had a rough sketch of a plan. I had none. I literally had no idea what or even who I wanted to be. This was a scary way to enter my senior year. My initial strategy was simply to hang with Cam and Jerry and have as much fun as I could between now and graduation. The year did not disappoint. It turned out to be another of the best years ever!

CHAPTER 18

✳ ✳ ✳

CLARISE'S COUSIN AND THE SPRING OLYMPICS

The first half of the school year almost seemed to vanish into thin air. Cross-country went pretty well; we finished first in the district but lost at area again. This time it was not my fault. I finished seventh at the area race, which was about thirteen places higher than I normally did. We finished third out of fifteen teams, but only the top two went on to the state race. Still, this was the highest the cross-country team had ever finished in school history, so we were pretty pleased. In addition to athletics, I had already been to two drama tournaments, and Cam and I had rocked first place in duet acting at both of them. Neither of us had met any girls, but I'd done well enough in the past not to worry about it too much. Besides these fun activities, I had taken the SAT again one Saturday morning at a high school in Dallas. I hadn't studied but improved my score up to

1,000. I don't know why I took it again, since I had already been accepted to Texas Tech. I guess I just wanted to hit the millennium mark. Anyway, the time had flown, and I found myself on Christmas break.

Cam had left the grocery store in Possum Fields and now worked at Kentucky Fried Chicken – or KFC as it's called now, for those of you who like efficiency! He had also started dating a freshman girl named Sandra, and she was a little cutie. He was staying at her house quite a bit, but I finally got some Cam time during that Christmas season when she traveled to Ohio to see her grandma. After our obligatory smoke session with Jerry at the Waynesville Market, we drove over to Clarise's house. She had called me and wanted me to meet her cousin. Cam and I drove over and parked out in the driveway. Cam looked over at me, and I had a sudden burst of pride. We had spent some time primping and working our turtleneck sweater combo outfits. Cam wore them regularly to cover up hickeys received in make-out sessions with Sandra, but I rarely sported them. However, the New Kids on the Block era was upon us, and a guy did what he had to do. Because of this, I had a white turtleneck with a black V-neck sweater, and a bolo tie as the finishing touch. I have to say, my hair had cooperated tonight, so I was feeling good. Cam had a black turtleneck with a white sweater on. We both felt and looked outstanding.

"Hey, man, whatever happened with Mindy?" Cam asked me.

"We messed around a little, but her dad caught me in her pants in the car out front, and that was that," I answered.

"Well, she was hot. You screwed that one up. Why aren't you tapping Clarise?" he asked.

"Good question. I guess we're just friends, and I figured I'll respond if she makes a move, but so far, she really hasn't," I said.

We bantered like this the rest of the way to the door. I rang the bell. The door opened.

My mouth dropped wide open. I quickly composed myself and looked over at Cam. He had made no effort to contain his shock. I swear, to this day I have never been more blindsided by a woman's beauty and sexiness than right then and there. This girl had hair so blonde it was almost white. She was wearing it up in a ponytail. Her eyes were dark blue, like an enchanted coal. Her black sweater hugged her curves like it was custom fit for her body. Her white cotton pants hugged her ass so tight you could see a faint impression of light blue panties underneath. "Damn" was all I could think. This girl was worth whatever I would have to go through to win her, and I hadn't even heard her speak yet.

"Hello, I'm Karen. You must be John and Cam," she said.

She knew our names! I think I got a hard-on just knowing she already knew who I was.

"Hi, Karen. I'm John, and this is Cam," I replied.

We both shook her hand, lingering longer than we should have. At that moment, Clarise came onto the scene to move things along, as she had obviously had to deal with blubbering fools around her hot cousin before.

"Come in, ya'll," she invited.

You didn't need to tell us twice.

"Let's go out back to the fire," Clarise said.

"Cool," I answered.

When we got outside, Clarise had prepped some chairs, and there was a cooler there. Once we all got settled around the fire, her mom brought out some hot dogs. I guess we were in for the night, and we had no intentions of going anywhere else. Of course, our plan had been to stay for thirty minutes or so and then head up to Dallas for teen night at one of the local clubs. We could still do that, but not until both of us had spent all the time we could with Karen.

"So, Karen, where are you from?" Cam asked.

"I'm from Coleman. Are you guys from Waynesville?" she asked.

"I live here in Waynesville, but Cam stays in Possum Fields," I answered.

I grabbed a hot dog from the tray and took a bite. Clarise handed a Miller Lite to me.

"Wow. Right in front of your mom?" I asked.

"She doesn't care as long as we don't drive," she answered.

Her mom went inside, and I quickly finished off the hot dog and lit up a smoke. Cam was in drill-down mode, and I could tell he had forgotten all about Sandra for the moment. Who could blame him? I realized I had missed my window and Cam had busted right through the door. He and Karen were in a real con-versation now, which meant bro code kicked in and I had to give up the chase, unless he failed.

I felt bad for about a minute, but Clarise was no slouch ei-ther. She was hot in her own right. Her eyes were sparkling in the light of the fire, and I felt like this might be the night one of us made a move. She moved her seat closer to mine, and we chatted and smoked together for the next few hours. Karen spoke to me some, but Cam was in full-on game mode. I wasn't really sure if he was on the verge of scoring or not, but he thought he was, and even getting close to scoring with a girl like Karen is a triumph! Anyway, Clarise and I snuggled up a little together by the fire, but I wasn't sure if it was the beer working on her, so I just enjoyed the night for what it was and didn't make a real move. I look back on that night and I regret that decision, plain and simple. After a few hours of fun banter, it all came to an abrupt end.

I had my arm around Clarise, and she was leaning in with her head on my shoulder. I wanted to kiss her really bad but thought there was a chance I was just stuck in a really sweet friend zone. I wouldn't be the one responsible for ruining that, so I did nothing. Cam, however, took advantage of his opportunity, and I don't blame him. If you had seen Karen, you wouldn't either. The fire was dying down a little, and the radio was playing Bon Jovi's "I'll Be There for You." I was watching Cam and Karen sitting there talking playfully. Suddenly, Cam moved boldly in for the kiss. Karen moved away at the last minute and stood up.

"Oh, hey. I need to go inside. I had fun, Cam, and it was nice to meet you, John."

Karen went inside, and we never saw her again. I felt really bad for Cam, but he'd had to take his shot. Please don't think bad of Cam for trying to cheat on his out-of-town girlfriend. You just had to see Karen and you would forgive him. I did the moment he tried.

Clarise then pulled away from me, and the night came to an end.

"Thanks, Clarise. I hope you have a great Christmas," I said.

"Thanks for coming over. I'll call you after Christmas. See ya."

We didn't bother to go through the house; we just walked around the side of the house to the driveway.

"Dude, did you see that girl. She's the finest girl I've ever seen," Cam said.

"I saw her. I've never seen a prettier girl. God, she was smoking hot, man," I replied.

"I screwed up, man. I really thought she wanted me to kiss her," Cam lamented.

"I thought so too. She was flirting with you. She definitely was giving off vibes. I felt bad when she pulled away," I said.

"I'm not sorry, dude. I had to take a chance," Cam said.

"You gonna tell Sandra?" I asked.

"Are you nuts?" he questioned.

"Don't tell her. I didn't see anything. I would have called you stupid if you hadn't tried," I said.

We got in the car, and I drove Cam home. I'd only nursed a few beers during the time we were there, so I thought I was good.

"See you soon, man. I need to go jack over Karen," Cam said.

"I wonder how many guys have issued that same exact statement," I said out the window as I drove away. I also remember thinking that Cam had the right idea.

Christmas came and went. I had a good time hanging out with Jerry and Cam over the two-week break. Once we got back to school, reality hit me pretty hard. I was now on my last semester of high school. I wasn't ready for it to end. I was set up to go to Texas Tech in the fall, like my old man had, but something felt off about that choice. My grandparents lived close to the campus, so I would have been able to see them a lot more than normal, but it still felt weird. Jerry had flat out said he wasn't going to college. I never understood why, but he just didn't talk about the future. I had approached him about going to Tech with Lonnie and me, but he wasn't interested. We had also approached Cam. Cam never gave a straight answer on the subject either, and I figured that it had to do with money. One day I walked into Drama class and Cam wasn't there. What? We always coordinated our skip days, so where was he?

Our Drama classroom was a large open area with several chairs, props, and costume stations. Most of the time, people just got in their friend groups in different sections of the room until the teacher gave an assignment. The classroom had an office in it as well. I walked over to the office, and it was empty. I opened the door and picked up the phone. I dialed Cam's number, and he picked up on the first ring.

"Hello," Cam answered.

"What's up, dude? Where are you? Are you sick?" I asked.

"No. I had a mission today," Cam informed me.

"What kind of mission?" I asked.

"I went to MEPS and joined the Army today," Cam said proudly.

"What the hell, dude? You're only seventeen," I nervously threw at him.

"I know. My parents signed for me. I am in the delayed entry program. I leave August eighth," he informed me.

"Wow, dude. I guess that rules out Tech," I said.

"Right. Sorry I didn't tell you. I didn't want you to talk me out of it," Cam told me.

"Well, if that's what you want, I get it. Take it easy, brother," I said as I hung up the phone.

What now? I really had thought I could talk him into coming to Tech. That possibility was closed now, and I just felt lost. I finished the rest of the school day with my head hanging low. Cam was going into the Army.

A few weeks came and went. Cam and I hung out more than ever, at least when he wasn't with Sandra. I could feel him slipping a little closer to the military with each passing day. It's funny, Lonnie and I had always been friends, and I should have been more excited about going to Tech and rooming with him, but for some reason, Cam was the one on my mind. In a few years' time, he had become my best friend ever, and I knew it was coming to an end. Clarise still called me, and I would go over there when Cam and Jerry were working. She had rocked my world when she told me her cousin Karen didn't kiss Cam because she was into me. Talk about missed opportunities! Clarise told me she would try to set us up next Christmas. I didn't argue. Besides the normal crew, I had a new friend. After about a year-and-a-half drought, I finally had a girlfriend. Her name was Cynthia. I could write a whole book covering the intricacies of our relationship over the next few years, but that is for another time. I only mentioned her here so you would know how my life was going. I had friends and a girlfriend, and yet I still felt scared and empty.

The emptiness grew, and I realized it was due to the future. I had been in command of my path for several years now. I had a great friend group and a magical world to experience at the creek. My brothers had moved on, and so had Beatle, but for some reason I felt tied to Waynesville and the creek. When Cam joined the Army, things changed, and a fire of worry was lit inside me that could not be put out. His seemingly rash decision to join the Army gave me courage to pursue an idea that had been growing since Christmas, when my mother had shamed me in a conversation about college. She had made clear that she was not happy with the way I had coasted through high school. She constantly reminded me about my national honor society brothers and their college scholarships. Last, she laid a large guilt trip on me about my dad having to work extra hard to put me through college because of my mediocre grades. When Cam joined the Army, it opened my eyes up to other possibilities. It showed me that maybe college wasn't my only option.

On February 22, 1990, a Thursday, I turned eighteen and skipped school. I met Sergeant Mason at the Army recruiters in Indian Lake, and he drove me to the Military Entrance Processing Station in Dallas – what Cam had called "MEPS." I had already taken the ASVAB (Army Entrance Test) during a school event I had attended to get out of class for a few hours and qualified for any job they had. Today was the physical, drug test, and job selection. I passed everything and found myself in front of the counselor to select an MOS (military occupational specialty). I knew I didn't want to commit to anything longer than three years. The counselor showed me a picture of a soldier on a hill with a portable shoulder-fired missile aimed at a target in the sky. I was hooked. I signed on the dotted line and swore an oath later that afternoon. I was in the delayed entry program like Cam, but I would leave a little sooner. In fact, I would leave for Basic Training on July 10. I was a Stinger Missile Crewmember. I drove home feeling a peace like I had never experienced. I only hoped that P.J. Decker would feel the same peace over this decision.

I got home that afternoon and decided it was time to rip off the Band-Aid. It wouldn't get any easier to tell my mom I was ditching college for the Army. I decided to just walk in and do it. She had brothers that had been in the military during Vietnam, so she had heard it all before. I just knew that this was the last thing she was expecting. I walked through the kitchen and grabbed a Coke. I then walked into my mom's room, where she was sitting on the couch reading a novel.

"Hey, Mom," I said.

"Oh, hello. How was school today?" she asked.

"I didn't go to school today, Mom. I went to MEPS," I said.

"What is MEPS?" she asked.

"I joined the Army today, Mom," I said.

"What? You didn't ask us about that. What about Tech?" Mom asked.

"Well, you said Dad would have to work overtime to make Tech happen. I was the only son to not get a scholarship, so I fixed it. Dad doesn't have to pay now," I informed her.

"That's not what I meant. You need to change this. You need to go to college," she said with tears coming into her eyes.

"Mom, I'm sorry you're upset about this, but I know it's right. I'm going into the Army. I need you to understand that," I said.

The rest of the conversation was just variations on this: her explaining I needed college and me hitting back with military plans. She finally let it die. I told my dad when he got home, and it was a much different conversation. In fact, I was shocked at how easily he said okay.

I told Cam and Jerry, and they were pretty shocked. Clarise

wasn't surprised. I told the new girlfriend, and she wasn't surprised either. They knew I needed adventure. We made it into March, and the school year was moving at light speed. At this pace, I would be gone before you knew it. I knew I needed a few more creek missions to ensure I had exhausted that area of my life. It was a week in March that slowed things down and gave me some much-needed fun that I still look back fondly on today. It was Clarise that opened the door for me.

"Hey, John, sign here," Clarise said while handing me the paper.

I looked at it. The paper read "Spring Olympic Team Sign-up Sheet."

"What is this?" I asked.

"It's a competition. Teams will compete each day this week after school and on Saturday in a series of events. It's a battle for pride. Each team has to have at least two girls, which I already have taken care of. Our team will be called the Creekers," she explained.

"What kind of competition?" I asked.

"Well, there will be softball, basketball, volleyball, and a whole range of other sports and activities. Are you in?" she asked.

I grabbed the paper and looked at her. She had a sparkle in her eyes that could only be described as innocence. I had never seen it anywhere before, and I have only seen it once since. I signed on line number one as team captain.

"This is all I need. I will get the team together. You won't regret this," she said as she ran down the hall to begin recruitment.

She was so right. I didn't regret it at all.

The next day, after school, round one of the kickball competition started. We were up against the Band. Yes, the high school band fielded a team. We beat them twelve to four, and we advanced to the next round the same night against the science club. We beat them twenty-one to two. We would face the Jocks in the finals, which would take place on Saturday morning. The Olympics were really fun, and hundreds of people were turning out after school to watch the games. We felt pretty good about our chances. Our two girls, Clarise and another girl named Stacey, were by far the best female athletes in the competition. The rest of my team was Lonnie, Jerry, Cam, J.D., and myself, plus three other dudes we let join the squad that weren't actual creekers. Two of these guys were freshman, and the final player was Josh, who was a sophomore. Besides the band, science club, and jocks, there were six other groups, not counting our own. I can't remember all of them, but I know drama had a team, and the New Wavers posted a laughable outfit that finished behind the band. The only other team I remember was the thugs. They were longhairs that called themselves the Rockers. They ended up faring pretty well overall in the event.

Each day that week after school was another big sporting competition. They organized the big team events each day after school so that only the finals would need to be played on Saturday. We did kickball, basketball, volleyball, and soccer. We made the finals in each of these. Besides these big events, Saturday would host several smaller individual or duo competitions, such as the egg toss, sack race, and even a pie-eating competition. We were going to face the jocks in all of the main sports with the exception of volleyball. Somehow the rockers had beaten the jocks in volleyball and were able to make the finals against us. Each day during announcement period the broadcast would give a recap of the event the night before. School spirit was at an all-time high that week. I'll never forget it. Whoever came up with the Spring Olympics was a genius. I hope they are still doing them!

Saturday came, and my team met in the rock parking lot outside the school. Jerry and I arrived together, as did Cam and Lonnie. J.D. showed up with his girlfriend Stacey and Clarise. I lit up a smoke with Jerry and got ready for the finals of kickball. I was worried about the jocks in soccer and basketball, because most of them were superb athletes. However, I felt like we could take them in kickball, and I was fairly certain we had a good shot against the rockers in volleyball. The two-girl rule hurt the jocks and the rockers, as they had picked girls based on looks and popularity, not athletic ability. Clarise and Stacey were all-stars already on the girls' varsity volleyball teams. Yes, Clarise was a freshman, but she was the best they had. Stacey was a sophomore who was also really good. The girls on the jock and rocker squads were beauty queens – very pretty to look at, but not much in the way of fierce competition.

"Hey, Clarise, you ready for some kickball?" I asked.

"Yes. That was so much fun the other day. I hadn't played kickball since Alex Bields," she answered.

"We're gonna kick some jock ass," Jerry exclaimed proudly as two of the jock team strolled by on the way to the field.

"Whatever, numb nuts," one of them shot back at Jerry.

Jerry and I laughed hard at that and put out our smokes. We all grabbed our stuff and headed toward the field. If we lost at kickball, the odds were it would be a long day.

I'll spare you the glorious details, but let me tell you it felt good to crush the jocks at kickball. We beat them by fifteen points. Did we take advantage of two people who couldn't play very well? Yes, but they picked their girls based on feelings. Our girls picked us with a desire to win. We were now in first place in the entire competition. That glory didn't last long. The jocks utterly destroyed us at basketball, and they managed to beat us by a single goal in soccer. They took the lead with only one major sporting event left, volleyball. However, there were several other events that could make a difference. There was dodgeball and the sack race, and others. Our all-star girls came through for us in volleyball, and we made the rockers look stupid. We beat them so bad two of their dudes actually got in a fistfight over whose fault it was. This victory put us into a virtual tie with the jocks for first place. Lonnie singlehandedly won the pie-eating competition, which made everyone wonder how someone so skinny could put away cream pie so fast. We didn't care as long as he won. In addition to this, I teamed up with Cam to win the egg toss prize. The jocks pulled out the sack race, the mile run, and the football throwing distance challenge. We were down by only two points, and we had to win the dodgeball match to win the competition.

We stood around the field of competition, which was the gym. The dodgeball matches went fast, so they held the entire tournament on Saturday. Like many of the others, it came down to the creekers and the jocks. The winner of this match would receive five points, so the jocks would either win the whole Spring Olympics by seven or lose by three. It all came down to this. We had about twenty minutes before the start, so Cam and I went outside for a smoke.

"Hey, dude, we're doing better than anyone thought we would, right?" I asked.

"Only because our girls saved us in volleyball," Cam answered.

"I know. Clarise looks really good in those shorts," I said.

"Yeah, she does," Cam replied.

"Hey, John, are you getting nervous about the Army yet? I sure as hell am," Cam declared.

I answered him with a slight, nervous laugh.

"You wouldn't believe how nervous I am, dude. You at least grew up in the Army, so you have a feel for what it could be like. I got nothing to base my expectations on but movies and World War Two stories," I answered.

"I know, but I'm just as nervous. We should have joined on the buddy program. I mean, we could have gone in together," Cam informed me.

"Well, you freaked me out when you just went and joined without telling anyone," I said.

"Man, I was just lost because you and Lonnie were going to Tech, and I felt I had to take hold of my future," Cam confessed.

"I get it, man. It's just three years. We'll be crushing Dallas at twenty-one soon enough," I said.

I finished my smoke, and Cam stepped on his to put it out. Four of the rockers were smoking dope in the parking lot, so I figured we were safe enough with the cigarettes.

"Let's drill those jocks right between the eyes and take home the trophy," I said as we walked in.

The team was waiting for us. We all hit the court. There were five balls directly at mid-court. The official put us all in our positions. He then stood in the middle and yelled "Go!" A mad dash was made for the balls at center court. Cam and I each got one, and three of the jocks did as well. I drifted back to my general area and took aim. It was punkish, yes, but I was going to take the easy option. I put the homecoming queen, Nancy Mills, in my sights. I fired at her center mass and scored. She pouted as the official escorted her off the court.

"That's screwed up," a nameless, large football player yelled at me.

"Then get some girls who can play next time, dude," I yelled back.

The scoffer launched the ball in my direction. I dodged and was able to just get out of the way to stay in the game. At that exact moment, Cam took out female player number two. Clarise picked up the ball aimed at me and launched it back at the jock, who narrowly escaped ejection by a freshman – and a girl no less. I looked up just in time to see two balls flying in a coordinated manner at Lonnie and J.D. These balls came hard and fast and drilled both of them. Our two, star players were out! I grabbed a ball and launched it back across the court at the mouth who had yelled at me. I drilled him in the face. He went down. The official warned me that face shots didn't count, so the dude got up and was still in the game. I could feel the hate in his gaze as his partners launched red balls fiercely at me. I was able to avoid the onslaught, pick one up, and drill him straight in the chest. He sneered at me as he walked off the court. While I had been dodging bullets from the knuckle draggers, Clarise and Stacey had been eliminated, and Jerry had been capsized as well. It was now just Cam, me, and two others versus six on the other squad.

The jocks got together and took out our younger players quickly. It was now six to two. Cam and I each had a ball in our hands. We started moving around in untraceable patterns. I launched a ball at a tall basketball player, and it just nicked his left knee. The official told him to leave. Five to two was better odds for us. One of the jocks took offense at his friend's ejection and launched an anger shot straight in my direction. I caught it. Now it was four to two. At that moment, I saw Cam launch a bullet at the chest of the starting quarterback, who thought he had caught it but stumbled instead and lost his balance. He went down in disgrace to Cam's rocket ball. The jocks were now up three to two. I threw a ball over and hit nothing, and right on cue, two balls came blazing in my direction from two different sides. Both of them drilled me and sent me to the floor. I walked off the court, leaving our hopes for victory in the hands of the Cam.

It was now three jocks to one creeker. Cam was very mobile, and he moved well across his side of the court. The stands were full, and Cam took center stage. He grabbed a ball quickly and launched it at a player, who dodged. Cam reached down, grabbed a second ball, and shot it right back to the same target, who this time had let down his guard. He tried to catch the ball and it bounced off his right hand. The crowd was going nuts. You would have thought this was an NCAA playoff game or something. Two to one, and Cam was on fire with the crowd behind him. I stood up in the stands and started chanting:

"Cam! Cam! Cam! Cam!"

The rest of the gym joined in, and the house was rocking. Cam was working the crowd, raising his arms and keeping the chant going, while dodging a nuclear attack of red bouncy balls. He now had two balls in his hands. I didn't know if this was against the rules or not, and neither did the official. Cam had a ball in each hand and launched them both at one player. The dude dodged one and got beamed by the other. Cam had taken him out! He was going to do it. The crowd were on their feet. I looked over at the jocks in the bleachers, and they were clearly sweating. They were supposed to run away with this competition, and no matter how this ended, they had been beaten at sports by the creekers and the thugs. This wasn't part of the plan, clearly. Cam ran around the floor dodging balls left and right. He wasn't firing back as well as he should have, because he was too excited by the roar of the crowd. He sent a ball over and just missed the fast, springy player on the other side of the gym. For one brief moment, Cam took his eye off his opponent and looked up at the crowd. That was all the other guy needed.

Cam looked back across the court just soon enough to see a ball heading straight for him at alarming speed. He jumped out of the way but did not make it far enough. The red menace caught his foot and ended the match. Cam fell to the floor, exhausted by the battle. The jocks yelled in victory, and the rest of the gym yelled with them. The match had been so exciting that everyone was cheering. When Cam got up off the floor, the cheers only grew louder as the people of the school gained a new respect for him – and everyone who dared to challenge the jocks. Clarise and I ran to Cam and hugged him. I had never been prouder of my friend or my school. This had been the best week I could remember. I looked at Clarise with pride as well, as she had outclassed all the other girls in the competition.

"You know, Clarise, this Spring Olympics thing wasn't such a bad idea, after all," I joked.

She smiled in my direction and grabbed my hand as she walked with Cam and me out of the gym and to the parking lot.

"You loved it, and you never thought we would get so close to winning it," Clarise said.

"No doubt, you're right," I admitted.

When we hit the lot outside, Cam's girl Sandra was waiting for him. He put his arm around her, and they walked off toward her mom's van.

Clarise kissed me on the cheek and said, "So, next time I ask you to sign something you won't have to think about it so long!"

I smiled at her, and she got in the car for a ride home.

"I have learned to trust you, my friend. Now, let's go have a few beers by the fire," I said while starting the car.

"Sounds good to me. And by the way, you won't be here, but the creekers will win this thing next year," she said.

She was right, they did.

✳ ✳ ✳

CHAPTER 19

THE FIGHT

The glory of the Spring Olympics gave us strength to carry us through the rest of the semester. By mid-April, every senior I knew was chomping at the bit to graduate. I was basically done, with two Study Hall periods, a Drama class, and Athletics taking up the bulk of my schedule. The remainder was Health, English, and Government. I was coasting to the finish line with barely any effort. Cam was hanging out with Sandra more and more, so I found myself hanging with Jerry on the weekends, when he wasn't working, or at Clarise's house. Most weeknights found me at Cynthia's house on her front porch, because her dad was a jerk and didn't allow her to have boys inside. Fires, front porches, and beer were fun, but they basically were placeholders for me while I waited for the uncertain future. I had peace about the Army, but it was such a different path than my dad and brothers had followed. I couldn't help but wonder if that was a mistake, although as I write I hear the voice of my

World War Two vet grandfather assuring me it wasn't. My pondering came to a quick end in the lunchroom one day in early May.

Our normal lunch routine was as follows: I would grab two burgers and two Dr Peppers. Cam bought the lunch of the day, which usually sucked, so I typically ended up giving him a buck for the snack machine in the hall. Lonnie brought a sack lunch that consisted of a peanut butter sandwich and some celery sticks. He also made use of the soda machine to buy a drink each lunch period. Jerry went through the snack line like I did and bought the dollar square pizza when they had it. On the three days a week that they didn't, he bought either the fish sticks or a burger. J.D. was more of a free agent; I couldn't ever pin him down on his lunch plans, as they were different every day. For this particular May lunch, I believe he had a bag of Lance chips, a fig bar, and a salad.

It may seem weird that I should remember this particular day after all of these years. However, the events of this day proved to be the start of a very peculiar period that still registers as one of the craziest in my life. It wasn't some huge event, but what transpired was so out of character for my friends that the three-week segment that followed still haunts me to this day. It started off with an argument over something so insignificant that it makes no sense. J.D., Cam, and myself sat there watching the following scene play out with mouths hanging wide open.

"Dude, why'd you take the last pizza? You saw me there behind you," Jerry said angrily to Lonnie.

"It's the luck of the draw, amigo, and your card sucked," Lonnie replied.

"That's screwed up," Jerry replied.

Now, we often had arguments between these two, so if it had ended there, this could have still been salvaged as a normal lunch period. However, this was not to be today. Jerry looked really angry, and he reached over to grab the pizza.

"Hey, dick. Keep your hands off the pizza," Lonnie said, while pulling it quickly away.

"You're a cocksucker," Jerry said with venom dripping from his tongue.

"What the hell, dude? When did you become such a pussy? If I'd known they'd see you throw a baby fit if you didn't get what you want, I'd have done this a year ago," Lonnie replied.

Jerry got up from his side of the table and walked around toward Lonnie. He slapped at the pizza and knocked it out of his hand. The pizza flew out of its packaging and landed face down on the cafeteria floor.

"Now you won't get it either, bitch," Jerry said with a grin and a half-laugh.

Lonnie was not happy about this turn of events and looked at me with anger but also confusion on his face.

"John, you said this guy was cool, but he's a shithead. I know you won't take offense when I whoop his ass," Lonnie said loudly so the entire table could hear.

"Oh, you're gonna whoop my ass, huh? That's a joke. I'll beat your ass and take a shit on your face when I'm done," Jerry threatened.

This was getting out of hand, and I noticed J.D. and Cam get out of their seats to position themselves to break up a fight if needed. I stood up as well.

"Hey, guys, we're all friends here. Let's cool it down a little," I said.

Cam agreed and joined my cause.

"Right, this has gone too far. Nobody's whoopin' anybody's ass today. Let's sit down and eat," Cam pleaded.

"No, it won't be in school, where I have to stop. It's at the creek, next War Games session in three weeks. I'm kicking your ass, and then we're done," Jerry said.

He gave Lonnie a shove in the chest and walked away.

"Oh, screw you. I'll be there," Lonnie replied.

Lonnie picked up his pizza and ate it. The three of us looked at him in disbelief over what had just happened – and the pizza.

The next couple of weeks were brutal, with threats being lobbed back and forth and Cam, J.D., and I trying not to take sides. As far as I was concerned, Lonnie and Jerry were both acting like dumbasses. Cam even asked me to intervene and whoop both of their asses to snap them out of this stupidity. However, the tension continued to grow. Every day they came close to blows, and the battle at the creek became the focus of our lives. People from around the school asked us about it and where it would be. Of course, there would be no one from school other than creekers in attendance. The only other person invited would be Snoopy from Indian Lakes. Fights at the creek were battles of honor, and no one was allowed to talk about them outside of the group. Beetle now worked at the Waynesville Market, so he had heard of it. He, of course, would have been allowed to come, but he never really wanted to hang out with me if my high school friends were around. I didn't blame him for that. This was the worst way to end a great school year, with a fight planned between two of my best friends.

I mentioned earlier that the tension was growing at an alarming rate. Each time they ran into each other, words of evil intent were exchanged. I had seen guys want to fight before, but never with such a long interlude between the catalyst event and the actual fight. For Lonnie it all seemed like a big joke, and he was laughing it off. He wouldn't back down from anybody, but he took it all in his stride. Jerry, on the other hand, was seething and practically foaming at the mouth. I could see evil in his eyes I had never noticed before. He really wanted to hurt Lonnie, not just throw a few blows to make a point, which is how most fights went. The two had even stopped sitting with us at lunch. Jerry sat at the table with Mason's group, and Lonnie sat with the band people. Just when it got to the point where none of us could stand it anymore, the Friday of the War Games actually arrived – except this time, there would be no teams coming to take us on. Instead, it would be a real battle between two creekers. I hated this and wanted to roll up into a fetal position and hide, but at least it would be over tonight.

The plan was simple. Lonnie would come to the camp with J.D., Cam, and me. Jerry got off work at 10:00 that night and would be there at 11:30. We would be at the New campsite. Jerry would travel up through the Old campsite and take the field between the two sites to come in the back way. When he reached the fence line, he would call out and we would send Lonnie to the middle field by the platform to wait for Jerry. Jerry would wait five minutes and then come to meet us, and we would walk together to the site of the fight. We could have just planned to meet at the site at a certain time, but I think Jerry wanted time with me before the event to get psyched up. I guess he thought of me as his cornerman, even if I disagreed with the fight and wanted it over as quickly as possible. What the two combatants didn't know was that the other boys and I had decided we would let them go at it about a minute to take the edge off the initial anger, and then we would intervene. I wasn't going to sit by and watch either of my friends get seriously hurt, no matter how stupid they were being.

It was about 9:30 now, and Snoopy showed up at the camp. We hadn't seen him in a while.

"All right, I guess this is gonna happen, huh?" Snoopy always had a smile and a cheery disposition.

"Yep, we need to get this shit over with," I said.

Lonnie laughed and said, "It won't last long. Don't worry, I will end it quickly and won't hurt the bitch too badly."

J.D. and Cam were tending to the fire, and Snoopy and I lit up smokes. Lonnie was sitting on his sleeping bag with his Walkman headphones in, getting into the zone for the coming battle. A sense of dread came over me as I smoked and watched him lying nonchalant on the bag. The dude had even brought Rec Specs, like he was getting ready for a real sporting event. I could tell Snoopy was bewildered by the coming fight.

"So, what the hell happened?" he asked.

"Your guess is as good as mine. Their normal, daily argument spiraled out of control, and here we are," I answered.

"Are you gonna let it happen? I mean, this is stupid, right?" Snoopy appeared as upset by the coming event as I was.

"Man, I know it's dumb, but it's been brewing for a long time. I figure if they get a little of it out of their systems, maybe that will quell the demon enough to get us through the end of school. They live on different sides of town and will probably never even see each other again once Cam and I are gone," I answered.

Cam joined in our conversation, while J.D. was lost in his thoughts, looking into the fire. The time felt almost normal as we tried to talk about anything but the fight. We were rudely pulled out of our bliss by a banging on the fence across the creek from us. Time had flown, and Jerry had arrived.

"Damn," I said. "Is it already eleven-thirty?"

"Eleven-eighteen to be exact," J.D. answered.

Lonnie got up and put his Rec Specs on. They were basically a clear eye shield with a strap that stretched around the back of the head. Lonnie didn't see very well without his glasses, so I remember wondering if these were prescription.

"All right, boys. I'll see you on the other side. Time to shut this bitch up," Lonnie said loudly as he flipped on his flashlight and headed out into the woods to travel to the designated waiting spot.

We would wait for Jerry to come into camp and then walk over to the fight spot with him. That would give me one more chance to try to talk him out of it.

For the sake of creek history, I must pause the story for a moment. To my knowledge, since I had become the sole remaining member of my family camping at the creek, we had planned four "ring of honor" fights, and three had actually taken place. Lonnie was involved in two of them, and I was involved in one.

The fourth didn't happen because the dude threatening Cam realized he wasn't going to leave the creek without a beatdown, and he withdraw at the last minute. This guy was named Cy. He was Sandra's previous boyfriend and just couldn't stand her being with another guy. The Friday morning of the planned fight, I approached him in the halls and told him Cam would win the fight. I had made up all kinds of shit about Cam and his ability to put opponents in the hospital. It was something to the effect that he was a black belt and fought in tournaments around North Texas. This was all a lie, as Cam didn't really know how to fight at that point in his life. Anyway, it was enough to make Cy reconsider. He told Sandra he was sorry and formally withdrew his fight challenge. Cam breathed a sigh of relief at this, and he was able to retain his honor at the same time. My work was done.

The three fights that did happen followed a specific pattern. The opponent was allowed to bring two guests, or cornermen. These were allowed so they would know we weren't planning to ambush anybody and they could count on a fair fight. We met at 11:00 p.m. outside of Jerry's house and walked to the field as a group. I remember seeing fear in one freshman's eyes when he saw me walk up to meet him and his group. He had brought Brad Johnson as his wingman. Brad was a pretty tough dude, but I had bested him in wrestling on many occasions, and he must have mentioned that to Lonnie's nemesis for the evening. Brad's eyes lit up when he saw me walk up to meet him.

"What's up, John?" he asked. "I didn't know you were involved with this. If I'd have known you were involved, I would have stayed home."

He looked over at the combatant and said, "If Decker's here, it's fair, plain and simple."

I looked at Brad, and we shook hands and started walking together to the field. We had been cool since junior high. I wouldn't say we were friends, but we always respected each other.

Once we got to the site, the fight would happen, and we would always stop it before anyone got really hurt. We would then close out the night being gracious hosts to the enemy with drinks and Doritos at camp. Creekers had a respectable three and nothing record going into the fight tonight. However, a creeker would lose tonight no matter what, and that was very sad.

J.D. and Cam stood together watching the fire and talking quietly among themselves as they watched Lonnie walk away from camp, through the woods toward the platform. Snoopy and I took a seat on the fallen tree and waited for Jerry to cross the creek and come into camp. I think we both wanted to stop the fight, and yet it seemed like this was something that needed to happen. I mean, the tension between these two dudes had been building since they met, and this might just be the release valve the steam needed. I checked my watch, and it had now been three minutes. Jerry should be starting on his way toward us soon.

Snoopy decided to make one last appeal to reason.

"Dude, you have to stop this. Friends aren't meant to fight. The creek will never recover from this," Snoopy reasoned.

"Man, school is over in a few weeks. Most of us will be gone, one way or the other. The creek will never recover from that. I think it may be over already. It feels that way to me," I said.

"Right, but fighting is just stupid, and it makes me sick," Snoopy pleaded.

"I agree. The creek god declares this will be stopped after a few blows. We can't let either get the upper hand with these two prideful bastards. We need to make sure honor is maintained but the beef gets squashed. I'm afraid the loser would be done for good, and the shame would haunt them. We can't let that happen," I insisted.

A few minutes of silence passed after Snoopy and I had spoken. I could still hear J.D. and Cam talking quietly by the fire. I looked at my watch once again. It had now been ten minutes since Jerry had first made the noise alerting us to his arrival. This was weird. I hadn't heard him crossing the fence or the creek.

"Jerry. What the hell, dude? Come on," I yelled across the creek.

"Enough already. Let's get this shit over with," Cam yelled.

I looked over at him.

"Where is he? He's five minutes late, and I haven't heard any movement," I said in frustration.

"You don't think the bitch would go attack Lonnie without us there?" J.D. asked.

"I don't know. I would have said no a month ago, but the past few weeks have caused me to change my opinion a little," I answered.

"He's always hated Lonnie. I don't know why, but he has," Snoopy remarked.

"Right," I said.

We got silent and listened for noises. The night was quiet.

"If he's not here in a few minutes, we're going to the field," I ordered.

"Agreed," Cam said.

We all stood very tense, staring at each other and the fire. I was starting to get scared, wondering if this was the start of a *Friday the 13th* movie or *Halloween*. The fact that I even had those thoughts showed that deep down I knew this whole situation was screwed up. Why had I agreed to this in the first place? Was I part of the problem? Did I actually want to see them fight? These thoughts ran through my head as I stared into the glow of the fire. At that moment, the peace of the night was broken. We could hear screaming coming from the woods. The words being yelled were unintelligible so far. I began to run in their direction. Cam followed, and I presume the others did as well. The words became clearer as someone ran through the woods in our direction. It was Lonnie. I was sure of it now. In the darkness, the following horrifying words rang out as moonlight tried to break through the thick forest:

"I killed him! He stopped moving! I didn't mean to. I didn't mean to, I swear."

The words were punctuated by wails and weeping. I had never heard such angst. I finally caught sight of the light. I stopped running, not wanting to meet craziness in the middle of the woods alone. I decided to go back to camp and make sure the others were okay. When I made it back, the others were huddled in a tight group by the fire. I knew I had felt the presence of Cam as I ran off, but he must have doubled back when I wasn't paying attention. The noise from the forest grew louder as Lonnie came into sight. He was now shirtless, and his Rec Specs were nowhere to be seen. He burst into camp and landed square on his knees, as if begging God to end the nightmare playing out in the moonlight in our woods.

He was yelling, crying, and generally losing all composure. He was on his knees crying and begging our forgiveness.

"I'm so sorry. I didn't mean to. He's dead. I couldn't stop. He hit his head on the platform. Jerry's dead!"

He repeated variations of this over and over, but I didn't stick around long enough to question him. I had to get to Jerry. I ran through the forest, leaving the others in my wake. It took about two minutes to travel what would normally take six or seven. I had never moved with such speed and purpose. I finally crossed out of the woods into the field. The platform was on my right as I entered the vast natural arena. I could see a few cows about fifteen yards to my left. The field was lit up well by the moonlight. I scanned the field for people or anything else. I saw nothing so far. I then took a right and headed for the entrance to the white rock creek that led to the Old campsite. As I closed in on the fence I needed to cross to get to the actual creek, I saw him.

There he lay, remarkably close to the edge of the field. Jerry was motionless. I went to him in shock as I felt tears starting to well up in my eyes. The moon shined on his face, and he looked very pale. I pushed him a little, and he had no reaction. He still felt warm, but I felt no rise in his chest. I heard the others entering the field behind me.

"John? John? What are we going to do? He's really dead."

At that point, Lonnie entered the fray again. He was back on his knees mourning over his actions and Jerry.

"I didn't mean it! I didn't mean it!"

Lonnie was hysterical as Cam worked quickly to comfort him. He grew louder and louder and more tearful. I slapped him across the face and begged him to get it together. Cam was now holding Lonnie and comforting him. Then, like something out of the *Twilight Zone*, Snoopy and J.D. started talking strategy.

"Do we bury him?" Snoopy asked. "We can deny he ever showed up, and no one else even knows we're here."

"I'd know. We need to pursue this by the book," J.D. said firmly.

"I won't bury him. That's bullshit," I declared. "We'll carry him to his parents and call nine-one-one. I'll take the heat," I told them.

Everyone was now huddled around Jerry in desperation, with the exception of Lonnie, who was lying sprawled flat out, face down in the middle of the field. I couldn't imagine what he was going through, having just killed a creeker. I remember thinking to myself, "How could the creek god allow this? How could I allow this?" It was now clear: everything was over, and what had taken years to build had been brought down in mere minutes. There would be no more ring of honor, no more capture the flag, no more Sudan Wall, and no more friend. Jerry was dead.

"Well, no use delaying the inevitable, it's time to go for help. There's no point in getting an ambulance out here. They'll just get stuck. I'll carry him home and tell his parents. This is gonna kill them," I said. "All right, guys. First off, there will be an investigation. Just tell the truth. They will have to come out here, so our camping days are over, as the owners of the property will now know who we are and where we camp."

I looked down at Jerry's body and tears began to well up in my eyes.

"Jerry, what the hell, man?"

I got down on my knees and put my head on his chest. At this point, I was streaming real tears. I slowed down and just prayed silently to myself. I could hear others in the background muttering, but none of that mattered. I had failed as their leader. I had failed to keep them safe. I was not the creek god's vessel; I was just a dumbass punk who was in over his head.

"Forgive me, God," I said as I sprang from my knees to my feet.

I reached down under Jerry and grabbed the back of his T-shirt. I then put my right arm under his head and down under his shoulders. I would sit him up and then pop him over my shoulder fireman style for the walk back to his parents. I lifted him up and prepared to bite the bullet.

"Ahhhh! Screw you! I got you! I got you! Creek god goes down, bitch! Down!!!"

Jerry burst from my grasp and up onto his feet. He was alive! I looked up at him in disbelief. He was hopping up and down like a jackrabbit, laughing and yelling! Lonnie was rolling on the ground laughing his ass off. The four of us stood stunned. Jerry was alive. What the hell? He was alive.

"What the hell, Jerry?" I yelled in anger.

"No shit, Jerry. That's bullshit," J.D. shouted.

"Screw ya'll," Jerry replied. "The fucking creek god goes down! All you bitches went down! Man, you idiots are stupid," Jerry screamed in the moonlight.

He bounced around the field in victory, like he had just won the lottery – or even the Super Bowl or something. The guy had just crossed my line. It wasn't the prank; it was the gloating.

I stood up and ran at Jerry full steam. I cocked my arm back and threw a haymaker in the direction of his right jaw. It landed, and Jerry went down hard. I jumped on top of him, reached up to start my ground-and-pound, and then felt arms holding me back, denying me the justice I craved at that moment. Cam and J.D. were talking to me, but I only remember the sentiment being shared – like "quit hitting him" and "get off of him." He had been out cold for a minute or so when I felt J.D. release me. The one punch had satisfied my anger. Then, from out of nowhere, sweet relief rolled in as I realized I didn't have to tell Jerry's parents or sister that he was dead. Relief also took over because it seemed the crazy feud was done as well. Lonnie was still laughing, although Cam had tried to shut him up. After a minute or two, Jerry was able to get back up and was still full of glee and triumph. He just wasn't as loud, and I could thank the haymaker for that blessing.

"John, you're no longer the king of initiation! I am! The creek god bullshit is over. I serve no one, and I am king out here. Your time has come and gone. It's time for beer," Jerry announced as he started heading back to our campsite.

Lonnie got up and followed Jerry back into the woods and out of sight as they both headed back to our camp. The rest of us – J.D., Cam, Snoopy, and myself – stood there in disbelief, looking straight at each other.

"He's right," I said. "I took the creek god thing way too far. I mean, he got me, right?"

"He got us all," said J.D.

With heads held low, one by one we headed back into the forest to return to camp. It was time to take my medicine like a man and acknowledge the best prank I'd ever seen. As I walked back, I searched the last three weeks in my mind. There had been no indication that the feud was fake or that the anger wasn't real. A few minutes later I saw the fire, and I went to congratulate the victor and new "creek god."

"Man, now that the fog of war has cleared, I gotta say, that was the shit! You got me so bad. That was genius! I'm sorry for slugging you, Jer," I said.

"No problem. It was worth it. It was so worth it, dude," Jerry answered.

Lonnie cranked up the tape player. "No One Lives Forever" by Oingo Boingo was the perfect song for the moonlit night and the situation we were in. J.D. came in and high-fived Lonnie and Jerry.

"Damn, Lonnie, I didn't know you could act like that. You deserve an Oscar. You really sold it," J.D. conceded.

"It was nothing. The darkness made it easy, but I am proud of my performance," Lonnie bragged.

"You should be," Snoopy replied.

We spent the next few hours discussing the prank and the planning, ignoring the real truth that this might be our last night together in the playground of our youth, and the creek was losing its grip on us as the night wore on.

Jerry informed us that the whole thing had been his idea to prank me and that he hadn't let Lonnie in on it until a day or two ago at school. He said he'd needed it to seem as real as possible for effect. So, as far as Lonnie was concerned, the fight was going to happen. He said he originally got the idea two years ago when we initiated one of Snoopy's friends from the private school. He said he realized at that moment that I took the pranks too seriously and that I needed a dose of my own medicine. This didn't make much sense to me at the time, because he had been in on the planning for all of the initiations. However, I didn't want any more fighting. It seems that he bided his time for the perfect opportunity, and then the pizza argument happened, and he decided that might be his last chance since I was leaving soon for the Army. He may have been right, but something felt off about his plan. I remembered seeing hatred in his eyes in the lunchroom that day, and I was sure it was real. He wasn't that good of an actor. I decided to let it go; it would look like I was a sore loser if I ripped up his story as it was being told, so I swallowed it. We all drank a few beers and went to sleep, and for the first time at the creek I dreamed of my own bed and the comforts of home. I didn't want to be at the creek.

On the walk back to civilization, I asked Lonnie when Jerry had actually told him of the prank idea. He said that he went to the field ready to fight. When he reached the platform, he saw someone coming from the fence line and thought it was Jerry breaking the rules and trying to jump him, so he prepared for the attack. He said he approached the figure slowly and confirmed it was Jerry. Here is the basic conversation as he told it to me:

"Lonnie, it's me, Jerry. Dude, stand down. I didn't come to fight. That was all bullshit."

"What do you mean, bullshit? Fight night's here. It's too late to back out now, bitch," Lonnie responded.

"I'm not backing down. I never really wanted to fight. I want to prank Decker, and this is the best chance we will ever get," Jerry told him.

"What did you have in mind?" Lonnie asked.

"John and crew are back at camp waiting for me to arrive, and they must be getting anxious, as I'm already late. In a few minutes, before they try to come here, you go running into the forest yelling about how something went wrong. How I jumped you in the field, and you fought back, and I fell and hit my head and died or something. I'll play the part here. Just make it incoherent but consistent. In the night, they may buy it," Jerry explained.

Lonnie told me he felt bad for lying the previous night about having been told a few days before at school, but he hadn't wanted to ruin the guy's moment. He swore to me that he hadn't known until a few minutes before he came running into camp. This coincided with the theory I had developed during the night that Jerry had basically chickened out on the way to the fight. He had come up with a genius plan to kill two birds with one stone – a plan that would both get him out of the actual fight and prank me in the process. Whatever and however it went down, his plan was genius, so I wasn't going to make any drama on the way back from camp. I guess I wasn't angry, and I can take a good joke, but I was hurt. Jerry was the one dude I had always stayed faithful to. I had never wavered when it came to him. I couldn't help but wonder where the animosity toward me came from.

After a good shower and nap at home, my head cleared. My only guess as to why Jerry felt the need to get back at me was that I had made out with some girls from his church at camp and once at his house. Maybe he'd had his eye on one of the two girls and didn't ever tell me. That's all I could conjure up. A few days later, I called his sister. She said Jerry always told her I was his best friend and she thought he worshiped me. This was confusing to me. I clearly had some issues to address with Jerry and his anger toward me, which I had seen that night at the creek. However, I didn't want to dig into it so close to his moment of victory, because that would make me look like a loser who couldn't take a dose of his own medicine. No, he had pranked me in a big way, and I would let him savor it for a while. Graduation was just a few weeks away, and before I knew it my whole world would change. My last few weeks of high school, and of living in Waynesville for that matter, were now upon me, and I was anxious but ready.

✳ ✳ ✳

CHAPTER 20

GOODBYE FLIGHT

can't really remember any of my final exams that May, but I know I passed them. Once I had signed up for the Army, I pretty much half-assed my schoolwork, even more than before, because I knew I had already been accepted. My graduation was all but assured, so I did just enough to pass. Could I have done better? Yes, but I chose to actually live rather than sit in my room studying my ass off for some scholarship or school status. I didn't do as bad as you might think. I actually finished in the top 25 percent of the class. I was in the 40s out of about 200. I guess my parents thought I should have done better. I could tell some teachers thought that as well. The six people I had been in Talented and Gifted with in elementary school all finished in the top ten of the class, and two of them were numbers one and two. I had been as smart as these people and even had better marks than some of them in the early grades. Somewhere along the way I was seduced by fun and decided

I wanted to live. I'm not saying these people didn't live – just not the way I wanted to.

As Cam spent more and more time with his girlfriend Sandra, I found myself hanging out with my new girl Cynthia. She was petite with long blonde hair. She had a rocking body and always had a killer tan. I guess I always kind of knew in the back of my mind that she was just a fun diversion for me. I tried to be serious and fall in love, but it just wasn't in the cards for us, no matter how much it might seem so in the future. In addition to Cynthia, there was a girl named Julie I was talking to. She was a soccer player, and I found myself going a few towns over to her practices every couple of days. What can I say? I was a jackass.

Julie was the kind of girl I could have married. She was not one to go out with just any guy that came along. I think that is what attracted me to her. She wouldn't agree to go out with me, but she did want to hang out and see where it might lead. I was unwilling to drop Cynthia on a possibility, so my relationship with Julie never moved beyond friendship. As for Cynthia, she was really falling for me. I told her I was going to Julie's practices, and she still stayed with me. I didn't realize what I had, and I look back now and see I was treating her badly.

As graduation day approached, our excitement grew. Clarise planned a graduation party for the creekers. There would be beer, fire, and smokes. Clarise was a great friend. She finally had a boyfriend that went to her church, but she made clear to him that creekers came first. She was the real deal, an angel of a girl that we didn't deserve. She took care of everything, so instead of a last session at the creek, we would be right next to it at Clarise's house. I even invited Cynthia so she could see Waynesville and experience the fun we had.

As I wrapped up the business of school and exams, I couldn't shake the feeling that something was off with Jerry. Cam and J.D. told me his story was bullshit. They believed he hadn't planned the prank but had simply chickened out that night and come up with a brilliant plan to cover it up. I still wasn't sure. Jerry and I were talking, but there was now some bad blood between us that I couldn't account for. I decided I needed to know why he'd felt the need to prank me, when I had never pranked him. Two days from graduation, I decided to go to his house and confront him. I didn't want to leave town with something negative brewing between us.

I drove to his house and asked for Jerry.

"Hello, is Jerry here?"

"No, but he'll be back soon," Trina answered.

"All right, can I wait?" I asked.

"Sure, just go up to his room. He should be home in thirty minutes or so," Trina said.

I walked up the stairs to his room. I went in and sat down on his bed, amazed at the trust Trina had shown in me. On the nightstand next to the bed was a book. The book had a black cover and was clearly a journal of some type. I stared at it for a minute or so. Finally, I decided to take a chance. I opened up the cover. It was Jerry's. As I looked through the book, I noticed everything was dated and that his notes were meticulous. I decided to go back to early May and see what Jerry had been thinking leading up to the fight. Strangely enough, all of May was gone. It was obvious that he had written much leading up to the fight, but nothing of May was left. Why would he remove that section? It was his journal. If you can't be honest with yourself, who can you be honest with?

I was satisfied that I would find nothing about the fight in this journal, but that didn't mean there was nothing I could glean from its pages. I decided to turn back a year or so at random. I found a page marked Thursday, April 20, 1989. The page read as follows:

I worked until 10 tonight. Walked home from Waynesville Market. Screw my homework. Not doing it. Screw college and Trina. Oingo. Going to bed.

This was nothing I needed to see, and I felt bad for reading it. The fact that he had ripped out pages from May of 1990 was enough proof for me that he was lying about the prank and the fight. I should have stopped reading there, but something drove me to look at one more day, and I'm sorry I did.

I flipped to the next page, which was marked Friday, April 21, 1989. The words jumped off the page:

Screw Lonnie! I will beat him with a bat. I will beat him up with a cat. I will screw him with a rat. John is a bitch. John just wants trim. Trina would have him. Trina won't do me.

Lonnie can suck me and needs to die. Did my homework tonight so it won't ruin weekend. Work is fun. Dad nice to me today. Smoked weed behind store. Going to bed happy.

I can't really describe my shock when I read those words. First off, I shouldn't have read them, but what the hell was wrong with this kid? I can't remember ever even really arguing with the guy, and yet I'm a bitch? This was so disturbing. You could see hatred for Lonnie dripping off of the page, and his feelings toward me weren't that much better. I had to get out of there. Dude was deranged, and it was clear I had never really known him. I put the journal down exactly where I had found it. I turned off the light and left the room. I walked down the stairway and said bye to Trina.

"Hey, Trina, I just remembered I have a few pages of homework to do. Tell Jerry I stopped by," I said.

"Sure will. Take it easy, John," Trina replied.

I got in my car and drove away. I won't lie: I was flustered. I had just realized one of my best friends didn't feel the same way about me. In fact, it was quite the opposite, and I would never know why. As I look back now as a father, I know he must have had mental troubles. It would surely have been diagnosed as anxiety and depression, but he was good at hiding it in public. The last time I saw him was the day after graduation, and it didn't go so well.

✳ ✳ ✳

A few years later, I came home on leave from the Army and decided I would go talk to him. My mom stopped me as I was prepping to go. She told me the horrible news that Jerry had run his vehicle off the road into the creek a few hundred yards before Alex Bields Elementary. It had been icy that night, and he had crashed his dad's truck off the bridge. He had survived the initial crash but died in the hospital three days later with a collapsed lung.

"You won't find them at the house. They sold it and moved away. After the car crash, they were just devastated and wanted to start over in a new place, one without so many memories. The whole situation was a tragedy," Mom said.

"Why didn't anyone tell me?" I asked.

"You were overseas, and we didn't want to upset you," she said.

It didn't matter, I was upset, and I still am.

I decided after leaving Jerry's house that I was done with him. The dude was clearly unstable, and I didn't want to rock the boat. I should have told someone about his sick writings, but thirty years ago we minded our own business, for better or for worse. I prayed for the guy and felt really betrayed, but I mainly just felt sorry for him. However, my overall mood was still pretty happy, and I made it to the last day of school with no other problems. As I headed to Possum Fields High on the final day, I decided to stop in at the Waynesville Market and get some gas. Beetle was working the register.

"Ready to graduate tonight, dude?" Beetle asked.

"Oh yeah. I've never been more ready. You coming to Clarise's tonight?" I asked.

"No, I'll be at your parents' 'pre-party' with my mom. Clarise and them are your thing, but I'll smoke a few with you before you go."

"Cool. See ya tonight," I said as I paid for my soda and gas.

My last exam came and went. I grabbed my remaining stuff from the locker and headed toward the car. On the way out, I ran into Lonnie and J.D in the hall. They were actually becoming friends.

"Hey, John, did you ever get answers from Jerry?" J.D. asked.

"I got answers, just not in the traditional way, and not the ones I wanted to see either. Not a big deal, dudes. I've just learned this week that everything ends," I lamented.

"Shit, we'll never end," said Lonnie as he reached out and patted my shoulder.

"Right. It's been good with you guys. I think we're gonna make it," I joked.

"I'll at least make it to the party tonight. I can't promise anything after that," J.D. said.

I continued through the school and out into the rock parking lot. I reached the car, and Cynthia was waiting there. I came up to her and kissed her quickly on the lips.

"Hey, girl, what's up?"

"Since we get out early due to exams, my mom can't pick me up," she informed me.

"Well, hop in," I said.

I started the car and drove to her house, which was about

two miles behind the school back in the woods. We sat in her driveway talking for a few minutes before she went inside.

"Thanks for the ride," Cynthia said.

"No problem, and don't worry about the exams. I know you aced them," I told her.

"Okay, I will try to stop, but I also have some bad news for you. My dad decided I can't go to the party tonight. I feel really bad, and I really wanted to see the creek you're always talking about," she said convincingly.

"Well, when can I see you again?" I asked.

"Call me this weekend. You'll still be here, right?" she asked.

"I'm here until July tenth. That gives us a little more than a month to see where this goes," I answered her.

"Well, don't have too much fun at Clarise's tonight, and I'll be at graduation if the parents don't stop me," she said as I started the car.

"I'll be there and will look for you after. I'll be good at the party. See ya," I yelled out the window as I backed out of her driveway.

I lit up a Marlboro Red for the drive home.

Later that day, I graduated from high school. I don't feel the need to bore you with the details of the ceremony. If you've ever been to one, you'll understand and appreciate my decision. If you haven't been to one, you will someday, and then you will understand. After the ceremony, I said bye to the last four years and many friends I would never see again. However, Cynthia was missing from the audience. I thought I might run to her house to see what was up, but then family and friends came out of the woodwork. After a few pictures at the front of the auditorium, my family and I were ready to go. I told them I would meet them back at the house. I walked to my car and drove home, not thinking that this would be the last time I saw the school for more than a year.

Jerry wasn't at the graduation either. This thought stayed with me the entire way home.

When I reached the house, cars were already there. I saw Beetle standing out front smoking. I joined him.

"Your mom made the poke cake, man," he said.

"Sweet," I replied.

The Jell-O Poke Cake was my all-time favorite dessert. It was basically yellow cake with toothpick-size holes poked in it while still hot. You poured hot liquid Jell-O into the holes. Strawberry or cherry were the flavors of choice in our house. Next, you put the cake in the fridge for a few hours, and then applied a thick layer of Cool Whip as icing. This cake is heavenly, and anything left after the party would be quickly consumed by the family.

"How does it feel to be done, dude?" Beetle asked.

"Feels really good. I'm starting to get a little nervous about the Army, but it's all good," I said.

"It is the logical extension for the creeker in you. The Army will be a launchpad for many adventures. I wish I had the courage to leave and chase the call of the creek god," Beetle added.

"You did. You went to college for a while, and the call drew you back here. I wonder if the same will happen to me," I said.

"No. You have a mission, a destiny beyond Waynesville. I am proud of you and the man you're becoming," Beetle said, sounding more like a father than a big brother figure.

"Thanks, man. You have been a big part of it. I never would

have had the creek without you. If it had been up to my brothers, the fire would have died a long time ago," I said.

"The fire never dies. Let's hang a few times before you leave. It's July tenth, right?" Beetle inquired.

"Right, but they said it could move to July thirteenth," I answered.

"Okay. So, we'll drink some brews next weekend," Beetle said.

"All right. Thanks for coming and for the graduation Marlboro carton. Midnight basketball at Shiloh Church next Friday. Don't be late," I said.

Beetle got into his ride, shut the door, and rolled down the window.

"I'll be there," he said as he slowly drove off into the night.

I strolled inside to thank everyone for coming and for any presents they had brought. Beetle was right about the poke cake, and my mom had actually outdone herself and made two. I saw Beetle two more times before ship-off day in July.

Later that night, I went to Clarise's for the party she was throwing us. It was fun. I basically drank beer and smoked cigarettes until 4:00 in the morning. Cam, Lonnie, and J.D. were all there, so we hung out laughing all night. Clarise was there with her new boyfriend from church, who was obviously very protective of her. Jerry was a no-show for the party as well as graduation. We all speculated as to where he was, but none of us bothered to walk a few houses over to check on him. He had really done a number on us as a group, even though I hadn't told them what I had seen in the journal. I simply didn't want to dishonor the guy or upset anyone. As I walked home, I decided I would find him tomorrow, and wherever I needed to go to make contact, I would. I just had to know why he had turned on me.

My first full day as a high school graduate was surreal. I didn't feel any different personally, but the world itself somehow felt bigger. My plan for the day was to confront Jerry about his prank and his journal. I know it seems like I was being a bitch about the prank, but our code had been broken. Creekers didn't prank each other once initiation was complete. Jerry and I were basically the originals of our generation, so I had to know what had led to it. I knew he usually went to work about 2:00 on non-school days, so I figured I'd hit his house about noon, before he was ready to leave. It was a nice sunny day, so I decided to walk it. Jerry's car was still in the driveway when I arrived, so I thought this might be the time. I rang the doorbell, and he answered right away.

"What's up, John? Over your scare yet?" Jerry said while laughing.

"Yeah, it was a good one, Jer," I replied.

Jerry stepped out onto the porch and lit a smoke. I did the same.

"Where were you last night? Did you not want to graduate with the class?" I asked.

"No, man. I screwed up my English paper and have to do summer school. I start next week. I'll be done the end of July," Jerry informed me.

"Shit, man, I didn't know you were having trouble in that class."

"Neither did I, dude," Jerry said with a laugh.

"So, is that why you weren't at Clarise's last night?" I asked.

"No, dude. I'm not hanging with Lonnie any more than I have to," Jerry said.

"I thought you guys were good, man, that your beef was all a charade," I countered.

"Nah, man. The beef was real. The fight was a charade," Jerry told me.

"I'm sorry you didn't get to graduate with us," I said.

"No skin off my back. I don't really give a shit as long as I get the diploma," Jerry said as he put out his smoke on the sidewalk leading to his driveway.

I sensed the mood changing, so I thought I'd better get my questions in now.

"Jerry, are you sure the prank was planned? The group thinks you got scared before the fight and came up with a clever-ass way to get out of it. Is that what really happened?" I asked.

"What? Is that what you shitholes think? Fuck you, like I'm not capable of having a plan? You think I'm afraid of Lonnie?" Jerry asked in a raised voice.

"That's kind of what I do think. I know you can plan, but I know you've had it in for Lonnie for a long time. And you broke creek code by pranking members. I have never pranked you, dude," I said.

"Sorry your feelings are hurt, but you got to toughen up if you're going into the Army," Jerry said as he grabbed a second smoke.

This last statement really pissed me off, so I decided to just come out with it.

"Jer, why did you call me a bitch in your diary?" I asked with a straight face.

"What the hell, dude? You read my journal?" he asked.

"Yes, and I know you hate Lonnie and make fun of me in it all the time as well. I think you wanted to fight Lonnie and me also, but you don't have the balls. So, you came up with a prank to save face and still feel like you got the upper hand. I get it, and I've accepted it. I just need to know what I did to earn this hatred. What did I ever do to you?" I asked.

"What did you do to me? Dude, I have listened to you talk about girls and other friends for years. You're an arrogant piece of shit that only cares about yourself and how much pussy you can score. It gets old, dude," Jerry mentioned.

"All right, so you can change your tune about not being scared. It is clear from your journal you hate both Lonnie and me, so you wanted to fight and just got scared at the moment of truth."

"Screw you, dude. I'll show you who's scared, bitch," Jerry yelled as he swung at me.

I blocked the blow and followed with a quick jab of my own that caught him by surprise. He went down to his knees, and I raised my fist ready to strike again if I needed to.

Jerry got back on his feet but was still wobbly.

"That's right, dude. I am tired of your shit and arrogance. Everything's gotta be about you. I won't put up with it anymore," Jerry said while still in a kind of daze.

"I thought we were like brothers, dude. I was just hoping you had a bad day or something, but you really do hate us," I said in wonder.

"Yeah, I do. Get of my property before I kick your ass some more," Jerry said in a loud voice.

"Dude, you need to get some help, some counseling or something. I'm leaving, so you won't have to attack me again, and I won't have to lay you out," I replied.

"Damn you. Bullshit creek god. Always living like a piece of shit and taking everything. You don't even work, bitch," Jerry said insultingly.

I had had enough. This guy's feelings were so deep seated I didn't know where to go from here.

"All right, man, I'm leaving. You won't have to worry about me again. Good luck on the summer school, dude. Don't call me, we're done," I said as I walked away from Jerry for the last time.

I never saw him again.

June went faster than I would have liked. I hung with Clarise a few times, but it just wasn't the same now that she had a boyfriend. I also hung out with Beetle when I could. We played basketball with forty-ounce beers by the graveyard at Shiloh Church. The court was off the road behind the church, so you couldn't be seen. If I had known about this place earlier in high school, I would have used it much more. I also hung out with Cynthia. I basically went to her house every couple of days and messed around with her. I tried to get her into the sack, but she had self-control, which, looking back, I am now grateful for. At the end of June, I said bye to her so I could focus on Cam and the family for the last couple of weeks.

"So, are we still together?" she asked.

"Look, Cynthia, I don't know when I'll even be back. I will miss you, but you gotta live your life," I said.

She was crying a little, but not too much. I think I must

have been the first guy she'd fallen hard for, which made me feel worse, because I didn't respect her as much as I should have.

"If I'm in town and you're not with somebody, we'll go out when I'm here if you want. Otherwise, I want to say we're single and just remember this as a great high school relationship. I'll miss you, but you're free," I said.

"But what if I don't want to be free? What if I want to wait?" she said with tears growing in her eyes.

"I can't and won't do that to you. I'm sorry, but you'll thank me when the pain is gone," I said as I started walking toward the car.

She came over and hugged me, harder than normal. I kissed her on the cheek and broke her grip on me.

"Bye, Cynthia. Live your life."

I got in the car and started it. I drove away with a small ache in my throat. Maybe I liked her more than I thought. Anyway, I still had some goodbyes to say. I didn't know it then, but Cynthia would play a pivotal role in the next few years of my life. Like I said earlier, this story is just the tip of the iceberg.

The pain of giving Cynthia up was subsiding, and I knew I had made the right call. Speaking of calls, she had stopped calling me and leaving messages by day three, so I think she was getting over it as well. The main thing missing so far this summer had been Cam. He was working and living at Sandra's house. Yes, it's hard to believe, but her parents let him stay there in the camper outside. Sandra spent most of her time with Cam in the camper. She was a good-looking girl, and Cam was eager to make her happy, so I can only imagine the fun he had that summer. I don't blame him for ignoring the boys when he was clearly having the best summer of his life. He was definitely trying to get all the life he could get before his August ship-out date. On July 5, he called me and said he had cleared the day to hang with me. I drove over and picked him up. We then made our way to Bayton Springs to buy beer. This was the go-to spot for underage drinking. They never carded people, and yet somehow they were never shut down. After getting the beer we headed out to Shiloh. It was a Thursday, so the church employees were already gone for the day when we arrived there at 2:00 or so in the afternoon.

We played horse and some one on one. Beetle was going to join us later in the evening, but we didn't waste any time. We drank a lot, and the basketball was giving us greater tolerance as we burned calories.

"So, man, how's your summer going?" I asked, even though I think I already knew the answer.

"Great. I think I'm in love with Sandra, and I'm going to propose to her," Cam said, blindsiding me.

"Dude, she's pretty and sweet, but are you sure she's the one?" I asked as calmly as I could.

"She's the one. She's perfect. I can't live without her, dude," Cam gushed.

"Okay, but she's fifteen, dude. She can't even drive yet," I countered.

"She'll be sixteen before I leave in August, and her parents will sign for us to get married. I can't wait, and I need your support," Cam pleaded.

"Don't your parents have to sign too?" I asked.

"I'll be eighteen soon after she turns sixteen. They won't need to sign," Cam insisted.

At this point I knew there was no talking him out of it. I thought it was a horrible idea, but I shut my mouth on the truth and spoke lies.

"All right, dude. I'm sorry I'll miss it. I'll be gone in a week," I said.

"We should have joined on the buddy program. What were we thinking?" Cam said.

I wasn't sure what "we" were thinking, but I knew what I was thinking. The Cam I knew and loved was still here, but his passion was now focused on the girl. No matter how good a friend I was, I could never compete with her. I just wanted the day to go smoothly, so I indulged his wedding plans.

"I'll be most of the way done with Basic by then. Send me pictures, man."

"I will. I will," Cam said as he downed another Miller Lite.

We finished up at about 3:00 a.m. that night. Beetle came and hung from about 8:00 to 12:00, and then Cam and I brought it home until the end. We were out of beer around 11:00, so the four hours gave us time to sober up. I dropped him off with a hug, and I could see Sandra standing out in the driveway waiting for him. I envied him at that moment, because I knew what he might soon be doing in the trailer. Anyway, they never did get married. Thank God. Her parents talked them into waiting until after Basic and AIT (Army individual training). Then Cam got stationed in Italy, and they talked the pair into waiting until he got back to the States. While Cam was in Italy, Sandra had a string of affairs. She slept with a number of guys, from what I have heard. Cam received the infamous "Dear John" letter in the middle of 1992, but he had heard about it from friends still in Possum Fields long before that. Cam went on to have a great wife, so it all worked out for him. I still consider him one of my top two friends ever to this day.

The day of departure finally arrived. I said bye to my brother Joel and to Beetle. Brett wasn't around for the send-off, but we had already said our goodbyes. My sister was proud of me for joining, I think, but she never really said bye, as she was thirteen at the time and living the life of a new teenager. My dad gave me a hug and told me he would come up to New Jersey for my Basic Training graduation. I thanked him for the good life he had given me. P.J. Decker was there as well.

"Well, you're growing up. This reminds me of my brothers joining in the sixties" she said.

"Mom, they were going to Vietnam. I'm going to New Jersey," I said to minimize her growing sentimentality.

"But you'll be a soldier, and there will be other wars," she said with tears welling up in her eyes.

"It's all good, Mom. Don't worry. I'll go with the Lord behind me," I said confidently.

"Okay, I love you, son," she said.

"I love you too, Mom. I'll write and call when I can."

I couldn't keep this conversation going any longer or I would break down. I stepped into the sergeant's car, and we drove away to MEPS and later that day to the airport.

I jumped on my first plane ride ever. It was a flight from DFW in Dallas to Atlanta. I would then pick up a connecting flight to Newark airport, where I would catch a bus to Fort Dix, New Jersey. As the plane left the runway, I couldn't help but think about what I was leaving behind: everything. I had a loving family and a great group of friends. I had had a girl up until a few days ago, and a magical world to camp and grow up in. Still, I knew I had taken it all for granted and hadn't learned the lessons I needed to learn from all of my experiences. I guess deep down I knew some drill sergeant was sitting there waiting for me as I had these thoughts, so lessons would be learned whether I liked it or not. My only regret was how it had ended with Jerry. I hated having to punch him, and his hatred for me honestly made me sad. As I look back now, it seems he took all the creek god talk more seriously than it was intended to be. I don't know, but I know he was on my mind as I rose above the clouds in the large aircraft. Within a few months, my mom was proven correct about her "other wars" comment, as Saddam Hussein invaded Kuwait and kicked off years of Middle Eastern conflicts involving America. However, I didn't know how these conflicts would affect me later in life, so I flew away from the sun with optimism and hope for the future. My thoughts then turned to home, Cam, and Beetle. What was I doing? I had joined the Army. I looked out my window into the sky and felt real emotional pain for the first time in my life. I wasn't the creek god. No one was. I looked at the back of the seat in front of me and then took a quick glance at all the people in the plane. I turned again toward the window and felt a tear fall from my eye. It was the first of many.

Get ready for the next installment in the John Decker adventure series: *American Days, Korean Nights!*

Coming in multiple forms in 2021!

AUTHOR'S NOTE

✳ ✳ ✳

I began this journey wanting to write a story about my life. I then realized that some things are better left in the past but that I still had a trove of fun life events that could be accessed to craft a good story. All but one of these characters are completely new creations, based very loosely on people I knew in the past. A few of these events actually took place, but they have been changed so much from reality that they are now completely fiction. The character who is not completely a new creation is Beetle. He didn't need fictionalization to become interesting! However, when he reads this, I hope he is able to enjoy some of the situations I have inserted him into. Based on our many hours of midnight discussions, I know that he will! Thanks for reading this. I have a ton of ideas, so I hope this is the first of many books.